KU-419-042

THE CHATHAM RATS

THE CHATHAM RATS

by

David Mariner

Dales Large Print Books
Long Preston, North Yorkshire,
BD23 4ND, England.

British Library Cataloguing in Publication Data.

Mariner, David
    The Chatham rats.

A catalogue record of this book is
available from the British Library

ISBN   978-1-84262-621-4 pbk

First published in Great Britain 1969 by Robert Hale & Co.

Copyright © D. McLeod Smith 1969

Cover illustration © Len Thurston by arrangement with
P.W.A. International Ltd.

The moral right of the author has been asserted

Published in Large Print 2008 by arrangement with
David Mariner, care of Watson, Little Ltd.

All Rights reserved. No part of this publication may be
reproduced, stored in a retrieval system, or transmitted in any
form or by any means, electronic, mechanical, photocopying,
recording or otherwise without the prior permission of the
Copyright owner.

Dales Large Print is an imprint of Library Magna Books Ltd.

Printed and bound in Great Britain by
T.J. (International) Ltd., Cornwall, PL28 8RW

The characters in this novel are entirely fictitious, and any resemblance to persons living or dead is purely coincidental. In using the nickname, The Chatham Rats, no disrespect is intended to any person, or persons, to whom the nickname may apply. If a destroyer by the name of *Wildcat* served in the Second World War, then that, too, is purely coincidental.

For

Margaret Mackenzie Smith

1

Major Troy stopped eating, listened, his chubby, dimpled hand creeping across the table towards the Luger automatic.

He got up slowly, silently.

If they *were* in the house, then they *had* come in the car which had passed some minutes before. An old trick. Drive past. Stop. Return on foot. It was all in the textbook. Theirs *and* his. So was Troy's next move. But alas, the window was three storeys up, with no convenient ledge.

He moved stealthily across to the door, gun in hand, flattened his body against the wall on the side by the hinges; and then he watched the handle ... saw it turn slowly ... then stop ... then turn again...

It crashed open in his face.

It was wrenched away in the same instant that the enemy sprang, trapped his arms, removed his gun.

The men in raincoats and soft hats could have been from Scotland Yard, the *Sûreté Extérieure* – any police force. But they were not. They were Gestapo. They looked human, and only their eyes revealed that they were not human. Nor were they animals.

They were *nothing!* And because they were nothing, they said nothing, and Major Troy had nothing to say to them.

They dragged him from the house, along the pavement, jammed him brutally into the rear of a black saloon. Two got in beside him, one on each side, and the two others got in beside the driver. All five had less than an hour to live.

It was almost midnight and the streets of Trieste were nearly deserted, except for the long convoys of heavily guarded military vehicles which were on the move or parked for the night. And from one such convoy a truck, carrying a Panzer Mk IV tank, was missing. The tank, weighing many tons, had slipped from its conveyer, damaged the conveyer's chassis, and extinguished its headlights. The accident had happened 'x' miles west of the city, but since the road was only partly blocked, no action had been taken.

The black saloon sped west, leaving the border city by the route the convoys had come. The road ran close to the north shores of the Adriatic Sea.

Being Gestapo, the five men remained stiff and alert, and the speedometer needle rose to the one hundred and fifty kilometre mark.

Being British, Major Troy yawned and fell asleep.

His next move was involuntary, head first,

and through the windscreen.

They had found the missing Panzer tank.

For once in his life, Troy left the scene of the accident without comment. He ran as fast as a damaged ankle would allow. No one followed. They had been stiff and alert, he had been inert; in that, Troy decided, there was a powerful moral.

His wristlet watch had been shattered, the hands destroyed. It was dark. He had no idea how far west of the city the accident had occurred. All he knew for certain was his general direction; it was either north or south! But if the latter, then he was at any minute going to fall into the sea. Instead he stumbled on to land as flat as an airstrip.

It was an airstrip.

Three huts and one parked aeroplane loomed up in the darkness, so did a sentry. Troy spoke to him quietly in German. The man approached with caution. The next move was in the textbook.

Clad in the uniform of the Wehrmacht, the Major made for the nearest hut. What he wanted was a car. What he found was the world's first guided missile, the radio-controlled glider bomb.

A description of that moment might well have been recorded in history, but it was completely overshadowed by another event taking place at that precise moment, and not too far away. That was the naval Night Action off Cape Tainaron, in southern Greece, to be known as The Battle of Matapan.

The date was March 28, 1941.

On the afternoon of March 27, Captain Guiseppe Durand, commanding the Italian Destroyer *Scorpio,* received the following instruction from the Admiral-in-Charge, Destroyer Flotillas, Napoli: 'Disengage from present operations and return to Napoli forthwith.'

No explanation.

But Durand was a man of honour with two brothers fighting in the famous Ariete Division, then in Libya, and he was well aware that the future of the Mediterranean sea power was going to be decided at any hour.

He signalled back: 'Urgently request reconsideration of instruction. Every Italian ship will be required if British Battle Fleet sails from Alexandria as anticipated.'

Not many officers would have shown Guiseppe's enthusiasm, and the Admiral, at Napoli, showed his sincere appreciation by offering an explanation:

Deeply regret cannot reverse decision. You have been chosen to carry out trials with new weapon in north Adriatic Sea on June

10. It is vital that you and your vessel remain in safety until that time. You are the only man suited for the task of observing and assessing the weapon's potential against warships and of offering constructive criticism on its performance to aid Luftwaffe in their experiments. The success of this mission may well decide the course of the naval war.

Guiseppe was flattered but annoyed. Nevertheless, he acknowledged in the affirmative and, at 17.15 hours, withdrew from the screen surrounding the Italian Battle Fleet, then south of Crete.

He held a course nor'west by west.

Daylight faded and night came, and with it the news that the British Battle Fleet had sailed from Alexandria at dusk.

Guiseppe was furious, and to make things worse his engineer officer reported that all was not well down in the engine-room. Could they heave to for one hour?

No, they could not! A reconnaissance report from an HeIII of the Luftwaffe indicated the presence of a British cruiser force screened by two destroyer flotillas.

At midnight flashes were observed on the horizon, then a flush of crimson.

Something was happening.

But Guiseppe's binoculars revealed only the windy night, ghostly wave-crests, and the sudden realisation that his ship was slowing down.

Ten minutes later *Scorpio* was stopped.

It was the engineer officer who decided the course of events. He pleaded with Durand to leave the bridge and see for himself exactly what was wrong.

Sasso, Guiseppe's second-in-command, was a man of great charm, but his appetite for war was weak. Left to himself on the bridge, he found himself sweating with tension. An imaginative man, it was not difficult to exaggerate the horrors of a closely fought night action; in fact, the Italian and British Navies, with or without imagination, would have found it difficult to exaggerate.

The captain had only gone three minutes when the searchlight slashed through the darkness and lit *Scorpio* from stem to stern. Her guns were trained fore and aft, useless for seven seconds; Sasso knew that, and the enemy could see it. There was no time to think. Night actions were fought at point-blank range. He who fired first, won.

All Sasso had time to do was clench his teeth, close his eyes, and bring his knotted fists to his forehead.

'Ahoy, there! Are you in trouble, friend?' The inquiry came from across the sea by megaphone, and it came in Italian with a strong Milano accent.

A miracle had happened. Sasso could have

kissed the Yeoman of Signals.

He grabbed his loud hailer instead and bawled: *'Scorpio,* here. We have engine-trouble. Can you stand by us?'

'We'll do better than that. We're coming alongside. Stream fenders!' the voice replied.

There were two things Sasso could do. He could call the Captain or stream fenders. He chose the latter because the searchlight, still blazing, was already coming alongside fast. But to stream fenders in a hurry, he had to stand the guns' crew down from action positions; and this he did.

In two minutes the fenders were hanging over the side; in three, the searchlight arrived alongside with a bump and a squealing of coconut fibres.

Sasso was now down on the main deck. Guiseppe was still in the engine-room. The Yeoman of Signals, who had the confidential books and messages in a bag, ready to destroy, returned them to the chart-table.

Behind the searchlight it was just possible to make out the black shape of a destroyer, whose crew seemed to abandon ship as one, leaping across the gap and on to *Scorpio's* deck along her whole length; and with strange, foreign cries – of welcome?

A tall figure, silhouetted in the blaze, landed just in front of Sasso, and bowed slightly.

'Hullo,' he said cheerfully. 'You'll have to

17

excuse my sword, but we ran out of ammunition and torpedoes sinking one of your cruisers. My name's Edward Dunbar, H.M.S. *Wildcat,* and those deplorable hooligans are known in naval circles as the Chatham Rats.'

For Sasso there was but one course left. He fainted.

2

With the descent of darkness the guns' crews had been stood down from Dusk Action Stations; which meant merely a minimal degree of relaxation in the ship's state of immediate readiness.

Lieutenant 'Professor' Rose, the Navigating Officer, removed his 'tin' hat, once-white anti-flash hood and gloves, and sighed with pleasure in the fierce wind of the destroyer's passage. For a Mediterranean evening, the temperature was extraordinarily cool, the sky overcast. Because the Captain had gone to the rear of the bridge to speak to Mr Chaplin, the Commissioned Torpedo Officer, Rose was conning the vessel with the relaxed air of a motorist who is happily following a queue of cars; for the Navigator was dead tired, not lazy, and the lethargy, shared by many of the officers and men of the Battle Fleet they were screening, was a psychosomatic reaction to the happenings of the moment.

These events were starkly outlined on foolscap:

H.M.S. *WILDCAT*
June 3, 1941
News Sheet

General: Intelligence reports indicate that German forces have extended their recent occupation of Greece to many of the strategically important Aegean islands, including those in close proximity to the Turkish mainland; while Italian Air Force units in the Dodecanese, to the east of Crete, have been joined by formidable units of the Luftwaffe. In Crete itself, 28,000 British and Empire troops continue their orderly withdrawal over the mountains to the island's southern shore, where they are being evacuated. But two thousand marines, fighting a rearguard action in the north, report heavy casualties from incessant air attacks, and crack German paratroop regiments who continue to be ferried in by plane and glider. Wehrmacht losses are said to be 'considerable'.

Naval losses include the cruisers *Gloucester* and *Fiji*, the destroyers *Kelly*, *Juno*, *Kashmir* and *Greyhound*. Details of survivors are not yet available.

In the Western Desert the British offensive, Brevity, has made no further progress, the plans for the evacuation of Egypt by way of the Suez Canal are already laid.

The Battle of Matapan, which ended the menace of the Italian Battle Fleet, stretched its historical finger into Alexandria harbour last night. The Italian destroyer *Scorpio,* which surrendered to *Wildcat* during the night action on the 28th March, weighed anchor and escaped under cover of darkness. It is believed that the Italians tricked and overpowered their guards.

Captain's comment: From bitter experience, we on *Wildcat* know *Scorpio's* Captain, Guiseppe Durand, to be a daring and resourceful officer and patriot, with two brothers serving in the famous Ariete Division, now in Libya. With conditions what they are in Egypt, I personally feel little surprise at this audacious escape, for it is known that there was no alternative but to leave *Scorpio's* crew on board pending their passage under escort to Suez.

The News Sheet had been edited, authorised and signed by Commander Edward Dunbar, *Wildcat's* Captain, and issued by Lieutenant-Commander Simon York, his First Lieutenant. Both were more than a little grumpy at the loss of their prize.

Silent in his brothel creepers, Dunbar arrived back at the Navigator's side. 'There comes a time when danger becomes a matter of degree,' he announced tiredly. 'Men are not machines. York and I have decided to give the lads a break.' It was typical of him to dispose one to believe that such a dangerous decision had been shared, although he alone took the responsibility, and he added: 'In favour, Pilot? The Coxswain's all for it.'

John Rose was feeling anything but magnanimous. 'You once said, sir – and I quote: "If there are any decisions to be made, we'll make them together. If it agrees with what I have already decided, we'll do it." End of quote. It's a good system. You have my blessing, sir.'

'Borrowed it from a Corporal of the Third Reich,' confessed the Captain, unabashed. 'Cheeky fellow. Managing Director now. Expanding his business interests fast, from the look of that News Sheet. Damn pity about *Scorpio,* though. Our old friend Guiseppe lapped up half my gin. "Aren't you worried about being a prisoner of war," I asked him. He drained his glass, belched, thumped it on the table, put one hand on his chest, the other in the air, and burst into song. Verdi's *Aida.* He fell asleep like a wound-down gramophone, drowned in Gordon's Mine.' With that last bitter comment he turned to the First Lieutenant who

21

had joined them in the darkness of the bridge. 'The Pilot agrees with your decision, Simon.'

'Good. I've already put it into effect.' York, too, was sceptical of the committee system.

The destroyer's loud speakers crackled into life. A bo'sun's whistle shrilled. 'D'you hear there! D'you hear there!' It was the gruff, metallic-sounding voice of Chief Petty Officer Morgan, *Wildcat's* Coxswain. 'Secure Action Stations! Secure Action Stations! The Port Watch will go to supper in five minutes time. Starboard Watch will go to supper at 21.30 hours. Cooks to the galley! Stand fast Starboard Watch. Starboard Watch close up at Defence Stations!'

The bridge speaker squeaked, crackled, and clicked into silence, leaving only the muted drone of the funnel exhausts, the repetitive 'pings' of the Asdic pulses, ever present as the underwater detection equipment searched ceaselessly for enemy submarines, and the distant thuds of gunfire from where the white flashes flickered back and fore along the horizon. The was Crete. Each flash was an instant tombstone.

'We're lucky,' muttered Dunbar. He didn't say why, he just said it. He wasn't a typical naval officer, for in Rose's opinion there was no such thing as a typical anything; but he was certainly the screen image of what a naval officer should be. He was tall, dark, slim, exceptionally handsome, with a permanent lean, hungry look which, only a week before in Alexandria's Hotel Cecil, had brought three lady sailors to the brink of ethical disaster with a prolonged hushed 'Coooo!' before remembering their chastity. Yet he was not conceited; on the contrary, he was astonishingly shy with strangers, with whom he displayed an awkwardness that told of the inner battle against that one weakness, or so Rose had divined. That facet also appealed to women. The crew called him 'our Edward', with respect and affection. His superiors called him 'that bastard, Dunbar', for Edward was as reckless as he was dashing in appearance – to them. But what was Dunbar really like, deep within? The answer to that, as with all men, lay in the filing cabinets of Heaven or Hell … and the door to each was ajar these days.

A few miles ahead, a chandelier flare exploded in the night sky and hung suspended: six tiny lights, pale-orange, tinting the belly of a cloud and illuminating a wide circle of sea with an eerie, shadowy brightness, against which the narrow stern view of the destroyer ahead was shown up in silhouette.

'Damn and blast,' swore *Wildcat's* Captain. 'It's that wretched HeIII again. Persistent fellow. Funny, though, how difficult it is to find ships in the darkness.'

'He's looking for the Battle Fleet,' York growled.

'He'll get a dose of dysentery if he finds it,' Dunbar forecast, and poked Rose. 'Come on, Pilot, a tour of inspection is called for. It'll get some of that excess fat off you.' Aside to York he said: 'We'll leave you to it, Number One. Keep an eye on Captain "D". He may alter course if the Luftwaffe get too close. Wouldn't want to be like the rear drummer who walked on when the band turned the corner.'

Somehow the quip annoyed the Navigator, and it certainly annoyed York, for he turned his bearded face away and squared up to the front of the bridge.

Rose grabbed his cap and followed Dunbar as the dull thud of a distant explosion explained the sudden crimson glow in the Cretan sky.

Forewarned, the Coxswain was waiting. 'Hullo, sir.' An ex-middle-weight, Chatham Division, to which the ship and all her crew belonged, his easy greeting, the tone, would to a naval stranger have categorised *Wildcat* as a 'happy' ship. 'It's a lousy night, sir. Want to do the upper deck?'

'We'd better. Mightn't get a chance later, Chief,' Dunbar was psychic.

Morgan turned and led the way aft in darkness, directing a courteous pool of blue torchlight on the deck behind him. Over his

24

shoulder he said: 'Lads are getting a bit edgy, sir.'

'I've noticed it in the officers. Just dropped a clanger myself,' murmured the Commander dryly. 'There are times when even the most celebrated comics fail to amuse.'

The Coxswain chuckled politely; clueless, of course. Rose felt better. His hand even strayed to his waist where the tyre pressures, he had to admit, needed attention.

Dunbar was thorough. He started among the depth-charge crew aft, made his way slowly for'd.

It seemed he had a photographic memory, for he spoke to each rating by name, obviously aware not only of the man's Defence Station but of his private problems as well. To Rose most of them were anonymous hooded shapes in the night.

Two-thirds of the crew were Active Service, regular navymen. One third were Hostilities Only – H.O's – but they had learned fast. Apart from Rose himself – and a few ratings whom had joined a few days before at Alexandria to replace the dead and wounded – they were all destroyer men; a race apart; who, with modesty, referred to their sleek, powerful vessels as 'the boats'; and not even the submariners shared their fame.

'Where's Freer?' asked a puzzled Dunbar.

'Sorry, sir, I had to swop him round.' The

Coxswain gestured at the after tunnel. 'Up there, sir, on the Oerlikon. But I'd scrub it, the ladder's filthy–' He broke off and added 'Christ' very softly in protest when Dunbar vanished upwards.

With the funnel exhausts muttering away, and the sharp hiss of the moving sea, Rose heard nothing below.

There were two distant flares in the sky, the far-away CRU-UMP! of depth charges – each caused a small metallic TWA-ANG! on *Wildcat's* elastic steel sides – and the never-ending flashes on the horizon. Only Dunbar's long look seaward, when he climbed down, revealed his growing concern.

But he said: 'That silly clot up there is Able Seaman Freer. Got married in U.K. the day he joined the trooper to come out here. Pleasant lad. Bet he hasn't even slept with her yet.'

'People just don't stop to think in wartime,' Rose sighed. 'I've seen some tragic cases.'

'Coxswain! Where the hell are you?'

'Here, sir.' Morgan arrived fastening up his flies.

'Put Freer down for a gunnery course,' Dunbar ordered. 'Anything. A.A.3, if you like. Dump him on the jetty with his bag and hammock immediately we get back to Alex. They'll fly him home with the C.W.

candidates if I give him a high I.Q.'

'But, Skipper, he's got less brains than that bollard!'

'So have rabbits, Coxswain.'

A gruff voice muttered, 'Rabbits?' thoughtfully, 'Aaaah,' after a pause, then, 'Aye, aye, sir!' with disgusting relish.

The long and the short and the tall; they were all there on board. And all the tragedy of man's inhumanity to man was there, too. Like Leading Seaman Yates.

'A hard case,' whispered the Coxswain. 'Under close arrest until we left harbour. Chucked an Egyptian taxi driver into the drink – the, er, Mediterranean, sir.'

'He agreed on fifty ackers when we got into the taxi,' Yates protested to his Captain. 'But when we reached the jetty, sir, he wanted a hundred and fifty.' A pause. 'Honest to God, sir, I never laid a finger on him. He just got out of his taxi and fell into the sea...'

Then there was Nelson. He was in the living quarters, beyond the blackout screens, in comfort. He had one eye, a chipped ear and half a tail, twenty razor blades – five on each black furry paw – and was balanced on his flexible feline spine, jack-knifed in two, one hind leg on each side of his head, green eyes focused on his organs of generation, perhaps puzzled by his enforced celibacy. He wasn't alone!

Then – 'Hands to Action Stations! At the double!'

When the Navigator burst through the port blackout screen he found himself in a vast cavern, its roof four thousand feet high and lit by six chandeliers which hung on slowly descending parachutes below tinted clouds that looked like dense, turbulent smoke. Six square miles of sea was its floor, and on the dark-grey, shadowy waters were six brightly illuminated, pale-grey destroyers, including *Wildcat,* all describing foaming patterns as they zig-zagged or circled independently to avoid the bombs which screeched down from the skies and lifted the sea, time and again, into glittering columns of white; and from each boat, rising lazily like flaming ping-pong balls, thrust the orange tracers of the 20mm Oerlikons, each upward shower streaked with the white tracers of the smaller and faster .303 Lewis guns.

Voices bawled obscenities. Shell cases by the dozen clattered and rolled on the iron deck. One voice yelled 'Fire at the flares, Cooney! Get the flares, man!'

The planes were invisible, but their screaming engines chilled the blood, and Rose stared at the sea and then at the sweating, hooded men who were lit for an instant by the brilliant flash of the after 4-inch, whose shrapnel-filled shell joined the others behind the flares to explode un-identified in the dull CRUMP! CRUMP! CRUMP! of a dozen others: then all the noise seemed to vanish again in the rush and whistle of more armour-piercing bombs; and when the foul fumes and sweating men were again lit by the flash of the 4-inch it was as if the guns' crews had been turned to stone, had lost their voices – except for one unknown warrior whose hushed words spoke for all in the second after a tongue of crimson flame seared sky-ward from a sister destroyer.

'Jesus wept!' the voice said.

It was Hell on Earth, of man's own mak-ing, and as Rose grabbed blindly at the bridge ladder he reflected bitterly that, in nearly two thousand years, man had learned nothing, and Jesus probably would, again.

But Dunbar was calm, composed, half-bent over the voicepipe at the front of the bridge passing helm orders to the Cox-swain, now at his action station on the wheel. 'Keep her on oh-four-oh, Chief... Hullo, Pilot. Got lost? That was Captain "D" who got it. Keep an eye on him, will you... Watch her head, Chief...'

Rose, who was also Signals Officer, noted the mild rebuke, extracted his instructions from the stream going down the voicepipes, and was turning aft when he heard and then saw the enemy.

It was coming in – unlike the Stukas which dived vertically – at a shallow angle right under a chandelier, and he recognised it even before the lookouts on either side of the bridge screamed in chorus: 'Ju88 at Green two-oh! Attacking! Attacking!'

Orange and white tracer swept across the sky as *Wildcat's* gunners and the gunners on three other boats saw it at the same time and brought it into their sights without taking their fingers from the triggers: but they were too late and the Navigator actually saw the bombs. Five. Five dark, deadly eggs, glinting in the flares' light, separated from the under-carriage of the twin-engined Junkers in the same moment that the German nose-gunner opened up on *Wildcat's* bridge and upper-works with his twin machine-guns.

Everyone on the bridge ducked for cover – except Edward Dunbar, who remained exactly where he was.

Rose had an irresistible urge to leap forward and grab him, for there seemed nothing to be gained by a second or two of fatal bravery; but time beat the urge, and he cried out in lieu– 'Look out, sir! Look out!'

The bombs were plain and ordinary, not 'screamers' like the Stukas used. They swept over the bridge with a noise like escaping steam. One nicked the foremast, left it five degrees off true, while one passed so close that the wind of its passage gusted coldly in their sweating faces. All five crunched in the sea. The plane was on fire. But the bullets: they were everywhere.

Dunbar was going to die. Rose knew it. As senior officer on the bridge at that moment he was even getting ready to spring forward and take command as the well of the bridge filled with whining, bounding projectiles, visible by their flame tracer. Nothing unshielded could live, and even the shielded died by ricochet; like Leading Signalman Brown who pitched face-down, soundless, motionless. One of the lookouts, kneeling for protection, sprang hideously into the air, crashed against the metal of the bridge chart-table and fell grotesquely twisted to the deck: it was muscular spasm, for he had died instantly, unlike Able Seaman Crowther who writhed in agony, hit in the thigh, groin and stomach.

A numbness of the cheek and arm was the only physical sensation Rose experienced; and then it was all over, the enemy plane blazing on the water. Five seconds, perhaps seven. But that was all.

And Dunbar was still there, half-bent above the voicepipe. 'Keep her steady on three-five-four, Coxswain. Yes, a Ju88 just straffed us. Some casualties, I'm afraid...You there, Damage Control? Let me have your report as soon as possible, please!... Hullo, Pilot, bin hiding? The Luftwaffe's getting

31

cheeky... Sick Bay! We have wounded up here.'

'And dead,' Rose butted in.

The tremor in his voice brought a glance from the Captain.

'You're bleeding, Pilot.'

'I was bleeding frightened,' retorted Rose, and gave Edward an up-and-down scrutiny. 'You're not – wounded?'

'Me, I'm immortal. Or didn't you know, Pilot?' The voice was a little tired and a little dry.

The gunfire died away as the last flare hit the water and fizzled out, but the deep distant thunder of guns came again from the Cretan beaches to port, and now to starboard where another 'cavern', faint on the horizon like a remote galaxy, was seen by the E.R.A. in charge of Damage Control.

'That's the stuff,' he said, stepping aside while two Sick Berth Attendants removed the dead. 'They've found the Battle Fleet, sir. About time that shower had a taste of this.' It was unjust.

'Captain "D" is calling you, sir,' shouted the relief lookout. 'There he is, sir.'

'Signalman!' But Brown, Rose remembered, had read his last signal in this life. He turned his binoculars on the tiny blue flashing light out on the beam, read it aloud to Dunbar. 'From Captain "D", sir. He says: "Have sustained superficial damage and some casualties. Have you been hit? Please reciprocate.'''

A relief signalman sent Dunbar's reply while the Navigator allowed his wounds to be dressed. The Sick Berth Attendant had obviously taken an honours degree in cruelty and Cynic philosophy. 'If you put a stick through the hole and turn it daily, sir, it'll heal up round the stick. Then you'll have the hole to prove you were wounded...?'

'I think not.' Rose was still fighting back nausea when, halfway up the bridge ladder, the radio operator collided with the damaged arm.

'Captain wants you on the bridge immediately, sir. A signal from Naval Intelligence, Alexandria. Most Secret.'

It was. Most. And read:

From D.N.I., Alexandria, to Officer Commanding *Wildcat,* repeated Admiralty, repeated C-in-C Mediterranean Fleet. T.O.D. 22.05 hours, 3/6/41. With immediate effect. Transfer all if any sick, dead or wounded personnel to flotilla leader. *Wildcat* to disengage from screening Battle Fleet and proceed with utmost dispatch to position 36°N by 22°E. Arrival to be timed at precisely 03.00 hours on 4/6/41. Stop engines and await contact. In event of enemy activity no action will be taken – repeat no action will be taken – unless enemy opens fire first. The attention of

Lieutenant Rose is drawn to the position and time of rendezvous. The insect will not sting.

Commander Dunbar looked closely at his Navigator, who in turn looked closely at his puzzled Captain. Then they both returned their eyes to the signal that lay under the hooded light on the bridge chart-table.

Edward said: 'And what does the position and time of rendezvous mean to you, eh?'

'I'm just a professor of languages, and that only needs an ear for music, sir. But it looks very much like a double code to fool any of our own ships who read it.'

Edward sighed, repaired to the voicepipe. 'What does 36 North by 22 East at 3 a.m. mean to you, Coxswain?'

'A blind date with a very, very fast blonde, sir...?' suggested the voicepipe tentatively.

Oh, but it were...

It was an Able Seaman, one of the lookouts, who came forward.

'Excuse me, sir, but it's the exact time an' position we captured the Italian destroyer back in March.'

'*Scorpio!*' Dunbar punched his open palm. 'Well, I'm damned! They recaptured her!'

'Or she didn't *escape* in the first place...?' asked the voicepipe.

The Chatham Rats, unlike their officers and bollards, were not solid from the deck up.

3

Because the wind had strengthened and *Wildcat* was travelling north-west at maximum speed, she seemed to tear through the night, her dimly visible fo'c's'le rising and falling as she covered the nautical miles in long bounds, like a greyhound in slow motion: each dip of the sharp, flared bow cut deep into the swell, lifting and turning the dark sea whitely to port and starboard, where it rolled endlessly away into invisibility.

Edward held his wrist in front of his face for some seconds, and for the umpteenth time. 'Ten to three,' he muttered, raising then the binoculars which hung on a thong round his neck. 'Can't see a damned thing... Anyone see anything?'

None of the lookouts had, and Rose checked the windy darkness for his own satisfaction. It was in the days before Radar, and seeing was believing, and perhaps to die.

The Captain went aft.

The bo'sun's pipe shrilled.

'D'you hear there! This is the Captain speaking. The ship is approaching the point of rendezvous. We are now fifty miles south-west of Matapan and deep within enemy waters. When we heave to, there is to be no noise whatever. Stand by your weapons and remain silent and alert. I don't know what is happening any more than you, but I don't intend to take any chances. If there's an opportunity, I'll transfer the mail. Last letters to Lieutenant Rose. Good luck.'

When Dunbar's voice ceased, the loud speaker remained on, making an exciting noise like frying bacon. Morgan's Kentish accent said, 'Right, then, sir,' in the background and then boomed in the night. 'Close all watertight doors and hatches! Hands will go to Action Stations in five minutes time. Mail will close in two minutes time. If I catch anyone smoking on the upper deck, I'll kick his fanny from here to breakfast-time. Got it? Right, then.'

The intrepid Coxswain was a little nervous, and Rose was glad; so was he.

At first he thought it was Dunbar who grew out of the darkness. But a voice said: 'Lieutenant Rose, sir?'

'Here.'

'A letter, sir.' The rating, whoever he was, stuffed it into the Navigator's hand and vanished. Stoker Petty Officer Moy announced himself and brought three others.

One of the most hateful, thankless and sordid tasks was censoring letters. Rose made a point of skimming through them, ignoring their sense and looking only for any contravention of the strict conditions of secrecy concerning the ship's location, et cetera. This he did now under the hooded light on the chart-table; or this he did with three. But when he reached the end of the fourth he read it again, slowly.

Like the others, it bore the ship's official address: H.M.S. *Wildcat,* c/o G.P.O. London.

My dear, darling Ann,

As usual I cannot tell you where we are or what we are doing. But even if I could it would not make any difference, because nothing seems real any more except you. It is like being in Hell and writing to an angel in Heaven. I know that sounds silly but it's true. Up till tonight I thought I would never see you again, but the Captain spoke to me and said he would try and send me home when we get back to our base. Isn't that nice of him? I'm so excited I couldn't sleep, although we've just had four hours rest. I had a shower and darned my socks and wrote to you instead.

I want you to know, darling, that you are the only person in the world who would make me leave *Wildcat,* because she is a lucky and happy ship for reasons I cannot tell you yet.

When I get home we will have our honey-moon as we planned. I try to understand why you cried and were afraid to make love to me before we were married because of your religion, but I would have died rather than make you sin and be unhappy. So it has been worth waiting, and now I know we will be together soon.

I have asked the Captain if I can come back after my course is finished and he said yes. Everyone tries to get back if they can, including the officers.

I do love you with all my heart and soul and I hate the war. We know London is being bombed and I worry all the time. God bless you and keep you safe for me. See you soon.

All my love, darling,
(Signed) Peter.
P.S. XXXXXXX

Lieutenant Rose turned over the blue air mail sheet. It was addressed to a Mrs Ann Freer, in London.

Not a passionate letter – but who could write a love letter knowing that a stoutish, flushed, balding, half-baked schoolmaster was going to read it?

Conscious of a movement behind, he turned. It was York. 'Haven't you finished the pornography yet?' He brought his fingers down sharply on the chart-table. 'Seal 'em up and forget 'em. If war's a tragedy, life's a disaster. These bloody letters broke my heart a long time ago. Now, come on, Professor, Skipper's waiting. We're nearly there.'

True or false, it was difficult to imagine anything other than a hammer and chisel making any impression whatever on the heart of Lieutenant-Commander York. An Englishman with a physique like a Scottish Highland Games athlete, he had grey, hazel-flecked eyes that could be very cold and very stern, a brown beard that obscured two-thirds of his face like a huge, magnificently-groomed, fur sporran; it had been grown to make a young face look older, but the war and the sun had already nullified its original purpose. His laugh, *when* he laughed, was as deep as it was infectious, but mostly his humour was as dry as the desert sands, and like the desert sands, people hesitated to cross him. He could mix his drinks, drink buckets. He was a man's man, enigmatic in matters affecting women, politics, the Arts, and Edward Dunbar. As well as being First Lieutenant and 'housekeeper', he was also Gunnery Officer, second to none in this fine art of remote-controlled killing. A disciplinarian – 'Swift' as the Navy termed it – he trained the guns' crews daily, even in action, and to perfection. His slogan: 'If it doesn't answer in the King's English, shoot it?' This, it was said, applied to the Scots, Welsh, Irish, Americans and Australians. But once he had said, 'We stay alive by efficiency and not by luck. We are a happy ship because we know we have that ability to stay alive,' and perhaps these words explained *Wildcat's* magnetism ... and then again, perhaps only in part.

The Navigator dropped Able Seaman Freer's letter into the post-bag as the loud speakers piped the hands to Action Stations. He checked their position carefully and reported to Dunbar who ordered a reduction of speed.

Wildcat wallowed exactly where the 36th Parallel is intersected by 22° of longitude east of the Greenwich meridian when the engines finally stopped and she lost way.

Asdic was clear, the loud speakers switched off, and the only sounds in the breezy darkness were the small moan of the wind in the signal halyards, the mutter of funnel exhausts, the rasp and burble of the cruel sea.

Their eyes searched and saw nothing. Their ears strained but heard no foreign sound. Half an hour passed. And sweat trickled unnoticed. Rose shivered; some clumsy fool had walked over his grave.

'SIR!' came the big whisper from a lookout. 'There's something right astern, sir.'

'Report properly!' York snapped.

'An object on Green one-seven-five, sir,' returned the lookout. 'Looks like a ship, sir.'

'Very good.' Dunbar crossed to the starboard side aft.

She could have been *Wildcat's* sister, had she not been a little larger, a little more streamlined. Her barely-visible raked silhouette stood above a white bow-wave.

'*Scorpio!*' Dunbar spat the word. 'Stand to! Stand to!' He swung on the Signalman. 'Challenge!'

As York bawled 'Stand by to open fire!' into the telephone, two white lights and one red, vertically displayed, lit up *Wildcat's* yard. They were duplicated almost instantly by the Italian destroyer that passed fast and close: so close that Rose took an involuntary pace to the rear.

In darkness, such an approach was irresponsible and highly dangerous.

York put everyone's resentment into words.

'Bloody idiot. Is he mad? I'll bet the flaming shortsighted ignoramus didn't even see us!'

'And he's doing every bit of forty knots,' Rose estimated angrily as *Wildcat* heaved drunkenly in the other destroyer's wake. 'God Almighty, if he'd hit us...' The answer to that one was superfluous.

'Signalman!'

A blue signal light winked far out in the night from the direction *Scorpio* had disappeared– '"Most terribly sorry we are late. Forgive my wash. Got chased by the Battle

41

Fleet. Ours! Will circle and approach you on port quarter," the Signalman read slowly. "'Stream fenders and prepare gangway. Will use own ropes. Fall out Action Stations and instruct your officers and men to stow all personal gear in their lockers and cabins. Officers and men should retain one towel. One change of underclothes. Toilet gear. Nothing else. Prepare to abandon ship. You have ten minutes. Please acknowledge.'"

'He *is* mad!' gasped the First Lieutenant.

'We'll damn' soon find out,' Edward vowed, and poked the Signalman. 'Make: Who the hell are you?'

'With or without the swear word, sir?'

'*With!*'

'Aye, aye, sir.' The Signalman steadied the Aldis lamp on the elbow of his free arm, and flashed.

The blue light flashed back.

The Signalman cleared his throat ominously. 'He says, sir: "Vice-Admiral Sir William Dormain. And who the hell do you think you are. Query."'

Edward Dunbar may have been immortal, but he wasn't infallible.

It was the second time in five hours *Wildcat* had been married at sea in danger and darkness, and the Navigator didn't like it one little bit. He reached Dunbar's side, amidships, where in front of them a small gangway creaked and groaned in its task of

42

bridging the gap between two wildly un-stable destroyers.

Behind them ranged along the deck, almost unseen in blue overalls, were *Wild-cat's* crew – some of whom had, back in March, taken *Scorpio* to Alexandria – each with a white rolled-up towel under his arm.

Morgan prowled, inspecting his charged. 'All got your frillies, my beauties? That's the spirit, then... No, Cooney, we're not going to scuttle her... And what have you got there, Freer, eh? Who the blazes told you to take an attaché case, then? Open it up! That's a good lad... Two pairs of pants. Three vests. *Six* bars of Fry's Cream. A pretty case for your toilet gear. A book. No, two books. Three pairs of nylons... What d'you think *you* are, then – a travelling sales-man?'

'N-no, sir – I mean Chief.'

'That'll be enough, Coxswain!' Dunbar called sharply. 'Tell him to stow it away and get back here fast.'

'Aye, aye, sir.' There was no resentment in the Chief's voice. He muttered instructions to Freer, whose feet pattered forward. Then Morgan passed aft, making noises like, 'Nylons. What next?'

A pair of shapely legs to fit them to? Ah, me... Really, Rose, old chap, you are a sexy old devil.

'What are *you* muttering about, Pilot?'

43

'It must be the funnel exhausts, sir. Me, I was just drooling.'

Heavy footfalls and York arrived breathless. 'Here he comes,' he warned. 'With a bit of luck he'll fall off the gangway.'

'Perhaps, er, Leading Seaman Yates...?' It was just one of Rose's more malicious thoughts ... and they were directed at the tall, all-white figure in sleeveless shirt, shorts, stockings and shoes who, followed by an all-dark figure with a pronounced limp, came striding along *Scorpio's* starboard side and turned across that small gangway, rigid fingers already at its cap's peak in salute to *Wildcat's* invisible quarterdeck – a tribute to Nelson's namesake from where they cut down, searched and found Dunbar's unfriendly hand.

'Hullo, Dunbar. I'm Dorman. Naval Intelligence, London. Get your crew on board *Scorpio* as fast as you can, please. Key officers and ratings first. Tell them to replace my men. We're taking over *Wildcat*.'

'And where exactly are you taking *Wildcat?*' Edward asked coldly – he hadn't even said 'How do you do' yet!

Against the lighter darkness of the sky Sir William's profile exhibited an aggressive nose like a kestrel's beak, and a nautical stoop from years of bending into the bottom drawer of his Whitehall desk for the bottle and glass.

'Your First Lieutenant will take her to Port Said and through the Canal,' he replied curtly. 'His instructions will be to remain at sea, unseen and unheard, for two weeks. Is that adequate?'

'And *Scorpio?*' York's voice had that quality of incredulity of a man who had just been stabbed in the back.

'That,' snapped Dorman, 'is hardly your concern, Lieutenant-Commander.' He half turned and indicated the all-dark figure behind. 'This is Major Troy. An expert in methods of sabotage. He will be going with you, Dunbar. But come, we will talk in your cabin.'

'Rose can take her!' York blurted angrily. 'Rose – the Navigator, here – he can take *Wildcat*. He knows the ropes.'

'Rose knows damn all,' Rose growled.

'Rose won't!' snorted Dorman. 'Rose happens to be vital to this whole operation.'

'*Me!*'

'You!'

But York wasn't finished. 'Then Lieutenant Gilcrest,' he persisted. 'He's in line for promotion, sir. He'll take *Wildcat* and be glad to.'

Everyone hated Gilcrest, an ambitious snob and 'a bit of a creeper'.

'No. And that is final.' Sir William turned away with Dunbar and Troy. For one awful moment Rose thought York was going to

45

detain him by force; but no, and the trio went off at the trot.

'Desk-bound bastard!' York snarled. 'Armchair bloody sailors!'

He slammed his fist into the metalwork.

'Well, at least you'll be out of the war for a bit,' Rose said in sympathy – and regretted it.

'What the hell do you know about it, you fat little intellectual! We don't need bloody school teachers fighting the war for us.' He raised a quivering arm at the ratings filing across the gangway. 'I've wet-nursed those kids. I've kicked their arses round this deck until their dim brains do what they have to do without thinking *how* to do it. That's the way to keep 'em alive. They're the best guns' crews in the Med. But what would you know about that? Nothing!' He walked a few paces away, paused, then looked back. 'We're a team, Professor. Me and them. Break up that team – *and you are dead!*'

Rose wasn't conscious of Morgan's near presence until the gruff voice spoke close to his ear. 'He's right, sir. And worse – we're boarding a strange ship with strange guns.'

'I think our First Lieutenant is in love with a bunch of scruffy kids, Coxswain. Wouldn't have thought he was the sentimental type, though.'

'Oh, he is, sor. Under all that hair he's as soft as a marshmallow. Brave, too. Er, not

46

like Lieutenant Gilcrest, sir.' Somehow there was deep meaning in those last words.

When the transfer was completed, Rose made his way aft, down the companionway, and ambled towards the cabin flats.

The limping character who approached from the direction of the Captain's cabin was Major Troy. And it was nice to meet someone whose eyes were on the same level, even if he was thinner, his hair curly, and his face tanned.

'Hullo,' he said. 'Frightfully sorry about all the mystery – but you'll see the point soon.'

'I fear,' Rose smiled bleakly. 'Not Cambridge, perhaps?'

'Oxford, sorry.' Barbarians that lot.

It appeared that Troy had left Dunbar's door off the lock, for it was slightly ajar. Eavesdropping wasn't one of Rose's many vices ... but it was Dunbar's raised in anger and saying terrible things enough to send any schoolmaster white-haired.

'A glider bomb. Somewhere between Bologna and Trieste. But you don't know exactly where. We've got to find it, you say. A handful of miles from the very heart of the Third Reich! Have you any idea what the Gestapo will do to us if they catch us on an Italian ship, masquerading in Italian uniforms? Spies and saboteurs get shot, you know – or hasn't London wakened up to the fact that this is a rough war!' If Dunbar was shy with strangers, anger had certainly banished his inhibitions.

'If the worst happens, you have the cyanide tablets,' the Admiral pointed out.

'Well, that's terribly decent of you, sir. I almost forgot.' Sarcasm of that order took guts.

'I'm not going to argue, Dunbar. I went to a lot of trouble to engineer *Scorpio's* escape. Not one other man knows it was faked, except the Prime Minister and the C-in-C, and he damn' near sunk us on the way here rather than give the game away. I worked on Guiseppe Durand day and night for three days before I could convince him Italy couldn't win the war–'

'And you think you won him over! A man with two brothers fighting in the Ariete Division! A man with a record for courage and daring and patriotism! My respect for British Intelligence is ebbing fast.'

'I don't like your attitude at all, Dunbar.' Dorman was desperately hanging on to his temper and dignity.

'I don't particularly like asking my men to commit suicide. And I know damned well you are removing York from under my command deliberately.'

A great big breath, and Dorman said, 'Now, look here, Dunbar, I *know* York's reputation. He's trigger-happy. One stupid shot would ruin this operation *and* lessen

48

your chances of survival. Oh, I didn't expect you to be reasonable; few men of your calibre would be; and that's why I'm prepared to disregard your confounded insolence. However, I am very well informed. I know about that disgusting party at Liverpool when you turned up after being posted dead. I've heard the rumours, too. Your fraternising with the ratings meets with my strong disapproval ... and Their Lordships'.'

The sting was in the tail, typically.

'I'm devastated.' That was all Dunbar said.

'However,' Dorman's voice went on coldly, 'you were picked for three reasons, none of them petty. The first – and again in spite of your damned impertinence – you happen to be the best man. We were also impressed by the way you handled *Scorpio* at Matapan. The third is pure chance: you happen to have a Navigator who speaks fluent Italian and German, even if he is a fat pompous ass.'

Dearie me, the old adage was painfully true.

'As a matter of fact, he happens to be a charming and talented man,' Dunbar countered icily – bless him.

It was time to knock.

'Come in!'

Dunbar and the Admiral were standing, wisely, with a mahogany table between them.

'Yes, Pilot?' Dunbar smiled through his obvious anxiety.

'The transfer of the crews has been completed, sir!' Rose reported to his Captain, with a new, sudden affection.

'They took their time about it,' Dorman chipped in. 'You'll kindly tell Lieutenant-Commander York to man *Wildcat's* bridge. I will slip in two minutes.'

On your face, I hope, Rose nodded silently, and retired on Dunbar's carefully concealed wink.

He was half out of the door when Dunbar's voice said, 'Sir, I appeal to you to let York stay. Defensively speaking, he *is* vital...'

Skirted by mahogany doors with partly slotted fronts and brass knobs, Rose trudged along the cabin flat, pensively, until, by an Act of God, a fresh-faced Lieutenant burst from nowhere and collided with him, head-on. This sudden and painful marriage gave birth to two of the Navigator's more spiteful thoughts: up on *Wildcat's* bridge it would be pitch dark ... and the Admiral's crew wouldn't know Adam from Eve.

But plan as one may, some damned thing always went awry; in this case it was that small gangway.

After a verbal and physical marathon, Rose hared across it and vanished into the Italian's superstructure, to emerge breathless, and two pounds lighter, at the rear of *Scorpio's* bridge, in time to catch a glimpse of Sir William and Edward arrive amidships at the precise moment Lieutenant Gilcrest, voice filled with a new confidence by the Admiral's fictitious promise of immediate promotion and a decoration, screamed out from *Wildcat's* bridge on schedule. 'Let go-o-o for'd! Let go-o-o aft!' When the wire ropes splashed into the sea from bow and stern, he ordered, 'Slow ahead, both engines!' This last order was stimulated by Rose's cry that the gangway was in, which it wasn't, because the Coxswain, the idiot, failed to coax his Captain across.

Wildcat's propellers churned noisily. She moved forward slowly. The small gangway, alone bridging the gap between the two vessels and now bearing Edward's fleeing figure, changed direction, taking on a new and dangerous angle between the British and Italian stanchions to which, alas, it was still securely tied.

The night was filled with cursing, grinding, tearing, snapping, and finally a loud splash.

A panicky voice yelled, 'Where's Nelson?' and another from the moving *Wildcat,* answered, 'Here. Catch!'

A black ball of fur soared across ten feet of sea. A rating yelped in agony in discovering it secreted no less than twenty razor blades.

'Full ahead! Port thirty!' and *Scorpio* was under way, turning.

'What the hell do you think you're playing at, Gilcrest!' Dunbar had arrived, breathless, livid, still partly blind after the cabin lights. 'York must be mad! He damn near killed me! What do you mean by getting under way!' Nowhere near finished, the verbal blast ended there. Edward's eyes were working again.

'*York!*' he exclaimed.

'Oh, sir, there's been a terrible, terrible mistake,' the First Lieutenant wailed. 'It – it was so dark, and, well, these destroyer bridges look so much alike.'

'You lying basket!' Dunbar's roving eye found the guilty party. 'You just *have* to be at the bottom of this!'

'I – I just don't know what came over me,' Rose stammered. 'It was – impulse. Like Yates and the taxi man.'

'Self-preservation, you mean. And I'll wager the Coxswain had no small hand in it, either. When the Admiral finds out he'll have you all drawn and quartered.'

'Sir, the Admiral *has* found out.' This from York, cheerfully.

That little blue light from across the sea was close to apoplexy. '"Heave to instantly! Am coming alongside!"'

'Dear God, there just has to be a snappy answer to that one…?' Edward sighed, looking around hopefully.

To the Signalman, York said: 'Oh, blow him. Make: Sorry, strange ship. Cannot find brakes.'

The Aldis lamp flickered bluely.

'A feeble retort,' lamented Edward, and begged the engine-room for more speed.

'You should 'ave told 'im t' get twisted,' advised a lookout with commendable loyalty.

'Esprit de l'escalier,' breathed the Professor sadly.

But smart-Alec Rose hadn't given a thought to Able Seaman Freer, and that would have been so very, very easy.

In appearance the Captain's cabin was little different from the one Dunbar had used on *Wildcat,* though a little larger, and more luxurious because its owner had an artistic temperament. Blue curtains covered the sealed portholes. A pale-blue fitted carpet showed off the brown polished woodwork of tables – there were two – chairs, bunk and wardrobe. On the centre table sat a green potted plant with yellow flowers; and on the bunk half-covered by a white sheet and blue silk coverlet, face upward and snoring heartily, the top half of his body clad in pillar-box red pyjamas, lay Captain Guiseppe Durand. He might have been an opera singer, for he was well built, if a little flabby, pale of skin, dark round the square chin which sagged in sleep, dragging open the red-lipped mouth; but he wasn't unhandsome, in an anaemic, hairy, heavy sort of way.

Lieutenant Rose approached cautiously, shook the 'enemy' none too gently by the shoulder. 'Hey! Captain Durand, sir!' Edward had said to treat him with the respect befitting his rank. 'Hey! Captain Durand! I have a message from Commander Dunbar...'

The Italian snorted, yawned, and said sleepily in his native tongue: 'Go away, Sasso! Or have you come to tell me the British dogs have been swept from Italian seas, eh?' The eyes then closed and the mouth wandered open. But it was the first indication of Guiseppe's true feelings.

'No, my Captain, but I have come to tell you that Mussolini has just assassinated Hitler and taken over the Third Reich,' Rose retaliated icily in like language.

The mouth snapped shut. Durand's small eyes focused on the Navigator's face. They were greenish-blue, off guard in the hazy moment of awakening, and in them, for but a fraction of a second, there was hate, followed instantly by a flash of anger when Rose announced: 'Commander Dunbar wants you to dress. You will be required on the bridge later.'

Contrary to instructions, the Navigator then walked to the chair where the Italian's uniform was draped, lifted the lot, walked back to the bunk, held the armful two feet above it, then dropped it on the puffy face. 'Your clothes, sir.'

The door slammed beautifully, too.

Below *Scorpio's* open bridge was the enclosed wheelhouse, a small place, ill-lit, always gloomy because the portholes were kept shut. It contained a spoked helm wheel and two slim brass pillars that were engine-room telegraphs. Usually, it was manned by three seamen with no particular qualifications, except in action when the Coxswain took over the helm, his eyes on a compass card, his mouth in front of the voicepipe that curved up through the roof and finished up in the region of Edward Dunbar's navel. At the helmsman's back, a door led across a dark and narrow passage into the chartroom, which also served as the Captain's sea cabin. It was here, in this small metal room, with a few Italian scenic pictures on the enamelled walls, an untidy bunk and scattered clothes, shelves of Italian nautical books – and some pornography – and a small central chart-table, that Major Troy briefed the senior officers and key ratings.

War at sea was a strange mixture of excitement, tragedy, fear and fun; but, at some times, there was a fifth ingredient called lunacy. This was one of those times.

Under the brown curly hair, Troy had sharp, hard features, not unpleasant because the steady eyes smiled along with his face. About him there was a subtle aura of toughness, but also a nonchalant mode of address more common to the R.A.F. than the Army, like, 'Right, chaps', or, 'Well, it's like this, old sport'. In fact, taken together, these two apparently conflicting characteristics marked him as a gentlemanly ruffian. As he talked, he leaned most of the time on the table, the upper half of his slight body pillared by a pair of wiry sunburnt arms in rolled khaki sleeves, eyes either on the papers, sketches and maps, or on the apprehensive faces that ringed him in a semi-circle.

He was humorous without being flippant and everyone took to him at once. He was also cogent. Nor did he mince words.

He had, he said, been in Yugoslavia organising food, arms and ammunition supplies for newly-formed groups of partisans. He had met their leaders. The Gestapo had put a price on his head. Prior to being 'pulled out' by a British submarine, he had been trapped in a room in Trieste.

Troy went on to tell of the car accident, of his finding the bomb. After that he had kept the rendezvous with the submarine and returned to Egypt. With him, he brought gloom and despair, he said, in the fearful knowledge of what that simple and devilish weapon could do to allied shipping.

'It is dropped from a parent plane,' he said grimly. 'It has no propulsion of its own. It's just a bomb with wings that can be glided down on to its target by radio. Our calculations show that it would hardly ever miss – even against fast ships.'

How could it be destroyed?

It couldn't. That was the even more fearful answer. It couldn't be destroyed. 'You can't,' Troy said, 'destroy an idea. But you can set the clock back a bit. A year. Perhaps two. We need time. That is what all this is about. Your lives in exchange for two years of time.'

A pin dropping would have made more noise than a two-ton girder when the Major said that.

Unhampered by argument, Troy picked up a signal and handed it round. It was the explanatory signal from the Admiral-in-Charge, Destroyer Flotillas, Napoli, to Captain Durand, outlining *Scorpio's* June trials with the bomb.

'That,' he smiled, 'is the little piece of paper that has brought us together. You captured it when you captured *Scorpio*. Without it, all this wouldn't have happened.' He laid it on the table where ten pairs of eyes stared at it with such venom that it might well have burst into flames.

There were so many unknown factors in the whole giddy idea – not least the treacherous Guiseppe whose presence was vital to fool the enemy at close range – that it seemed to York, who had just won a prize for sickly smiles, incredible that success could be achieved, and he said so; but added: 'Mind you, my lads could destroy the airfield installations, the prototype bombs, and the technicians whose brains thought up this little toy. But how do we find the airstrip?'

One ray of hope came in Troy's admission that the Luftwaffe had probably moved their experimental base after they'd found the bodies he'd left lying around. His friends, the partisans, had reported unusual activity in the Dalmatian Islands, near Zadar, on the Yugoslavian coast. He was also certain that *if* they fooled the enemy, they would probably get a clue to where the plane was based anyway. *If* they fooled the enemy, and the enemy was the Gestapo, and they were not fools. 'They'll be suspicious of *Scorpio's* escape from Alexandria,' he warned. 'They'll be along at any minute to have a close look at us. As the only man who can speak Italian and German, Lieutenant Rose is our best hope of success. I will act as security officer. Rose will guard the words. He will also send a signal to Mussolini. He will also be our ventriloquist. Captain Guiseppe Durand, with a gun in his back, will be our puppet.'

Finally Troy said: 'The enemy's original intention was obviously to use *Scorpio* to tow a spray target at high speed, at which to aim their bomb. When *Scorpio* was captured, they probably detailed another ship to take her place. Our job is to coax them into changing their minds yet again and to use Guiseppe. Not so difficult. They need him...' He drifted into silence then, picked up another signal. 'The first move in this game was to engineer *Scorpio's* escape. The third one is to fool the enemy under close observation. The fourth is to persuade Mussolini and Hitler to use Guiseppe. To turn *Scorpio* north to the Adriatic Sea.'

'And the second?' Edward asked intuitively.

'This was the second,' Troy admitted, handing the paper out to the waiting hands. 'That signal made you all a very intimate part of this operation many hours ago. It was sent in order to convince the enemy *Scorpio's* escape was genuine. Captain Durand sent it with pleasure. It gives you some idea how important all this is. Read it.'

The signal of betrayal was dated the previous evening and read: 'From Captain Durand to Admiral-in-Charge, Destroyer Flotillas, Napoli, for urgent transmission to

Luftwaffe Command. Have sighted British Battle Fleet and four destroyer flotillas. Position: 34°N by 25° 15′E. Steering north by east off Cretan beaches. Enemy speed at 20.30 hours: 20 knots.'

4

No one on board stopped running during that last hour before dawn, except for two breathless minutes in order to listen to Dunbar outline the mission, and that consisted of what John Rose already knew; nothing more.

Troy took charge of security, seeing to the urgent removal of all *visible* traces of each man's British identity. Clothes worn for the transfer of ships, mostly overalls, were put in sacks, weighted with cable links, then dropped over the side. Everyone dressed in the Italian uniforms taken from *Scorpio's* former crew, who were now, according to Troy, safely imprisoned on a British liner east of Suez.

What daylight would bring, no one knew. What the future held, no one knew either. It was a game of chance played with some very dubious cards. A few minutes was all it had taken to turn friend into foe, enemy into friend, to swop sides in the most devastating war in history; but, all told, they had no friends at all ... and each vibrant revolution of *Scorpio's* powerful screws thrust them deeper and deeper into the heart of the Axis empire.

The immediate danger was unfamiliarity – not only with the Italian's weapons, but their nautical way of life as well. These two facts made the First Lieutenant sweat physically during that last hour. On arrival on the bridge he was sour: 'Most of the equipment is bloody inferior to start with. Some uniforms are two sizes too big. Anyone with half an eye can see we're a bunch of Chatham Rats. And as for you, Professor, let me tell you I'd have been heading happily for the Red Sea now if you hadn't poked your nose into what doesn't concern you!'

After this monstrous display of ingratitude he glared at Edward. 'And why, may I ask, are we heading due west, instead of north?'

'Because we're doing exactly what Guiseppe Durand would do *first,* after escaping from Alexandria and foxing the invincible British,' Dunbar explained dryly. 'We're going home. To Naples. Via the Straits of Messina.'

'But I bloody well don't want to go home. To Naples. Via the Strai-' He broke off there and narrowed his eyes. 'What do you mean – *first!*'

Edward withdrew a folded paper from the breast pocket of his fine white silk Italian shirt. 'Read it before Rose translates it into the language of Rome.'

The First Lieutenant opened it up cautiously.

It read:

My Prime Minister and Illustrious Leader. It is with humility that I am able to report that our magnificent destroyer *Scorpio* has outwitted the British and is proceeding with all speed to home waters. Anticipating your extreme pleasure at this news I would only ask the favour of your consideration to allowing me the privilege of altering course north for the Adriatic Sea to fulfil the mission communicated in March and for which I am most suited. As my only desire is to serve my country and gain no personal prestige from the events which have occurred, your agreement in this matter would be reward enough and in keeping with our proud naval traditions.

Simon York carefully folded the document, looked up, first at the Navigator, then at Edward.

'What a load of old flannel,' he said. And it was.

But that signal was Troy's fourth and vital move.

At 05.40 hours Rose had it transmitted. It was addressed to Il Duce, by way of the Admiral-in-Charge, Destroyer Flotillas, Napoli, with a courtesy copy instructed for the Royal House of Savoy; this later addition being advised by Guiseppe, and his first – possibly treacherous – act. But he threw his hands into the air and cried. 'So you do notta trust me. But I say again: in the circumstances it is in accordance with protocol. If it had been omitted, they would instantly suspect you.'

It worked both ways; no way of telling which. No point in making threats. Yet. For if *Scorpio* sank, Guiseppe was sunk. It was a question of how brave was Guiseppe?

'Now we wait and we pray,' said Major Troy, tucking a Luger pistol inside his shirt and down into the waist-band of his trousers. 'My favourite weapon. Doesn't kick-up like the Colt. One trouble, though: the bullet tends to go straight through the body, sometimes missing the vital organs. Back of the head's the only sure place.'

Well, it didn't sound like a threat; though Guiseppe *was* present, and Troy's eyes weren't smiling.

That incredibly slow dawn on June 4 took one year off Rose's life. Nothing happened.

Daylight came, and with it a blue sky and a bright sun. *Scorpio* held her course, a few points north of west. But the Straits of Messina were still three hundred miles ahead.

In order to stall for time, and conserve oil, Dunbar reduced speed to twenty knots. Even so, by noon they were well out into the Ionian Sea, which is that part of the Mediterranean formed by the toe and heel of Italy to the west and north, and Albania and Greece to the north and east. And at noon there was still no reply from Benito Mussolini.

At 12.22, one of the lookouts reported a speck on the horizon. A few seconds later he screamed: 'Aircraft! Bearing Red four-five...!'

The alarm bells shrilled.

'Full ahead, both engines!' It was almost possible to imagine *Scorpio's* stern go down, for the forward surge made the unwary take a slow pace to the rear.

'Stand to! Stand to!' How Rose hated those cries, voiced by the captains of guns.

Metal telephone in one hand, binoculars raised to his eyes with the other, Edward had his face handy above the voicepipes. 'Hold your course, Coxswain! Yes, it looks like more than one plane. Long way off, though... No one to open fire except on my order, Number One. Got that clearly?... Get Captain Durand on the bridge, please!'

He glanced silently round the bridge, faced front again when he saw all was well.

The distant speck divided slowly into six twin-engined bombers. 'Six Ju88s, sir!' They were approaching on *Scorpio's* port bow.

Rose glanced up at the control tower – a grey metal 'mushroom' behind and above the bridge with slots to observe the enemy and direct the fire of the main armament. A Gunner's Mate was up there with three men. So at that moment was Trigger-happy York, greedy eyes visible.

Heavy footsteps announced Guiseppe's arrival, Troy behind, Luger in hand.

The Major was taking no chances.

Dunbar stood to one side so that the Italian could join him. Troy backed into the open front of the bridge chart-table, stood there, invisible from the sky but not from Durand's nervous backward glance.

'Aircraft closing fast, sir!'

Rose sighed, pulled on his anti-flash hood, put on the Italian helmet. It felt like a bucket.

He moved involuntarily closer to Sub-Lieutenant Reece-Davis – generally known as Stubby – a slim blond and a perfect gentleman.

The only ones unprotected were Dunbar, wearing the missing Sasso's commander's uniform shirt with gold, three-bar epaulettes, and Guiseppe, wearing his four-bar epaulettes and braided cap.

Edward was talking casually all the while

to telephone and voicepipes, being his fraternal self. 'Not long now, Coxswain. Yes, they look belligerent, I'm afraid. Too early to tell. But stand by to alter course... All right, everyone. Look natural. Not too much alarm, please. And hold your fire.'

The Ju88s were flying at fifteen hundred feet, growing larger and more sinister when they suddenly altered course and passed to port, moving fast from bow, to beam, to quarter, where they swept round *Scorpio's* stern and flew back along the starboard side.

On Rose's other side the Signalman was standing ready, the lamp resting on his raised elbow, eyes alternating between the Navigator and the planes.

There was an evil quality about those black crosses.

Sweat trickled down the inside of Rose's hood. Something was odd ... but what?

'I've got a funny feeling,' whispered Reece-Davis. 'Notice the direction they've come from?'

'I have.' It was Troy, and the Luger was pointing at the back of Guiseppe's head. 'There are a dozen airfields nearer, but those planes have come from Italy. And they haven't come by chance. Not straight to our position way out here. What do you say, Guiseppe? I bet His Majesty was surprised to get a copy of that signal...?'

The Italian remained silent.

The aircraft were a mile out on the starboard beam, now three thousand feet up.

Then - and Rose bawled 'Look out!' – the nearest broke formation, banked, dived straight for the bridge. The others followed. One after the other.

Screaming engines drowned everything but Dunbar's voice. 'Hold your fire! Hold your fire! Hold your fire!' He just *had* to be immortal to make that decision.

Rose's stomach started to contract.

The planes were ten seconds away. In ten seconds *Scorpio* would be a flaming hulk. That fact was etched on every tense, sweating face; those seen – those unseen, too, because a 20mm cannon opened up amidships in panic. Then another.

Edward went mad.

He bawled up at the control tower. York was nowhere to be seen. In desperation he grabbed Rose's helmet en route to the rear of the bridge where he flung it down at the gunners.

'Cease fire! Cease fire! Cease fire!'

At the same time Guiseppe flung himself at the side of the bridge and waved arms and cap frantically at the attacking 88s, yelling as he did so in incomprehensible Italian.

The noise was deafening. The planes were not quite one behind the other but had strung out, each selecting one sixth of

Scorpio's length. Thirty bombs. Even if half hit it would blow her up.

Rose's eyes were on the belly of the leading plane – on the Perspex dome where the crouching front gunner was plainly visible – on Troy who, absurdly, turned the Luger towards the enemy – and on the burst of orange tracer climbing like a string of fireflies from *Scorpio's* now silent guns.

Two seconds.

The high-pitched banshee wail of twelve nose-diving piston engines became an unbearable scream as they slammed across the ship at masthead height.

Radio aerials swayed, halyards cracked like whips, and every paper and chart on the Navigator's table took to the air in the hurricane slipstream.

But no bombs and no bullets.

The Ju88s climbed steeply away.

'I feel sick,' Rose announced.

Reece-Davis said nothing; but his hands, one on each side of the compass binnacle, were white like his face.

A rough hand caught Rose's shoulder.

It was Guiseppe. 'Tell them to wave! The guns' crews! Everyone one!' he cried in Italian. 'They are your allies!'

Guiseppe was right. The first test had come and they were all looking like a bunch of frightened Chatham Rats instead of Italians. Rose translated. Dunbar gave the order.

The Ju88s came again ... and again; three more times they came – from starboard, from port, from starboard – and each time was a lifetime. The Italian armies had been beaten in Greece by ill-equipped Greeks, by Britain's 8th Army in the Western Desert, and their navy had been defeated at Matapan. All this showed in the sheer contempt of this mock aerial attack.

But there was a fine limit to the First Lieutenant's endurance. Hair and beard like a porcupine with fury and the breeze, he appeared like a toad from the top of his mushroom, one hand cupped to his mouth, the other fist shaking at the receding planes. 'Just once more, you – you bastards. Just once more. Just once. *Please!*'

'Hold your hair on!' Edward barked.

But, shrewdly perhaps, the Luftwaffe turned away, and a light flashed from the leading plane.

'"Why did you open fire. Query,"' the Signalman read, and turned a puzzled face. 'It's in English, sir.'

Edward frowned at the Italian. 'You don't speak German. They probably don't speak Italian. It's just possible you would use English... Well, Captain Durand?'

'But of course,' Guiseppe smiled.

'Of course – yes! Or of course – no?' snarled Troy.

The Italian's eyes wandered to the Luger

first, then climbed slowly to the Major's glistening face; in them, Rose again saw the hate.

'Of course – yes!' he hissed.

'Better hurry,' advised Reece-Davis. The planes had already completed two impatient circuits of the ship.

Dunbar said: 'Make: We opened fire because we were afraid you had mistaken our identity.'

The Signalman hesitated.

'Send it in English!' Troy had the Luger pointing at Guiseppe's head. 'If they attack, I pull this trigger.'

The Aldis lamp came up on the arm.

'It's a trick of some kind. But what kind?' Dunbar watched Guiseppe as he said it, hoping perhaps for just a hint of mockery in the heavy, pallid features, his hand out at the same time to stop the Signalman.

'Stop!' It was Guiseppe's hand which stopped the Aldis trigger being pressed. The sweat ran down his face in rivulets. 'You send that signal and you will die.'

'I think he's still lying,' Troy said with menace. 'He's stalling to make the Luftwaffe more and more suspicious.'

'I do notta want to die,' the Italian declared with dignity. Two strides got him to the chart-table. He held a book out to Rose. 'We use this when we signal with the lamps.' It was a simple bilingual code; easy if one was used to it; but Rose wasn't, and it took nearly half a frantic minute to compile the message and hand it to the Signalman.

The Aldis flashed.

'It's too bloody late.' Rose glanced helplessly at Dunbar. 'We should have answered at once.'

'You should have gone through the books on your table,' Edward answered tersely. 'What the hell have you been doing since you came on board?'

'What have I–' Rose went speechless with indignation.

'Stand by to open fire!' Edward called.

This was answered by an eager, trigger-happy thumb.

They waited. But there was no acknowledgement. The Ju88s made slow passes over *Scorpio* from every angle. On one pass Rose even saw the cine camera. And what were the guns' crews doing? – waving as Dunbar had ordered, or lounging as they'd been taught that morning, or were they too tense, too alert and eager to serve York – too British?

Very soon now, somewhere, perhaps in Napoli or Rome, or Gestapo Headquarters in Milano, someone was going to study that film and start figuring the answers.

The planes reformed and flew away. No one it seemed had made a mistake except Guiseppe, and he made another very big one by laughing softly.

With all Troy's wiry strength behind it, the Luger sank deep into the ample Italian tummy, and it folded.

'Here endeth the first lesson,' announced the Major biblically. 'Anyone for lunch?'

Lunch was a dull affair, with food, and the *Scaloppini* had the same effect on the Navigator as the portrait of Benito Mussolini which hung in the very comfortable wardroom, aft.

The general complaint was of 'more wine than damned ammunition on board – and no spirits! And have you seen the hen-house and the pigsty? Phew, what a pong!'

So Guiseppe liked his bacon and eggs fresh – so what?

'No cow,' lamented the Paymaster Lieutenant, 'and I do so hate tinned milk on my porridge.'

They hadn't a nerve between them. Not one. Insensitive lunatics, that's what they were. The whole lot! All of them!

Rose went for a nervous stroll on the upper deck.

It might have been that he was still on *Wildcat*, had it not been for *Scorpio's* 'continental' look. She had things on the top of the funnels that looked like black berets pulled rakishly to the rear. Very chic. 'Well, sir, actually they serve the same purpose as padding in a bra, if you see what I mean, sir?'

Ask a silly question...

In common with most destroyers of her day, she had a built-up forecastle which supported two twin 4.7 inch gun turrets, called A and B, the latter being behind the former and slightly raised, that looking aft from between the anchors and cables at the bows they looked like pale grey stepping-stones to the high bridge behind, where York's 'mushroom' stood just in front of the tripod foremast with its single yard for halyards. The mess-desks were underneath the two forward turrets, entered by canvas blackout screens to port and starboard where, just behind the bridge structure, the after end of the fo'c's'le fell to the main deck, which was low and close to the sea and ran her full length, housing the powerful engines and supporting two raked funnels, both surrounded by 20mm cannon ack-ack defence weapons, the torpedo tubes, two sets of four, another 4.7 inch gun turret, known as Y because there were three in all, and then the mainmast, raked at the same angle as funnels and foremast and carrying the after end of the radio aerials. And finally the quarterdeck, with its gadgets for storing and dropping depth charges.

Apart from her two funnel tops, *Scorpio*

had no frills to speak of, next to no comfort for 'the common herd', her kind having been built for one purpose: combat: as history has shown, usually against exceptional odds.

The decks were 'iron' decks. She was heavily armed but lightly armoured and therefore vulnerable; but she was very fast indeed, manoeuvrable, and, even to a seasoned old salt like Morgan, an exciting, lethal, adult toy.

But Rose was thinking of the Junkers 88s, for they would have reached their base in Italy by now and delivered that cine film.

As he walked aft carefully – carefully because the guardrails surrounding the ship were lying flat to the gunwales, the vessel being cleared for action – he picked his way round the gun platforms where the Defence Watch was closed up but stood down. Some of the crews watched the sea and the sky, others lay flat out in the sunshine on the iron decks or were propped up against a handy bulkhead. They looked alarmingly British, in more ways than one.

It was natural that the enemy would be suspicious, without any subtle help from Guiseppe Durand; but that suspicion would make them more than ever wary, more than ever observant.

In his talk with the crew, Edward had said: 'Basically, our task is simple enough...'

But under the surface the task wasn't so simple. *Scorpio* needed up-to-date enemy code books for communication with the Italians *and* the Luftwaffe; not only for the experimental trials with the glider bomb, but in order to try and plumb the enemy mind and foresee danger; and such code books would have to be supplied in person by someone or other. They might want to inspect the ship, check Durand's identity, perhaps even provide an escort north to the shallow waters at the head of the Adriatic Sea ... and Guiseppe was very well known in Italian naval circles.

One could fool some of the enemy all of the time, and all of the enemy some of the time; but not all of the enemy all of the time. Someone had said that before.

He was moodily wondering if any perceptive member of the guns' crews shared his seedy apprehension when Able Seaman Freer's name was mentioned near by.

The casual inquiry was made.

'He's up on that cannon, sir,' a hairy Rat pointed.

It was just curiosity; and love was a sin?

The platform beside the fore funnel had a grey searchlight, with shutters like sun-blinds, and a 20mm twin cannon.

Freer was wearing a filthy navy-blue Italian seaman's uniform, anti-flash gloves, and the protective hood was down round his

75

neck like a bib. The face was fresh, rosy, boyish, with a dark mole on a chin it would have been sacrilege to shave. Blue eyes peered inquisitively from under the deep Italian helmet that concealed fair hair and the head-band of the telephone ear-pads; York's link with the gunners. His shoulders were pressed into the semi-circular arm-rests at the back of the twin cannons, whose long slim barrels faced a blue and choppy sea.

'Anything in the ear-phones?' Rose asked pleasantly.

Freer lifted an ear-pad. 'Pardon, sir?' When the question was repeated, he smiled. 'One of the lookouts thought he saw smoke on the horizon, sir.' He produced a cloth, held it out. 'You've got your hands dirty on the ladder, sir. Better give them a wipe.' To an officer, this could have been sarcasm, had the observation not been made with frowning concern.

'It would need a tin of Vim,' Rose chuckled, wiping his hands. He handed back the cloth and looked out to sea. 'The, er, Captain told me about you. Looks like your trip home will have to be deferred. Sorry about that.'

'And you read my letter, sir.' It was said candidly, a little tiredly, and the cheeks were like Rose's. Literally.

'I, er, don't usually. It was, well, only because I knew. That is, you see, well, I was

76

with the Captain last night when he spoke to you.' How difficult could life get?

'It doesn't matter, sir. About the letter, I mean.' He reached forward with a dirty embarrassed hand and fiddled with the cartwheel gun sights. 'I don't mind missing the chance, sir. It's just ... her...' His words tailed off. A big breath and he said: 'You've only recently joined us, haven't you, sir?'

'Two weeks ago. No, slightly less. Alexandria. Your other Navigator went, er, home on a course...'

They went on talking for some minutes. Freer was an H.O. Educated at a very ordinary school, he had been working in an office in London and studying economics at evening classes, where he had met the girl he had married. If Edward had been right, the only thing Freer had been gifted with that other men hadn't, was an exceptional will, a fact borne out by the grubby photograph of an irresistible human angel with dark and dancing hair.

'We'll get you home somehow,' Rose promised in conclusion. 'God knows how – but somehow.'

Freer nodded. 'Thank you, sir. But I'd like to come back. After my course. But I'm not complaining, sir. There are others worse off. Did you know Petty Officer Moy lost his wife in an air raid?'

Rose knew. He also knew of other tragedies

... but somehow Freer's case was different. Then he noticed that the blue eyes were still on his face, but they seemed to have emptied of all feeling. Freer was listening to his ear-pads.

'Something up?' Rose asked.

'It's a stand to, sir. Warships on the horizon—'

But those chilling cries were already ringing out on the decks below. 'Stand to! Stand to! Stand to!'

The alarm bells shrilled.

Rose all but fell down the ladder, his arm still being in a sling, and he picked himself up only to go head first over a damn fool ready-use ammunition locker.

Leading Seaman Yates picked him up. 'Careful, sir, we've lost four officers already this year like that.'

'*And* a taxi driver!' Rose snarled.

5

The three warships were tentatively identified as British destroyers, a long way off, all but invisible on a grey-blue, shimmering horizon. Their narrow, pyramidal appearance told they were approaching to intercept.

Edward appeared worried, walking back and fore a few times across the front of the bridge prior to settling impatiently by the compass and voicepipes. He dared not reveal his identity. Too many tongues would wag. The Gestapo had big ears. And perhaps he shared the Navigator's presentiment that truth and reality were about to happen, like a pit disaster on a balmy spring day. The hoped for signal from Il Duce, ordering them northward, had not yet arrived, and the huge island of Sicily, with its network of hostile air bases, was just five hours away. Once there, it would be too late to stall, and to pass through the Messina Straits would be futile. But it was, Rose decided, the more immediate perils that bothered Edward, like the heavily guarded Axis convoys that ferried supplies east to Greece and Crete, and to General-leutnant Erwin Rommel, the Desert Fox, whose presence completed the entire south side of a full circle of enmity.

Yet, at that moment, there were but three British destroyers and *Scorpio* ... and enough!

It was 3.14 p.m.

'Asdic clear, sir!' – its monotonous ping ... ping ... ping heard and yet unheard, like background music, as too were the drone of funnel exhausts, the surge of the bow-wave.

A cottage loaf, white, fleecy, serene, hung

in a bluebell sky. 'Wind: Force 4,' Rose noted against his calculations. It was blowing from the south; a beam sea, causing the destroyer to roll through an arc of twenty degrees.

The others on the bridge were the Signalman, speaking to Sub-Lieutenant Reece-Davis – they stood at the rear in a three-sided box affair full of rolled flags and pendants – the two lookouts, Major Troy and Captain Durand, the latter with a flabby hand on his stomach and a wary eye on the former.

There was no panic: *Scorpio's* 4.7s could out-range the British 4-inch, and her speed was greater. But it was important to 'stay in character', to appear Italian.

'They're ours, all right,' York called down.

Dunbar waved acknowledgement. 'We may have to fire a few shots, Number One. But for goodness' sake don't hit them.'

'Me? Never!' The First Lieutenant sounded hurt at the very suggestion.

Edward waited awhile. He was sipping coffee a white-coated steward had brought him. He was a terrible man for his coffee.

At last he said: 'What would you do now, Pilot?'

'Retreat!' Rose at his laconic best.

Edward smiled in agreement.

'Starboard ten!'

'Ten of starboard wheel on, sir!' chanted

the voicepipe. The it asked: 'It couldn't be Captain Butterworth and the 37th Flotilla, sir?'

'I hope not. Not *him*. But it can't be, Coxswain; what is it – seven boats in the 37th?' This was followed by the helm order: 'Midships! Port five! Hold her on three six-oh degrees!'

Morgan's voice confirmed the order, then argued. 'There's nine in the 37th, sir – unless they've lost two.'

'Surely not. Anyway, we can only see three.'

This mysterious conversation was typical of the senior officer and senior rating. They did it all the damned time.

'Who is Captain Butterworth, sir, and what do you mean – I hope not. Not *him?*' Rose asked inquisitively.

Edward sighed. *Scorpio* had just completed a ninety degree turn and the enemy was now astern. 'In the Mediterranean there are at present three lunatics,' he disclosed. 'There's this Captain Butterworth, he's Captain 'D' of the 37th. And there's a young chap called Reg Ashley, but he's submarines. Then there's me, Pilot ... and if that's Andy Butterworth over there, you had better clear away the life rafts, because he taught me all I know.'

'Warships dead ahead! On the horizon, sir!' cried a lookout.

'Three more on Red four-five!' screamed another.

'Which makes nine?' asked the voicepipe.

'The three astern are crossing fast to Green four-five!' York yelled down.

Scorpio was very suddenly in the centre of a vast but rapidly diminishing triangle. The first three destroyers had clearly held their audience while the other six had crept round below the horizon in opposite directions. Escape lay only in running the gauntlet between any two of the three opposing groups. At the best it would be six to one; and the odds? 'Against a cross fire from two hundred or so 4-inch shells and sixteen torpedoes, Pilot? It's Andy Butterworth, all right. To a T. This may mean spilling more British blood.'

'Ours or theirs?' Laconic Rose again.

They all knew that the 37th Flotilla had been on a do-or-die run to Malta with five merchant ships. Signals to the C-in-C mentioned 'vicious' air attacks all the way. The sorely-needed supply ships had all been sunk. That, Edward said, would explain Butterworth making a 'vengeance' sweep north on his way back to Alexandria. 'He'll be mad crazy after that lot.' Edward was such a comfort.

But there was to be no angry, hurried, concentrated attack. 'They're reducing speed, sir,' York called out. 'They're going to make us sweat. They've got us by the short hairs an' they know it. Sadists; that's what they are. That's the British for you. I'm bloody glad I'm Italian.'

He got a nasty sour look from Guiseppe.

But Dunbar was grim. 'Engine-room! I want revolutions for maximum speed. Every last knot. And I want smoke. Lots of nice, oily, suffocating smoke. Right? Good.'

The deck underfoot trembled as *Scorpio* increased to full power. Her delicately sliced bow-waves climbed to fo'c'sle height, breaking white and green like some beautiful Atlantic sea as it curved away. Dense smoke, filthy black, thick with unburnt oil, belched from her raked stacks, bending aft and out over her tumbling wake, to expand fast into a long cylindrical cloud a hundred feet broad by as much high.

Chief Petty Officer Morgan moved the helm one degree to starboard; just one; that the vessel's course was not straight, but turning, almost imperceptibly, and as time passed the smoke screen formed a vast quarter circle, and then half a circle, and finally, after seven minutes, they reached the smoke screen's beginning, and the circle, two miles in diameter, was closed.

On his 'battle' chart, Rose had drawn a triangle. At each corner he placed the enemy. In the centre with a pair of bow compasses he drew a circle to represent the smoke. In the centre was *Scorpio,* but not idle; Dunbar was laying an inner circle of smoke.

Simon York climbed down and lumbered across the bridge. 'All this is very pretty, and all that. But what the hell am I supposed to do now? I can't see a thing.'

'You wait,' Dunbar proclaimed, 'And hark if you like. But me – I'm making a cloud.'

The First Lieutenant frowned, turned aft, walked a few paces, stopped, shrugged and spoke to the deck-boards. 'He's making a cloud,' he said. 'Hmmmm.' Then a puzzled glance at Edward's back. 'What, pray, am I harking for – the Herald Angels?'

It wasn't.

The whistles came before the distant thuds of gunfire. They came all of a sudden, all over *Scorpio's* home-made pond, some near, some far: a piercing, discordant chorus of unnerving whistles which ended one at a time and some at a time in a hundred or more scattered puffs of smoke and the familiar CRUMP! CRUMP! CRUMP! of exploding anti-personnel shells. And more came until the whole circle was filled with drifting shell-bursts, like small tufts of dirty cotton wool, none higher than seventy feet, few lower than twenty, all spraying their deadly shrapnel over a wide area of sea like showers of pebbles. One burst astern of them, harmlessly; but it only needed one to burst over the bridge.

'All anti-aircraft guns' crews take cover!' blared the loud speakers. 'Take cover! Take cover!'

A glance over the after end of the bridge revealed deserted decks, except for Nelson, who strutted slowly down the port side.

'He ought to have a telescope under his arm,' muttered Reece-Davis, adjusting his helmet over a pained face.

The barrage lasted one minute. Then silence. Then it came again for one more minute. The purpose was to unnerve the Italians. To make them break for freedom. But the only Italian on board wasn't unnerved.

CRUMP! CRUMP! CRUMP! – to port, to starboard, ahead and astern. Everywhere. The din of sea, ship and shells was appalling. Vibration made Rose's battle record look like a doodle.

The elements were no help. As *Scorpio* executed her second sweep round a rapidly contracting circle she swayed, tossed and pitched as her slender bow turned into beam seas, cross seas, cheeky following seas, and head seas that brought showers of spray drifting over A and B turret and across the bridge, where it drenched their clothes, rattled against the metalwork with occasional shrapnel.

But all this helped to reveal the purpose of Edward's private cloud – and no god ever worked with greater zest. On the Beaufort Scale the wind was still Force 4, or thirteen to eighteen miles an hour, and blowing from the south. The smoke screen was steadily moving north with it. So was *Scorpio*. It was a small advantage designed to transfer the initiative to the British destroyers ... for they were waiting, and if they waited too long, not only would the wind expand and disperse the cloud over a vast area, but *Scorpio* would be slap in the centre of the Axis east-west shipping lanes.

'Shut off smoke!'

When the foul gaseous vomit ceased, the screen was one mile in diameter, higher and thinner than before, dented on the south side by the wind.

Four minutes passed and no shells came.

Dunbar lifted the telephone. 'Stand everyone to, Number One! Torpedo and depth charge crews close up! No, Mr Chaplin, just a precaution. I'm expecting a close range torpedo attack at any second.'

He replaced the instruments. 'Keep on your toes, everyone! Watch the smoke. Both sides... Damn and blast, my coffee's full of sea water!'

Tragic.

Scorpio circled, still at maximum power.

Five ... six ... seven minutes.

'Enemy in sight! Red seven-oh!' cried a lookout.

She was a big Battle class destroyer, pale-grey and beautifully raked, ghost-like in the thinning smoke and travelling at speed. Her battle flag – a huge white ensign – stiff in the wind of her passage, flew from her yard.

There was no warning other than the lookout's cry. In that small circle there was no time at all; time only to glance up; to feel afraid; to see the sun glint on the cold steel of one, two, three, four torpedoes as they spat out from the Britisher's midship tubes, splashed into the sea seconds apart, and vanished; and as the last hit the water the attacker keeled steeply to port in a tight, high-speed turn to regain cover, and every gun on board her opened up.

Those guns were half a mile away. One thousand nautical yards. Too near to miss.

But miss they did.

Orange and white tracer curved over the sea together with three broadsides of 4-inch. They pulverised the surface a hundred yards short of *Scorpio* at near muzzle velocity.

Flame tracer ricocheted off the waves, sparked away in all directions. But most went straight in. All lifted the water into a grey drifting mist; and one, a 4-inch, half spent and toppling, leapt at them, went right through the after funnel like a dinner gong.

When the spray settled, their assailant had gone.

'Torpedo tracks to port!'

'Hard-a-starboard!... Midships!... Meet her!... Well done, Coxswain.'

Scorpio had turned on the same course as the approaching underwater missiles. Two foaming tracks like white ribbons in the blue passed slowly up the starboard side. Two passed to port. The ship was moving almost as fast as they were.

'We'll just follow them,' announced Edward. 'If my guess is right, it won't do a bit of good, but there's just a chance that no one will be on the other side of the smoke where they're heading. If, maybe, perhaps.'

Half that made sense. Torpedoes, if they miss, travel a long way. Captain Butterworth would know that.

A furry head appeared out of the control tower.

'What d'you think of that lot, then?' York called down. 'They call that shooting. One lousy shell through the funnel. And that was a fluke. No wonder we're losing the flaming war!'

Butterworth's star pupil swung round indignantly.

'Oh, come off it, Number One. That was Andy B himself. His gunners couldn't get the elevation when he turned like that, that's all. I bet he hits us next time?'

'I told you this could be fun,' Troy chuckled.

'Ha, ha, bloody ha,' Rose growled. 'I'd give a year's supply of marijuana for a dull lecture-room and a bunch of smelly students.'

'Steady on two-eight-oh, Coxswain... Get an eye on those torpedo tracks, now.'

'They've just gone into the smoke over there. See, two or three degrees off the bow,' Reece-Davis pointed.

A Telegraphist panted alongside Rose, laid a bunch of signals on the soaking table. 'The top one, sir.' A furtive glance about him, and he left fast.

It wasn't from Il Duce. It was from the Admiral-in-Charge, Napoli; and read: '10th Destroyer Flotilla approaching your vicinity screening convoy. On your present course contact should be made at 16.00 hours.'

Dunbar read it.

'That's in twenty minutes,' Rose informed.

The Italian Captain revealed that the 10th Italian Destroyer Flotilla consisted of six boats.

Edward shrugged. He had other problems. 'Hoist the Italian battle flag!' he called.

The Signalman dived into his flags-and-pendants corner. Bar-taut in the salt-edged breeze, the huge green, white and red battle flag climbed up to the yard.

A few hundred yards ahead lay the inner

perimeter of the smoke screen.

'You fight under *my* flag, huh?' Guiseppe wasn't pleased.

'We will not bring shame on it,' Edward promised.

The smoke closed around them.

Dim in the haze, A turret swung its twin 4.7s to starboard, B turret to port.

'Open fire independently when enemy is in sight,' Edward said into the telephone. 'Try and keep your fall of shot just short of them, please.'

Snatches of sea and sky were already visible as he laid down the instrument. His face showed his own doubt that the trick of following the torpedoes would work.

'Stand by to open fire!'

Scorpio burst out of the smoke.

'Destroyers to port!' screamed a lookout.

'Three to starboard!' cried another.

The yellow flashes of gunfire were almost invisible, so bright was the day. Butterworth *had* anticipated Edward's move.

Those chilling whistles, and then the sea erupted into a dozen sparkling fountains of white water as shells exploded beneath the surface over a wide area.

'Open fire!' Dunbar called angrily. 'What the hell's the matter with you up there! Open fire! Open fire!'

That was important, if only to put the enemy off their aim; but *Scorpio's* gunners remained stubbornly silent because the enemy was British.

Edward made the only decision possible.

'Hard-a-port!'

At maximum speed the ship answered her helm instantly, leaning over to starboard, and over, until the bridge deck lay at an angle of forty degrees from the horizontal, and her long stern skidded through the water as she turned to regain the safety of the smoke.

One salvo shrilled over the bridge, followed by rapid broadsides as the opposing gunners found the range; but that sudden turn threw them off, and the sea where they might have been became a forest of shell-bursts.

The third broadside was over, the next straddled them, and the ship then gave two small shudders in quick succession. They had been hit.

The Damage Control telephone buzzed. But no one answered. That turn was so steep that Troy and Rose collided and all but collapsed on top of Reece-Davis, while Dunbar was trying to make himself heard above the barrage to a wildly gesticulating York – 'Tell the damn' fools to fire their guns! For God's sake, York – *make them!*'

'What do you think I am – a magician? They won't even answer me on the phone. I'll have them all court-martialled. The lot!

All of them!'

Scorpio righted herself on Edward's curt order.

Only one man pressed his trigger before the smoke enveloped them. That was Y turret. It didn't silence the enemy, who fired again and again into the screen where *Scorpio* had disappeared. But she wasn't there, for wily Edward had executed another turn and was steaming round the circle, through the smoke, as an alternative to going back into the circle.

'What happens if one of the destroyers cuts through the screen at right angles to our course?' Troy asked.

That question was already in everyone's thoughts, made them strain their eyes and ears. It was like listening for a pin to drop when standing two feet from a mill wheel.

'Stop engines!'

'There is something wrong?' Guiseppe had taken a pace forward in alarm.

'We listen,' said Edward. 'It's our only chance.' He put a telephone in Rose's hand. 'The hydrophone operator will give you approximate range and bearing of our late allies,' he went on. 'You plot them, Pilot. There may be a gap we can snake through.'

Although her engines were stopped, *Scorpio* was still under way, moving fast, and would in fact travel well over a mile before steerage way was finally lost.

Noise and vibration melted away, leaving a peculiar leaden silence in which the battle flag flapped and the wind of their passage wailed eerily, cold on Rose's tensely damp face and sodden clothes.

Nauseating, faintly brown and stinking of crude oil, the smoke swirled about them.

On the telephone, the small hard voice of the rating operating the ship's listening device gave the bearings of the British destroyers: he could hear them now that the threshing of *Scorpio's* own screws had stopped.

'It's a bit difficult,' he admitted 'They're in groups, sir. There's one group near by; about a quarter of a mile, I think...' As he went on, Rose plotted them on his chart.

But the pit disaster was sixty seconds away, the fuse triggered by the buzzing of the Damage Control telephone.

Dunbar answered it. He spoke to the Chief E.R.A. for a few seconds, then hung up. Over his shoulder, for general consumption, he said, 'We've been hit twice, I'm afraid. For'd and abaft the torpedo tubes. Bad luck. One dead, four wounded. The after director, one searchlight and a twin cannon knocked out.'

'I'd better see if I can help.' Troy ran aft.

But Rose only heard him subconsciously, as he did the Sub-Lieutenant's words of condol-

ence and the urgent voice of the hydrophones' operator – 'Destroyers approaching!'

One dead. Searchlight. Twin cannon. That
was all Rose heard.

'W-who's dead?' he gasped.

Edward cast a backward glance. 'One of
the able seamen manning the twin cannons,
Pilot.'

'Hasn't he got a name?' Rose snarled.

Dunbar turned, frowning. 'I'm sorry,
Pilot, it was Able Seaman Cooney.'

The limpness of relief, shameful in itself. 'I
– I, er, just thought...' But not one was ever
to ask the Navigator what he had thought.

'Oh my God – *look!*'

They wheeled round. It was Reece-Davis,
arm outstretched, eyes big and round with
horror.

At that precise moment *Scorpio* was
travelling at twenty knots, her speed decreas-
ing, passing through a patch where visibility
was up to thirty yards; and fifty yards away
they saw a bow-wave, curling whitely, hardly
discernible in the thinning smoke whose oily
content was streaked amber by the slanting
rays of an inquisitive sun: and in those para-
lytic seconds the British destroyer's forward
structure took shape in grey outline, her
turrets and streamlined bridge compressing,
bending the wisps of smoke, that it streamed
from her whole length as she hove into full
view, seventy feet away, travelling at speed:

approaching at an angle of forty degrees she was actually trying to turn away even as they saw her, going hard over to starboard as *Scorpio* herself was at Edward's urgent command.

Too close to do battle, or to turn – for when destroyers turn they skid: both vessels were almost parallel, facing opposite directions, skidding sideways, listing terribly and towards each other, crushing the sea between them into a frothing, broken mass as their raked lengths tried to make that wholly impossible turn

The crash stunned the ear-drums.

Loose guardrails, boats, davits, gun barrels – every projection on the port side of both vessels locked together in that horrific moment: but they were still moving in opposite directions at a reduced but combined opening speed of eighteen knots, and every fixture that failed to unlock was brutally uprooted in one piercing, abrasive, metallic shriek.

Sailors were sprawled all over the British decks, some face down, their heads in their arms. The officers on her bridge, as on *Scorpio*, clung to anything handy.

All this Rose saw and heard inside five seconds; then both vessels were stern to stern, the Britisher receding, her undamaged starboard side coming into view as she continued her right-hand turn, away from *Scorpio*.

The Navigator's glance out on the beam where she was heading was automatic. So was his cry of anguish.

Barely visible, phantom-like, the raked silhouette of a second destroyer was racing through the screen – and the first was turning straight into her path.

A sharp, violent crack like near thunder rolled across the water. The second destroyer didn't even lose way: it just sailed through the first, which stopped abruptly, both parts of her severed hull leaning different ways. Her stern, screws still revolving, tilted slowly to the sky, hovered; then to sink, to slip fast under the sea.

The swirling smoke became a funeral shroud, swirling round the gaping forward half, itself already tilting to reveal a broken funnel, the mast, bridge and forward turrets, from which men were leaping, crying out as they did so, or screaming, because some were mutilated, dismembered...

'There'll be a gap in the enemy defences to the north, gentlemen,' Edward said quietly. 'What you have just seen, a glider bomb can do equally as well.'

Scorpio gathered speed.

From somewhere ahead came the erratic drum-beat of distant guns. But they could be silenced, or evaded, unlike the faint pathetic cries of mangled drowning men astern; from those, for Professor John Rose, there would be no escape; not in distance nor in victory.

'It wasn't your fault, Pilot. I have sharp ears. I heard the hydrophones's operator myself. There was nothing that you or anyone else could have done.' That was Edward's last word on the matter.

The putrid smoke had filled every hole and crack on the buckled port side, and still poured thinly from them a full minute after emerging into clear sunlight.

Five miles away the sea was lumpy with Axis supply ships, four already on fire, others altering course this way and that to avoid the shells and torpedoes of the attacking 37th – for Andy Butterworth had found a bigger and better target on which to reek vengeance. His destroyers were right in among the enemy, braving a cross-fire from the merchantmen's decks but frustrating the helpless Italian 10th Flotilla now on the perimeter of the scattering convoy and unable to retaliate without hitting their own heavily laden charges.

Guiseppe threw his palms in the air.

'That is-a Captain Baroni. Son of an imbecile's imbecile! A fool's fool! All-a these things and more is-a Baroni!'

A panting Telegraphist delivered a flimsy sheet of paper. Rose handed the long-awaited signal to Edward.

It was suspiciously brief.

Proceed Catania. Signal port authorities
your estimated time of arrival.

If Edward had had any sense at all, he would
have waded into battle to help Butterworth,
then returned to Egypt.

He did neither.

He altered course south, away from the
battle, then turned west for Catania, the
biggest and most heavily defended port on
the east coast of Sicily: a port known to be
packed with Rommel's supply ships, their
warship escorts, and protected by airfields.

Edward leaned on the chart-table.

'I have a hunch we might just be about to
get those code books we need,' he muttered
pensively. 'Tricky, though. Tell you what,
Pilot, you'd best work me out a course and
speed to bring me into harbour after
everyone's asleep. Say midnight. And when
you've done that, go below, get the steward
to iron and press your best Italian suit. Then
take a shower, have a meal, and snatch some
sleep.

'I'm going somewhere?'

Edward shook his head gravely.

'Not necessarily, Pilot, but it may be a
trap, and you are the only one among us
who can deceive the Gestapo face to face.'

'I've got shocking news for you, sir.'

'What's that, Pilot?'
'I couldn't deceive a ten-year-old Italian Sea Scout.'

6

Scorpio glided along, rolling less in the lea of the land, her funnel exhausts purring like a big cat.

For nearly a minute no one on the bridge had spoken a word, all eyes except the look-outs' being directed ahead, peering, wondering.

Catania, the town itself a little to the right of its tideless harbour, was supposed to be blacked out. But careless lights showed here and there. Well to starboard stood Mount Etna, towering blackly against the sky, the cloud of deadly gases from her active volcanic heart glowing pink ten thousand feet up around her shoulders. Had the wind been from the west, ash from the crater would have covered the ship like fine dust.

'Time, Pilot?'
'Eleven minutes to midnight, sir.'
'Revolutions for five knots!' Edward ordered. 'Coxswain on the helm! Steady on two-seven-oh, helmsman!... Tell everyone to stand to, Number One!... That signal gone

to Sir William, Pilot?'

'Ten minutes ago, sir.' It was in fact the second signal sent to Dorman, and confirmed merely that all was well. So far. The first had gone immediately after their clash with the 37th Flotilla, informing the Admiral of Dunbar's decision. The reply had said that the Battle Fleet, with its formidable carrier strike force, was seventy miles to the south-east. The one code-word *Wasp* to the C-in-C would bring an air strike within twenty minutes – if the need arose.

Hurried footsteps brought Surgeon Lieutenant Cruikshank. He was really surgeon for *Wildcat's* flotilla, but Captain 'D' had insisted on him staying with Dunbar for whatever lay ahead. 'I'm going to have to operate on young Pascoe,' he informed curtly. He was thirty-five, far too thin, already balding, foul-tempered most of the time; but who could blame him?

'Can't it wait?' Edward asked.

'It *could* wait – but he'll be dead by dawn. Gangrene. The right arm has to come off. Now.'

'Okay, Doc, we'll try and not make a noise.'

To this incredible reply, Cruikshank said 'Thanks,' and left, leaving behind a faint smell of disinfectant. That bad-tempered man was the only one who, in thirty hours, had had no sleep.

'Stop engines!'

When *Scorpio* lost steerage way the glasses revealed the dark line of the stone-built harbour breakwater against the lighter sea. At the entrance were two boom defence vessels, like minesweepers, each attached to the heavy anti-submarine net, now closed.

Every contingency, or as many as could be imagined, had been allowed for. It was the first time Rose had known the committee system to work.

On the chart-tables were signals, written in Italian, and he selected one. Using the Aldis himself he flashed their identity, and added: 'Captain Durand requests permission to enter harbour?'

The reply came back at once.

'"We are opening boom. Follow pilot cutter on receipt of his signal. You may use your searchlight."'

The second signal was designed to obtain for *Scorpio* an isolated berth, to avoid the danger of being ordered to tie up alongside another ship. 'Have sustained superficial damage and casualties resulting from clash with enemy destroyer force in which one enemy vessel was sunk and another severely damaged. Request anchorage where repairs can be effected. Use of acetylene welding equipment necessary. Danger of explosion a possibility.'

A white lie.

'"Follow pilot cutter,"' repeated the winking light.

One of the vessels ahead drew open the boom. A small triangle formed by the red, green and white navigational lights of a motorboat appeared between the minesweepers.

'"Follow me!"' it flashed.

'Slow ahead! Port five! Midships!' Edward paused and glanced round. 'All right, gentlemen, here we go.'

He conned *Scorpio* round until her bow pointed at the motorboat and between the boom vessels.

'On searchlight!' It was the searchlight beside Freer's 20mm cannon whose powerful beam seared past the bridge.

'Major Troy and Captain Durand on the bridge, please!'

Telegraphists waited by the radio. Guns' and torpedo crews, warned to utter silence, were out of sight but handy to their weapons. A, B and Y turrets were trained fore and aft, their non-belligerent position, but not locked in place. Each man inside those turrets was keyed up, alert for York's command to fight their way out of the anchorage if need be.

The thick, dusty beam of the searchlight was stationary, directed on the water just ahead of the receding motorboat, but its powerful glow lit the heavily armed boom vessels to port and starboards as *Scorpio* slid through the gap in the net; a net made of thick wire which closed slowly behind them. Whether, if they had to escape, the re-inforced bows would successfully cut that net was a matter for concern.

Three camouflaged merchant ships, fun-nels smoking, decks packed with row upon row of military trucks and tanks, came into view in indistinct outline against a back-ground of darkness. They passed between them.

York gave a low whistle.

'Look – at – that!' he pointed.

A Littorio-class battleship hove into sight, then another, one on each side. The grey, sinister giants appeared to be asleep: the white figure on the fo'c's'le would be the anchor watch, the one amidships the quartermaster.

'Don't move, my darlings, don't move,' York whispered. He turned his face at the Captain. 'Just one torpedo – in each, sir. They – they'll never know where it came from. Just one teeny weeny tin fish. In each. Please?'

'Sit! Good boy,' said Edward.

Then came two Abruzzi-class cruisers and – yes – three Zara-class. The First Lieu-tenant's head followed them from the port bow, to beam, to quarter, by which time he was biting his fingers to the knuckles, an illusion caused by the depth of beard.

There must have been twenty destroyers, tied together in groups of five, then more merchant ships, all fully loaded, and three tankers.

'They've been here since Matapan,' Dunbar speculated. 'What a waste. Acting as ack-ack boats for Rommel's supply ships. The C-in-C would like to know about this. Pity.'

The First Lieutenant maintained a sulky silence.

A light winked on the motorboat. '"I am stopping. Drop anchor and ride on short cable on my present position."'

'Slow astern! Cable party on the fo'c's'le!'

Scorpio came to rest, close to the beach on the inner side of the harbour. Men from A turret slipped the anchor. They also removed the locking pin from one of the special cable links that joined the shackles, ready for a quick get-away, one rating being left with a sledge hammer to 'break' the cable.

The motorboat departed, but another came out from the harbour installations a mile to the right. It circled them twice before making for the blue gangway light, under which hung a Jacob's ladder; there, abreast the after funnel, Rose waited with Guiseppe.

Everyone else hid near by – except one Telegraphist. He stood behind, waiting for that one code-word, *Wasp!* Not that it would do any damned good.

'I hope you won't do anything silly,' Rose advised.

'You are fools,' Guiseppe growled. 'You have eyes but you see nothing. You think our ships are asleep, but they are watching you.' And Troy's Luger was watching him.

'They looked asleep to me;' but Rose wasn't so sure.

The motorboat, a naval type with cabin and cockpit, bumped the destroyer's side, swayed stationary. The blue light made the upturned faces of its five occupants look like coronary cases.

'Gestapo!' The word came from Guiseppe.

They seemed hesitant to board. One flashed a powerful torch along the super-structure, where it lingered momentarily on the three gun turrets, the 20 and 50mm guns.

Across the port side the E.R.A.'s Damage Control ratings started work on the buckled deck, and when the torch went out the small flashes of acetylene torches filled the darkness.

Two men ascended. One was big, the other was bigger.

'Kapitan Durand?' It was the big man who spoke. 'I am Colonel Lenz, Gestapo. I do not speak Italian. We will converse in the language of the enemy.' His voice was toneless, devoid of any feeling whatever. Like his smaller twin – who had books and a fat envelope under his arm – he wore a lightweight suit and soft hat, both buff-coloured, and the face was square, heavy, the eyes obscured by thick rimless glasses that reflected two blue bulbs.

Guiseppe didn't like the Gestapo.

'We have been in battle. My men, they are tired. One is dead. Others are wounded. Why you come, huh?'

The rimless glasses focused on Rose. 'Who is this?'

'My Navigator. Lieutenant Piccioni.'

'Do either of you speak German?'

Two heads waved cluelessly. One lied.

Lenz turned to his twin. In German he said: 'It is Durand, all right. And the little pig is obviously Italian, too. Did I not tell you the British would not have the guts to pull off an impersonation of this magnitude?'

'Try the forecastle and the Sick Bay,' suggested the other. 'I will remain here.'

Lenz took the books, handed them to Rose, and addressed Guiseppe. 'You will take me forward, please!'

He didn't, however, wait to be taken. He was off. But not through the blackout screen into the mess-decks. He went up the ladder and along the deck leading past B and A turrets to where, Rose knew, a very

British rating stood with a hammer. That knowledge made every pore on the Navigator's body open like sluice gates – and he threw the books at the Telegraphist and raced after Guiseppe who cried at Lenz, 'I do notta understand?'

'Then you have nothing to fear,' Lenz threw over his shoulder.

A shadowy figure drew back into the deep darkness behind A turret as the agile Colonel leapt the breakwater and arrived among the capstans and cables.

Rose could have fainted with relief; the rating with the hammer was no longer there! But the sensation was doomed.

Half-bent from the wait, Lenz side-stepped along the cable, shining the torch on every link. Then he stopped, right above the one which had been designed to break in two. In that link there was a hole, a quarter of an inch in diameter, where the locking pin had been removed.

The Colonel straightened slowly. 'You thought perhaps you might have to leave harbour in a hurry?'

A kick on the ankle untied Guiseppe's tongue.

'But no, my Colonel,' and up went the palms. 'Why should I want to leave, huh?'

'You broke your cable when you escaped from Alexandria,' Lenz said softly, thoughtfully, and slowly turned his back. 'Supposing that escape had been planned. Supposing the great Kapitan, who has, we know, two brothers fighting with the Ariete Division… Supposing he turned traitor…' For the second time he let his words drift into silence. Remained silent. Then he whipped round – 'Major Troy! Where is he?'

No warning.

Only the darkness saved them, for when the torch flashed in Rose's face he fended it off and covered his confusion at the same time.

'Major Troy,' Guiseppe said. 'I do notta understand.'

The torch went out.

'You are not very convincing Kapitan. But we will see. First I will look at the wounded you talk of.'

If the Colonel was quick, Rose was quicker. With a 'I will-a warn the doctor,' he skipped over the breakwater.

'*Wait!*' Lenz had good lungs.

But Rose hadn't intended to go far, and he was thus far when he obediently stopped. 'That you, Coxswain?' The whisper brought forth the shadow from behind A turret.

'Sir?'

'Quick,' Rose breathed. 'Tell the Skipper his Nibs can't speak Italian. And warn the Doc. And the mess-deck. Fast!'

'You'll never fool him on the mess-deck, sir – it's like Hag Fahmy Ali el Feishawy's bloody café on a Saturday night, sir!' and the Chief was gone.

The approaching Colonel flashed his torch where Morgan had been, and again at the Navigator's innocent face. But he said nothing. Then the only question was – had Guiseppe? Two can whisper, and the Italian had had the same chance.

In the centre of the canteen flat, an area immediately inside the blackout screens, was *Scorpio's* Sick Bay. Waiting patiently at the door stood Commander Sasso, the very spit of Edward Dunbar.

Colonel Lenz ignored him and barged in.

Ten by twelve feet, the Bay was spotlessly white, filled with the stench of chloroform, three two-tier bunks, and a table to live or die on; and on it lay the unconscious body of Ordinary Seaman Pascoe, covered by a blood-splattered sheet and hemmed in by Cruikshank and four attendants, all robed in white and masked. An S.B. Petty Officer acted as anaesthetist, with a drip and a wad.

They remained bowed over their patient as Lenz stood on tip-toe and tried to see what was going on. An elbow removed him.

He then strutted round the wounded who lay on the bunks, stopping beside a rating propped by pillows. The lad had a broken shoulder.

'You have been badly wounded?' Lenz asked softly.

The lad looked across at Rose.

'He does notta understand,' Rose said.

'No?' It was probably the only genuine atmosphere anywhere on the ship, but the Gestapo Colonel refused to believe. He returned his eyes to the bunk. *'Try!'* As he uttered the word he drove his fist into the bandaged shoulder.

A scream of agony is the same in any language.

No one moved.

The operation had stopped.

Edward was white, trembling visibly, making a superhuman effort to control his temper. So was Cruikshank, and he had more reason, for in his hand was a surgical knife.

Oddly, it was Guiseppe who spoke first, the words unrehearsed, uncoerced.

'For that I will personally throw you off my ship.' To prove that he meant it he made to advance on Lenz.

Dunbar deterred him with a hand.

'If he as much as touches one other patient, I will personally help you, my Captain,' and Edward meant it, too.

The Colonel said nothing. He moved slowly to the last two-tier bunk, on the opposite side of the table, and stopped. On the bottom bed – because there had been nowhere else to put it – lay the dead body of Able Seaman Cooney, covered from head to foot with a white sheet. And under that sheet, forgotten by all until that moment, was the irrefutable proof that *Scorpio's* crew was British.

Cruikshank glanced urgently at Dunbar. The knife in his right hand made a small pattern with its point on his robed left arm. His lips drew back to form the syllable 'Tat,' barely audible, then formed into a circle to produce 'tooo.'

Edward stiffened.

Another clumsy fool walked over Rose's grave.

The watery, magnified eyes were watching them from under the soft hat. Lenz had stood, staring at the mound under the sheet for some seconds, and now he'd half-turned, head a little on one side; it was the attitude of a puzzled man listening intently, conscious that something had been said, that some vital message had passed unheard by him.

'It is the man who died,' Cruikshank informed in a passable Milano accent.

Again the eyes moved from one to the other and back to the Doctor. 'Or perhaps ... Major Troy?'

'We do notta know any man of that name,' Edward denied. 'You look for such a man – yes?'

The eyes turned downward towards the sheet. 'Yes. Yes, I look for such a man. He,

111

like you, seeks a glider bomb, the property of the Third Reich. He is a British saboteur. He has done more damage to our cause than the entire British Army. Once he escaped my hands – *but only once!'* As he barked the last three words he ducked and flung back the sheet.

Young Cooney didn't look dead. He lay on his back, boyish face serene, hands folded across his chest ... and on one of his arms – God forbid! – was a blue heart pierced by a red arrow, and the words, 'I LOVE MARY!'

That soiled Gestapo hand was reaching to touch the dead when Cruikshank sprang.

His hand came down – *slap!* – on Lenz's shoulder, gripped, swung it viciously round, dragged it sideways away from the bunk, and slammed both shoulders up against the wall.

Quivering, one thirty-second of an inch from the German throat, was the surgical lance.

'You rape my country by your presence,' Cruikshank hissed softly. 'You enter my theatre with your filthy clothes and your germs. You have notta the good manners to take your soft hat from your soft head. And now you insult our dead. If you are notta convinced we fought the British, then I will convince you pig!' He glanced back over his shoulder at one of the attendants, nodded at the floor.

An enamel dish, as big as a roast tin, was retrieved from under the table, brought forward, held under Lenz's nose. In it, gangrenous and putrid, awash with warm blood, was Pascoe's shattered, amputated arm.

The Nazi face folded up in revulsion.

Rose's stomach climbed to his throat like pepper, hotly remained there, then froze solid when a cultured English voice from behind said: 'It looks human, and only the eyes reveal that it is not human. Nor is it an animal. It is *nothing!*'

It was Major Troy, Luger in hand.

'A jolly good show, gentlemen. I have heard nothing better on the London stage. But, alas, the game is over.' He paused and smiled in his own inimitable way, said cheerfully: 'Hullo, Colonel, we meet at last, eh? How nice.'

The astonished Cruikshank drew back.

'You are Troy?' Lenz looked puzzled, stunned by the suddenness of the showdown. And yet, behind those thick lenses there was a malignity such as the Navigator had never before seen.

'What the hell are *you* playing at!' Edward exploded. 'Damn it, man, we might just have got away with it!'

Major Troy sighed.

'Maybe. But you wouldn't know,' he argued. 'They don't ask questions the way we do. They play with you, like a cat a mouse, and watch your face for the answers. That's the way they operate *before* the torture, isn't it, Colonel? You'd leave the ship letting us believe you hadn't seen that tattoo. But up on the hillside there are two 8-inch coastal batteries. You can see them with the night glasses. They are trained on *Scorpio.* That's why we're here. On this isolated spot. Once the motorboat was clear, they would blow us out of the water before you broke the cable.'

'You will not leave his harbour alive,' the Colonel predicted calmly.

Troy raised the Luger until it pointed at Lenz's forehead. 'Not, er, in normal circumstances,' he smiled. He had a funny sense of humour. 'But in fifteen minutes, my revolting Colonel, the circumstances in this harbour will be far, far from normal.'

'Fifteen minutes?' This pensive question from Guiseppe was accompanied by a worried, quizzical frown.

Troy, for the first time, took his eyes off Lenz, nodded sadly at the Italian. '*Wasp,*' he said. 'And I know this place is full of your friends, so I really am most frightfully sorry, old chap.'

It was the unguarded moment. Troy's perky nod, his glance, the typically nonchalant remark: that was the Gestapo's moment and the blurred movement, the flame and crack of the black automatic came as one.

Troy died on his feet.

Lenz dived round the table, hopped over the body as it hit the floor, went through the door as Edward ducked and caught the discarded Luger and sprang after him.

At the starboard blackout screen, an ex-middle-weight, Chatham Division, was having a sneaky look at the gangway when he heard the muted shot, swung round, saw the fugitive and lashed out at the square chin.

The blow spun the German, but he recovered, collided with Edward, then dashed forward into the mess-decks, only to find that the hatch up to the fo'c's'le was closed.

None of the dozen men had time to act.

For an absurd ten seconds Edward chased his quarry over and round scrubbed tables and blue-grey lockers and in any one of those second could have shot him dead; but he didn't.

Because the mess-decks were entered from two sides, Lenz chose to leave by the other side where, in shadow, Nelson was playfully dissecting a live Italian cockroach.

A feline scream and the Colonel fell heavily. An oath and he struggled to his feet, barged on: but he had mislaid his glasses…

Rose found the Coxswain. Together they crept aft, their way lit by the small flashes of the acetylene torches. They picked their path through the Damage Control Party, who were hammering, welding, manhandling sheet metal under the E.R.A.'s obscene directives.

They reached the torpedo tubes where, across on the starboard side, the second Gestapo officer paced under the blue gangway bulb, his uneasiness betrayed by the way he glanced about him into the shadows. He was, perhaps, a man of extraordinary vision, for a 20mm cannon was trained on his back.

'What now, sir?' Morgan asked.

'We wait.' Rose motioned him behind the bulkhead, raised his wrist and waited for a timely acetylene flash. 'Allowing for the C-in-C to think up a good lie as to why he should suddenly attack Catania without prior air reconnaissance, two minutes.'

'Would the Commander-in-Chief lie, sir?' There was a shocked note in Morgan's voice that was too good to be true.

A Signalman edged between them, breathless. 'Lieutenant Rose, sir. Air raid warning *Red*, sir. And there's a storm warning from Alex, sir. Force 7-8. Prognosis for the next twenty-four hours – *bad*.'

Air raid sirens commenced their undulatory wailing, and when they died away there was darkness and silence, for the careless lights had winked out one after the other, as did the E.R.A.'s acetylene torches.

'An aircraft, sir.'

The drone of one piston engine passed high overhead. Something sparked in the sky and a single flare blossomed seven thousand feet up over the town and harbour installations. Then another, nearer. Six in all.

Not a gun had fired. Town and harbour, beaches and hills, all lay brightly lit. But a thousand guns were elevating skywards, listening to the distant drone of the flare-dropper as he turned back in his obsolete Swordfish biplane to exercise his prerogative of selecting the best target before the whole greedy lot arrived. A change in pitch and tempo of his engine told that he had done so.

Then, on all sides, red, orange and white tracer reached silently for the sky, to be followed a tenth of a second later by the thuds and chatter of the guns that had fired them.

It was Rose's signal to act.

He ran across the deck and caught the German by the arm. 'Come quick! There has been a terrible accident,' he panted. 'Follow me!'

He skipped off, this time through the starboard screen, and into the canteen flat where Edward stood wringing his hands and staring down at Cruikshank who had in his not so tender arms the head of an unconscious Colonel Lenz.

'What has happened?' There was deep distrust in those narrowed Gestapo eyes.

'He fell.' Edward, eyes like a sick spaniel, unclasped one of his hands and pointed upwards. 'From there. All the way. On his head.'

Rose could still hear the whack of the Luger butt.

'I think his scull is-a fractured,' lamented the Doctor, and glanced up. 'It is better we get him ashore for X-ray.'

As one, on cue, Dunbar and Cruikshank hoisted the Colonel to his feet, swung him round, bows aft, legs trailing, then charged through the screen, along the deck, to lay him finally face down, head over the ship's side above the motorboat.

Dancing behind, the other German tried to intervene as Edward called, 'Catch!' to the horrified upraised hands from the boat's stern sheets in the same instant that Cruikshank, the Colonel's ankles firmly in his hands, shoved.

It was normal and natural that Lenz's 'twin' should bend and peer over the ship's unguarded side to see where his Colonel had gone, abnormal and unnatural that he should dive head first after him, which he did with just the tiniest bit of encouragement.

'You forgot your hat,' Rose called as the

Coxswain hauled up the Jacob's ladder.

It drifted down on to the writhing mass of bodies.

'Englander dogs! You die for this. Die! Die! Die!'

But Edward, having dusted himself down, had trotted off, and the Navigator reached the bridge a second or two behind him.

The motorboat curved round *Scorpio's* bow and receded inshore. Flares, flames and gunfire – all three lit the harbour. An oil storage depot had been selected by the flare-dropper and blazed fiercely, flaming oil from ruptured tanks flowing down the beach like Etna's lava. Shrapnel plopped into the sea or clattered tinnily on the iron deck. Some of the Fleet Air Arm pilots bombed, but those carrying torpedoes had to hedge-hop the harbour breakwater before releasing their loads and were flying so low as they weaved to escape that they drew a cross-fire, damaging not only to themselves but to the enemy's own ships, and the whole anchorage was criss-crossed with tracer. Black smoke, laced with the flames of internal fires, poured from two ships, thinning and spreading with the increasing wind to form into a flare-tinted haze in which guns flashed and bombs erupted.

B and Y turrets whirred as they turned on their mountings, and when they stopped, their 4.7s were pointing at the hillside where the two 8-inch coastal batteries were plainly visible.

Only A turret, with Simon York firmly in the gunlayer's seat, declined to follow suit.

Edward picked up the phone.

'Bet you ten quid you don't make it first time, Number One...?' A pause. 'Oh, all right, moneybags, I'll make it twenty.'

Lieutenant-Commander York lost. He had to fire three salvoes before the motorboat exploded in flame, splinters and spray.

7

The W/T office was no larger than a bungalow's bathroom. A wall radio filled half of it. Cigarette smoke filled the other half. A sweating Telegraphist transmitted signal No. 1, but the tapping of the Morse key was drowned by the crash of extraneous gunfire.

It was to Gestapo H.Q., Milano, absolutely true, and read: 'Code books and documents received. Regret to inform that motorboat conveying Colonel Lenz and party received direct hit during British bombing raid. Captain Durand awaits your further instructions.'

Signal No. 2 was to Dorman, giving brief details of the circumstances surrounding Troy's death; and the air raid had long finished when at 02.05 hours, his reply was received:

'The death of Major Troy has come as a blow to those of us here who knew his skill and purpose. Because his primary objective was to destroy the men who conceived the glider bomb, and no trained replacement is available, it has been decided to abandon the mission. With deepest regret, I must therefore instruct you to return to Alexandria forthwith.'

There was one other paragraph conveying the news that all but three Swordfish had landed safely at Malta, whose geographical presence to the south had made the night attack from the Fleet carriers possible. They would rejoin their ships in daylight.

A black depression descended on the Chatham Rats. It remained until 03.35 hours, when Lieutenant Rose, using his newly acquired code books, deciphered a signal that he was sorely tempted to tear up and throw away – because it came from a one-time chicken farmer, now regarded as the most sinister and ruthless of Nazi leaders. He was the head of the SCHUTZ-STAFFEIN or S.S.

It was read aloud:

'"From the desk of Heinrich Himmler,

Prussian Gestapo H.Q., Berlin. To Captain Guiseppe Durand, commanding the Italian destroyer *Scorpio.*

'"Your plain language signal addressed to Il Duce and requesting reconsideration for duties with the Luftwaffe, was given into the hands of Reich Marshal Hermann Goering, who is responsible for this facet of missile development.

'"The decision has been taken to allow *Scorpio's* participation in the experiments, and full instructions on less immediate matters will be communicated in due course. You will therefore proceed into the Adriatic Sea and north to the island of Dugi Otok, in the Dalmatian group, and enter the anchorage shown under reference E24 on the chart supplied by the late Colonel Lenz. Oil fuel will be made available there. The test will commence on Monday, June 9.

'"Certain alterations have been made to our original schedules, and the airstrip has been transferred to the islands as a result of the intervention of an agent of British Military Intelligence, known to be a Major Troy. This man was thought to be dead. Information has now reached us to the contrary. To eliminate any suspicion we may falsely entertain on your integrity, your brothers Carlo and Oronzo have been relieved from duty with the Ariete Division and taken into our custody at the airstrip. If the tests are successful, they will be released unharmed.'"

On reading that signal, Edward sent for Reece-Davis and the Coxswain. He gave orders for Guiseppe to be locked in his cabin under guard. He also gave orders that each man should be issued with a voting slip on which he would write YES or NO. YES – I volunteer to proceed with the mission. NO – I wish to return to Alexandria. This procedure was right and proper, for as Dunbar said, 'Whoever sent Lenz to check on our identity, will be waiting at the other end to make quite sure. Our chances are not good.' That was an understatement.

At 05.00, Rose himself delivered the result of the vote.

Yes, we obey the Gestapo: 119
No, we return to Egypt: 1

Edward smiled. 'You can make that two, Pilot. Nobody asked me, neither.' His perception was better than his English.

In the matt, damp greyness of first light, when the smallest wave has a strange, intangible quality, when the fears of the night seem less real, *Scorpio* weighed anchor.

The wind cracked the halyards, flattened clothes to every contour of the human form, tore smoke from funnel tops, sent it scurrying low across the floating scum and wreckage.

No pilot boat had come. No reply had been received from the shattered harbour installations.

They passed bodies, face down, floating. They passed men in boats who searched without hope. One cruiser listed. Only the control tower of another showed above water. Of the two battleships, one was down by the stern. Vague in the mist, supply ships still burned, their ammunition exploding with dull thuds and geysers of smoke, sparks and flame. A minute alteration of course brought them safely past a mast with a yard, protruding above the surface like the Cross of Calvary.

The sea reared whitely along the break-water. Black storm cones were up on the shore mast to warn that only fools should venture forth. But the boom was open for a small freighter, which entered with much gasping and spitting and a toot of relief on its whistle.

A series of whoops, and *Scorpio* passed out.

Huge seas met them. But all the holes and cracks had been sealed. Watertight doors were shut. Emergency lifelines were rigged on deck. All was secure for heavy weather.

As they turned north, hugging the coast-line for maximum shelter, a signal was sent to Dorman announcing the decision to proceed. The reply was brief: "'I trust that rumours regarding your Captain's immortality have some basis in fact. But good luck and God's speed.'"

Dare-devil William had a sense of humour!

To the Navigator's amorous mind, Italy looked delightfully like a shapely leg wearing a high-heeled shoe. Tucked under the arch was the Gulf of Taranto where, at the north-east corner, lay Mussolini's most powerful naval base of the same name, but separated from the 44-mile wide Strait of Otranto, gateway to the Adriatic, by the long peninsula heel. But Edward expected no trouble. 'Getting in is easy,' he said, sipping his coffee. 'It's getting out: that's the problem.'

During the afternoon they reached Cape Rizzuto, altering course then due east to cross the mouth of the great Gulf and reach Italy's heel. The manoeuvre brought the full force of the gale and a ghastly sea angling in at forty-five degrees to the destroyer's centreline. Each wave towered to foremast height. The horizon became the sea that was coming and the one that had just gone.

Oilskins were worn. Hot food became a memory. Cold food wouldn't stay down.

In spite of it all, York trained his guns' crews, some of them pea-green. He was still sore about their disobedience of orders the day before.

Bows under, decks awash, her whole length veiled in driving spray, *Scorpio* plunged on, her mess-decks drenched, her crew sodden, and little Nelson, in his tiny yellow cork life-jacket, was a wet, skinny travesty of his fluffy self.

'Meee-oow,' he complained.

'Aw, shurrup!' growled a seedy Rose.

'I think he wants to go to the bathroom,' whispered Reece-Davis shyly. He and the Navigator were staggering at a standstill in swishing water at the entrance to the canteen flat, watching the noisy convolutions of the sea through the starboard blackout screen.

'He'll just have to cross his legs,' Rose answered with cruel disinterest. 'Anyway, what the hell difference does it make where he goes.'

'He's a clean-living creature,' a hairy Stoker muttered resentfully and dropped to his haunches. 'You're a clever, clean pussy cat, aren't you, my pet?'

'Meee-oow.'

Rose and the Sub-Lieutenant exchanged eyes.

The Navigator didn't care much for cats, he was really watching the men up around the forward funnel. Able Seaman Freer among them. They were just loafing, the only enemy being the weather.

Freer's safety had become an obsession.

So had Nelson's desire to defecate in his usual scupper; and that scupper was aft beyond the emergency lifelines.

They watched a huge sea slip inboard where, in front of them, the built-up fo'c's'le curved down to the low main deck. Travelling at speed it hit the boat's davits and gun shields, sending jets of spray as high as the funnels, then swirled on aft, round the torpedo tubes, finally to pour from the ship's sides and stern in a steaming torrent. Each one was preceded by a jolt and shudder, accompanied by a waterfall of noise, and followed by hoots of boyish laughter as someone got wetter. It could be fun.

The deck had been clear for nearly half a minute when a black and yellow body streaked out from between the Navigator's shaky legs – and the sea had been waiting.

The cat had no chance. Water enveloped him, bore him aft like a piece of flotsam, and the laughter changed to cries of despair.

The Chatham Rats had lost their beloved cat.

But no!

'There he is! See him – he's jammed under the depth charge racks!' screeched a rating.

Brave Freer started to climb down.

'Stay where you are!' bellowed Reece-Davis. 'There's nothing we can do yet. Stay put!' It was wise advice.

But the boy ignored it. He jumped down, ran aft.

Scorpio climbed a sea, hovered half-way to the sky, then crashed down into the trough.

Water roared past their faces.

Freer, swept from his feet, arms and legs flailing, vanished in foam.

There being no guardrails, the starboard side was just a wind-swept, heaving ledge. No destroyer man would have acted without prior thought.

'Come back, sir!'

But Rose was off, wading aft at best speed.

The storm took his breath away, sent him reeling. Bullets of spray rattled on his oil-skin, battered his face and hands, numbed and blinded him. Perhaps he was too late, he didn't want to think, he stumbled on, heard the waterfall roar as gushing water surged to his waist and removed his legs; feet first, he went straight under the torpedo tubes and stuck fast. No woman had ever looked twice at Professor Rose, and Freer was going to have his honeymoon; that was the only frenzied thought in his stupid head as he reached the quarterdeck and saw Freer's bedraggled head. The lad was over the ship's side, hanging by his fingertips.

It only needed one more wave, and Rose felt *Scorpio's* bow reach for the sky to produce it.

With the strength of fear he ducked and caught the boy by the arms, dragging him brutally on deck and across to the comparative shelter of casing below the stubby mainmast, got his wounded arm hooked through a metal fitting as water engulfed them.

A ton of sea clawed at their bodies. Freer began to slip. The fitting was sharp, angular, and Rose had forgotten that the arm he'd put through it was wounded; and now he remembered, but his cry of agony was converted into a desperate 'Catch my feet!' and Freer did – just – as he slipped away and the pain made the sea and the scudding clouds revolve.

When the stern lifted, the deck cleared.

With one arm he got Freer upright as a rope came snaking down from above. It was Reece-Davis and four men.

Some more rope was hauled down, the loose end flung back up. Freer was hauled up in the bight.

'Meee-ooow!'

'Where?'

'There!'

And there Nelson was, still jammed under one of the depth charge racks, out of reach because he vanished again under water and so did Rose.

'Hey, Pilot! Don't risk it!'

The Navigator glanced up. The rope, wet

and new and hard, slashed across his face. Fear exploded into anger. 'You clumsy ape!' He grabbed the end, tied it round his waist, gave it a spiteful jerk that all but brought the Sub-Lieutenant down. 'Pay the bloody thing out!' he snarled up. It was Nelson or nothing.

He dived across the deck and arrived slithering on his belly. The cat's home-made lifejacket had saved what was left of his nine lives by catching on a projection.

But Nelson was frightened, lashed out with his razor blades at the helping hand. Rose smacked his nose. Nelson spat back. Then he was free, in the Navigator's arms, and the rope dragged them back under foaming water.

Eager hands reached down. Nelson went up.

Seven seconds passed.

'What about me, then!'

But hands patted Rose's back as he threw a leg over the top and sat gasping astride the wet and perilous edge of a cannon shield, lacerated hands dripping blood.

'Oh, very well done, sir,' cried the Sub-Lieutenant. 'That was the bravest thing I've ever seen.'

The Navigator was in agony but flattery was a stranger.

Nelson purred in Reece-Davis's arms.

Freer's face was aglow. 'Oh, sir, it's someone like you who ought to take the Major's place,' he said.

'Uh' Rose opened his mouth to protest as the sea and sky again started to revolve; and the iron deck was ten feet below. Desperate hands tried to catch him...

The night train to London travelled smoothly. Rose lifted his head from the pillow of his First Class sleeper as the attendant entered. 'Well?' said Rose. But the man just stood there, his thick glasses magnifying the cold and watery eyes. At last he said: 'We know you are British. We've known it all along. But we are going to use *Scorpio* as a living target.' Then he melted away, and in his place stood Buckingham Palace, glittering in sunshine. And the King, in full uniform of the Admiral of the Fleet, a little princess at his side, came forward, pinned on the D.S.O. 'It's an honour to meet you, Hardy. Nelson has spoken so often about you,' he smiled graciously.

Then the little princess produced a bo'sun's pipe, blew it shrilly, opened her mouth wide and bawled: 'D'you hear there! D'you hear there! Hands to Action Stations! The ship will enter harbour in thirty minutes time. Cable Party will be required to secure oil barge.'

Head throbbing, Rose sat upright. What was *Wildcat's* Coxswain doing on the London train?

The door opened and the light clicked on. It was York and Cruikshank...?

'I – I expected the sleeping-car attendant,' Rose frowned. 'What are you doing in Italian naval uniform?'

'I told you it was concussion,' Cruikshank bragged.

'How's the hero?' grinned the First Lieutenant.

'Who am I? What time is it? Where are we?'

York sighed, shook his head sadly. 'Our Navigator. Isn't it marvellous, Doc? Where are we, he says.' Another sigh, crafty eyes on Rose. 'We're here, Professor. At Death's door. Dugi Otok. You fell on your pretty head, remember? On Thursday. Now it's Monday. Breakfast time.'

'The ninth. Hmmm. That means the Cambridge Easter term ends today, then,' Rose muttered.

'He's not fit,' Cruikshank urged. 'You'll just have to trust Guiseppe. That sedative must have been a wee bit too strong. But his confusion will wear off soon.'

'Not if that first glider bomb hits us in two hours time, it won't,' York prophesied morosely.

This, of course, was an outright lie – for the day was in fact Sunday – and, though it did get the Navigator out of his sick-bed in

132

two-point-five seconds, it was a typical example of York's insatiable appetite for the baser type of mean, cruel humour.

8

Sunday, June 8, 1941. It said so in the open page of the log lying on the bridge chart-table.

The time 7.9 a.m.

Met Office forecast: 'Winds light, variable. No cloud cover. Temp at noon: 90°F. Prognosis for next twenty-four hours good. (Moonrise: 23.50 hours.)

A synopsis, written in Reece-Davis's flow-ing hand, covered the events of Friday and Saturday. Major Troy and Able Seaman Cooney had been buried at sea on Friday, it said. The journey north had otherwise been without incident except for a Cant.506B which had shadowed them on Saturday but flown away in the afternoon. York had had the mainmast cut down and thrown over the side: this increased the fire power of Y turret and other weapons, previously restricted to limited arcs by what was described as 'a piece of vertical junk'.

A glance aft revealed that the radio aerials were now hitched to the forward funnel.

There were other things too; like gun training stops being removed, thus allowing port ack-ack guns to fire across the ship to starboard, and vice versa. All of it spelt *trouble*. So did the atmosphere on the bridge when Rose was well enough to perceive it. Everyone was nervous, and it showed in the uneasy pacing, the surplus of small talk, and in Edward's polite but curt acknowledgement of the Navigator's presence. 'Sorry to get you up. Subby will put you in the picture.'

It wasn't necessary for the Sub-Lieutenant to do any such thing, because, whatever the outcome of the next few hours, *Scorpio* was trapped: trapped at the head of the Adriatic Sea. It was the moment when the hero should have said: 'Not to worry, gentlemen, we'll make it back somehow.' But Edward didn't. He *knew* they wouldn't. Three days of living with that knowledge had made his face lined and tired.

A thousand yards ahead, the island of Dugi Otok looked more like a stretch of rugged, wooded coastline, an illusion created by the topography of the area; for the chart showed the Dalmatian group to consist of no less than five-hundred-plus semi-submerged mountain ridges, lying close and parallel to the alpine coast of Yugoslavia: elongated islands, appearing to overlap, each separated by narrow channels – known locally as KAN-

ALI – and teeming with T- and L-shaped bays as well as fish.

They steered into this maze of waterways between two towering headlands, altered course again towards a gap in the cliffs that was marked E24 on Lenz's map.

Guiseppe arrived on the bridge, accompanied by Petty Officer Adams, York's dapper, 'swift' and efficient Gunner's Mate, who saluted, turned over the body, and climbed up to the control room.

The Italian looked pale and puffy, shadowy about the eyes. 'He drank himself silly,' Reece-Davis whispered. 'Hasn't eaten a bite since Catania.'

'Slow ahead!' Edward called. 'Steady on two-seven-four, Coxswain!' A glance over his shoulder at the Signalman. 'Hoist the quarantine flag!'

The yellow flag climbed to the yard, signifying to those on shore that *Scorpio* had contagious disease on board.

Barely moving, they entered the channel between the cliffs, and a small T-shaped bay opened before them. Sheltered deep in the hills it was a place where placid water mirrored the inverted images of sandstone rock of pale sunlit gold, foliage of oasis green, and off-white houses with red roofs which either cluttered a foreshore fronted by drying nets and silent fishing boats or were dotted about the slopes, their uniform squareness softened by abundant trees. There were no installations, no piers; and ships could tie up to the steep face on each side of the village, where man had hewn a dusty road from the soft, perforated rock at deck level. Two black U-boats already lay alongside, their oval conning-towers level with the highway. But the three E-boats – the German version of British motor torpedo-boats – were at anchor, spaced around the harbour. An ocean-going tug with a black hull and white upperworks was weighing anchor. Tied alongside it lay an oil barge.

Scorpio slowed and stopped, turning then on her screws, in her own length, until her sharp bows pointed the way of escape. Edward was taking no chances.

The engines stopped, and the hot vibrant decks ceased to throb, and silence embraced them, broken then by the loud splash and rumble of anchor and cable. But on this occasion, from bitter experience, the rating with the sledge hammer was stationed out of sight in the cable locker.

And again the silence and shimmering heat, filled now with the buzzing of venturesome flies, come out from shore to investigate the pale-grey stranger who had churned up a wide circle of milky, silt-stained water.

Seven pairs of binoculars were already scrutinising the hills and houses and the enemy, then turned nervously on the church with the red spire where a bell started to toll.

'Right, gentlemen,' Edward said softly. 'We have one day to find a clue to that airstrip. One night to act on it and destroy the enemy. At eleven a.m. tomorrow, they will drop the first glider bomb in history. I don't want to be under it.'

'Do you know what your chances are?' Guiseppe growled.

Edward faced him.

'Let's put it the other way, Captain Durand. Let us say the chances are five hundred islands to one against finding your brothers. In time. Alive.'

It was the cruel truth. Face desolate, the Italian turned heavily away. He was a man with two enemies, and no friends. In any other circumstances, it would have been sad.

'Reception committee,' York said it quietly. A wry grin and he returned his eyes to the binoculars.

The tug's anchor had reached the hawse-pipe, and she turned slowly to begin her approach, her signal lamp flashing. 'He wants to know which side you want the oil barge, sir?' the Signalman called.

Dunbar's hesitation was marked. 'Tell him – starboard. But didn't he ask about the quarantine flag?' He had put it up specially to discourage visitors from the Gestapo.

'No, sir.' A pause. 'Shall I go ahead, sir?'

Edward nodded. Rose translated.

York frowned at his Captain. 'Something up, sir?'

'Why, dearie me, no, Number One. Whatever made you think that? Everything is find and dandy – except of course that we as yet see no Gestapo anywhere about, and I can't convince myself that they are not still suspicious, especially after Colonel Lenz having been suspicious, and especially because the aforesaid did not turn up to make his report on our spotless integrity – if that is the word to describe what spies pretend to have and haven't. But apart from that, don't you worry. These are matters for the immortals.'

'You'll forgive my big mouth, I hope,' York growled.

Edward took the Navigator's arm. 'Our cue, Pilot.'

They emerged through the blackout screen to find the Cable Party ranged along the deck, all looking the picture of bored Italian indifference. They waited to receive the barge. Edward borrowed a cigarette from the Petty Officer in charge, lit it, pushed his cap flat aback. In his role as Sasso he lounged as the tug approached slowly and obliquely, and laid the barge alongside with perfect precision. Heaving-lines there thrown, caught, bent to the wires, and the wires exchanged inside two minutes. In fact, the tug was already backing away as the Cable Party secured them to *Scorpio's* bollards. Apart from a few words Rose had flung at the Italian seamen, not a further word had been said; but the swarthy Tugmaster raised a friendly hand in farewell as Edward, desperate for a clue of any kind, said, 'Quick, Pilot, tell him to hang on and we'll pass him across a case of wine!'

The invitation was put.

One hand cupped to his mouth, the Tugmaster leaned out of his bridge, a big smile on his face. 'I accept with–' He not only broke off, but vanished as well for an arm had hooked round his face, jerked him back and out of sight behind the daylight sheen on the stormproof glass. And on the arm, clearly visible, had been a red band, with a black swastika on a white background.

'Gestapo.' Edward said it absently as he watched the tug continue to back away. 'What was the Tugmaster saying, Pilot?'

'He was just accepting your offer.'

'But the Gestapo didn't want him to, Pilot. Now, that's interesting.'

The Navigator had several questions, but Dunbar moved away, returned the Petty Officer's salute, dismissed the Cable Party, flicked his borrowed cigarette over the side with a grimace of disgust, used the nearest telephone and spoke to York: 'Tell the E.R.A. to commence oiling right away, Number One. I want it competed by sunset. Yes, I saw what happened. No, the Gestapo made no attempt to come on board to check our identity. Yes, I agree it's odd. It looked to me as if they didn't want to be seen at all. Yes, we'll leave the quarantine flag up. It'll discourage them if they do change their minds,' he finished, and hung up.

He turned to approach the Navigator, stopped, cocked his head in a listening attitude, then scanned the bay.

So did Rose, for he too had heard the deep-throated rumble of throttled-back aero engines, and an all-round glance revealed that all three torpedo-boats were under way, circuiting the harbour in different directions, with the unmistakable purpose of closing on the destroyer.

Guns' screws were still closed up, unseen but not deaf. One head appeared above a gun shield. Then another.

The Captain dived for the torpedo tubes, grabbed a telephone headset – 'If anyone shows himself or opens fire I'll have him shot!'

Edward meant it. The heads vanished.

They were just big motor launches, low in the water, with wide flared bows designed for speeds in excess of forty knots. Because they were covered with camouflage patterns of blue and grey, their sleek E-boat outline was, to the eye, slightly distorted; though not distorted enough to conceal at close range the two fixed torpedo tubes, one on each side of their enclosed cockpits, nor the two-pounder gun, four twin cannons, and two belted Spandaus, all abaft the stubby radio masts, and all manned by crouching gunners.

They approached from the rear. One anchored twenty yards off the port quarter, another the same distance to starboard. But the third nosed its way close along the destroyer's side, from stern to bow, before finally coming to rest a dozen yards in front of them.

One after the other they cut their powerful aero engines, and blue exhaust fumes drifted in the sudden stillness.

Edward was rigid, fists clenched. He relaxed carefully because the E-boat crews were now studying the ship with binoculars. He slouched over to the telephone, spoke to York, hung up.

Guiseppe's voice boomed out from the bridge.

'Has the German Navy lost its manners? Do you always greet your allies with loaded guns?' Both questions were put in Italian, then on receiving no reply, repeated in English. He sounded genuinely angry.

The cockpit door of the E-boat to starboard slid back. A young naval Lieutenant stepped forward on the bows, stood feet astride, hands on hips. The arrogance in his pose was heightened by the arched, Nazi-style cap and the iron cross that hung from a ribbon on the white shirt. His delay in replying was sheer, calculated insolence.

'You have lost your tongue?' Guiseppe snarled.

Again the insolence as the Nazi hands came up with deliberate slowness and cupped round the mouth. 'Good morning, Kapitan. You have no need to be afraid. We are here to protect you from the British.'

'I do notta see any British. But I see your guns trained on my ship.'

Rose could have sworn to a leer on the German's face. 'Nor I, Kapitan... At least, not with my eyes... But with my nose, perhaps...?' Another pause. 'We would not, uh, want you to be captured again, now would we?'

Under his cap, Rose's big throbbing headache was now joined by his heart. The insult made he and Dunbar exchanged glances. Together they stared up at the bull figure of Guiseppe at the rear of the bridge.

How much more could the Italian take?

The German had now put his hands back on his hips, and was clearly smirking at the angry silence.

That silence didn't last long.

The Captain's intake of breath came at the same time as the whirring of A, B and Y turrets turning on their mountings, guns at the same time depressing until all three E-boats were covered.

'I'll shoot York,' Edward breathed.

The German was rigid, hands now dropping slowly to his sides. Behind him, the crouching gunners had crouched a little lower. One of the Spandaus turned its muzzle on Dunbar and Rose.

But there was no angry bluster from *Scorpio's* bridge. Guiseppe's voice was very cold, very calm, very clear.

'You will perhaps kill Commander Sasso and Lieutenant Piccioni,' he said. 'You may even kill me before I can duck from sight. But your bullets will not penetrate half an inch of steel... You have a choice, Lieutenant. You have five seconds to make it.'

The German made it in three.

He spun round, spat an order in German that brought his gunners erect, their gun muzzles tilting to the sky. His next order cracked out across the water, and the other three torpedo boats followed suit.

He then faced the bridge.

'I have made *my* choice, Kapitan Durand.' That was all he said, and not even distance could mask the hate.

Rose winced as the door of the cockpit slammed shut.

The German gunners were bickering over cigarettes before Edward got his limbs to work. Then, as the turrets trained back fore and aft, he turned stiffly and took the Navigator's arm. 'Phew,' he said. 'So help me, I'll shoot York *and* Guiseppe. Blast it, couldn't they see he was bluffing?'

'*You* looked a little rigid, sor.'

'I don't want any cheek from you, Pilot.' But he took the Navigator's arm gently and steered aft towards the quarterdeck, an action explained by the one desperate word, 'Coffee!'

'I don't like this set-up,' Rose proclaimed.

'What don't you like about it?'

'The U-boats and the E-boats in a harbour where there are no installations and no boom defences to protect them from the hated British. Isn't it unusual?'

'It's probably a holiday camp for U-boat crews,' Edward said. 'After all, we have places like this where our chaps can rest up. A British submarine would have the same chance of finding them as the proverbial needle in the haystack. It's also quite natural for us to have an E-boat escort. We are about to take part in an important experiment.' He glanced sideways, added, 'Were,' and read Rose's mind. 'I know your next question, Pilot... What, you are about to ask me, did the E-boat coxswain mean when he said: "I have made *my* choice," to

Guiseppe. Well, I noticed the emphasis on the "my", too, and it immediately flashed across my mind that it could only mean Guiseppe *had* a choice. And that choice could only be – to betray us and save his infernal brothers.'

Edward stopped at the head of the wardroom hatch.

'But that would mean they know we're British,' he went on. 'And that's not possible, Pilot. You've just seen why. We could blow those E-boats and U-boats out of the water and be out of this harbour inside three minutes.'

Rose put his hypothesis carefully. 'Supposing the enemy know we're British, but pretended not to know…?'

'That would be damned silly. If they know that, then they also know we're after the airstrip. And I have the clue I needed. I also know how to penetrate this E-boat screen.'

He paused and frowned. 'What's bothering you, Pilot?'

'It's just that I had a dream,' Rose admitted lamely. 'About the late Colonel Lenz. I think they *do* know we're British. How I don't know. But I have a good memory – you know that, sir. And I keep trying to think. Because I know there is something we've forgotten. Something they know and we don't. Something like that. Some reason for them to act this way. But my head. It's splitting…'

York would have scoffed. Not Edward, though. He just smiled sympathetically, and would have gone down the steps into the cabin flat, had not one of Rose's Telegraphists, pale-faced and breathless, raced up those steps.

'The radio, sir! We can't get the Admiral's routine call from Alex. The Germans, sir – they're jamming the whole wave band! From up there in the hills, sir!'

But, whatever the reason, there was no turning back.

The day fled, like death was at the end of it. Nothing stirred. Heat shimmered. Flies buzzed. Out of sight, men worked, sweated, cursed, drank gallons of tepid water.

At dusk, in the chartroom, reports were complied.

Edward, head bowed, hands on the table, arms and part of a grim face in the light, listened, nodded, advised, ordered, and scribbled on a pad.

At the end of thirty minutes he possessed a complete and detailed account of *Scorpio's* fighting potential, from the oil fuel situation, down to the last potato in the Paymaster's stores. Every shell and depth charge had been fused. Every man had been supplied with a glass of wine on completion. Cruikshank affirmed that casualty stations had been set up for'd and aft, and stretcher parties organised. Young Pascoe had survived his operation and was doing well.

When the last report was received, Dunbar thanked them.

'I'm very much obliged to you all,' he said. 'Somewhere about dawn we will have to fight our way out of here. The exact time will depend on when you get back from shore, Number One. But tomorrow will be a long day. And tomorrow night I want to get through the Strait of Otranto under cover of darkness. Get all the sleep you can. Thank you, gentlemen.'

Thus the first meeting ended at 20.00 hours on the Sunday evening.

The second meeting followed immediately, and was held for the benefit of those men who had not been present when Edward had formulated his plan.

It was brief, dramatic, and attended by twenty-one men of Trigger-happy York's crack naval commandos – or his Boarding Party, as he preferred to call them. All gunnery school ratings, they were trained in close combat techniques, and all had been blooded with a naval brigade at Dunkirk.

Technically it was a platoon, formed by three self-contained sections of seven men. A thick-set Petty Officer, called 'Goosey' Gorman – he couldn't walk, he strutted about – led Section 3. Dapper, ramrod-stiff Adams led Section 2. And Section 1 was led by the platoon commander, 'T-h'York himself, with 'Taxi'Yates as second-in-command.

How they all squeezed into the chartroom would have astonished the Herring Canners Association. They left their Service revolvers, Lewis guns, tripods and belted ammunition, radio and other devilish equipment in the canteen flat below, and turned up bareheaded, wearing dark-blue overalls with little or/and nothing else. Funnel soot darkened their faces. They were the toughest-looking characters on two feet, whose idea of relaxation was dismantling a heavy field gun, manhandling it over walls, up cliffs, down slide wires, then assembling it and firing it, all within one minute – so they said; and the Navigating Officer, who felt like a stoutish virgin in an encampment of lecherous Bedouins, could well believe it.

The First Lieutenant, overall open to the navel to reveal a chest like a wet hearth-rug, wiped the sweat from his brow, said, 'Christ, it's hot,' put his head down and wriggled in last, causing Rose to pop out into the passage like a piece of soap.

Rose stood on his tiptoes with little avail.

He heard Dunbar say: 'Our clue to the airstrip's location is undoubtedly the tug. The Tugmaster seemed pleasant enough. But too pleasant and friendly for the Gestapo's liking. That means he has information of importance. As the First Lieutenant said, an airstrip would need aviation fuel and other necessary equipment. It could be carried by ship. Or it could be towed. Probably from Zadar, on the Yugoslav coast... Anyway, that's our hunch. We have no alternative but to follow it.' He paused and raised his voice. 'You there, Pilot?'

'Just, sir.'

'It's twenty-five to. Better do it now.'

'On my way, sir.'

The Signalman was waiting on the bridge in darkness. The E-boats were still there, almost unseen.

'The tug's over there, sir. Near the village.'

'We'll make: Please come alongside and remove oil barge. How long will you be.'

The Aldis lamp flashed as Rose dictated each letter in Italian. 'Twenty minutes,' came the answer.

Rose hurried below, where, not wishing to interrupt, he stood at the door behind Yates' broad back.

York was speaking:

'...so our task is to capture the tug before moonrise and get it out of this harbour while the Skipper creates a noisy diversion... Any questions?'

'Once we're on the tug, sir, it'll be too late to come back. So supposing there's no clue to the airstrip?'

149

'Why, then we just take up residence on the islands until the war is over, Gorman... Any more damn' fool questions?'

No one had.

'I heartily disagree with your decision not to take the cyanide capsules,' Edward reproved. 'All you do is affix them to whatever part of the body you can get to quickest. There's sticky tape in the tin... Come on, Number One, set the example.'

'I'm not stopping them,' York retorted indignantly. 'They can take them if they wish. Personally, I think it's a lot of bilge water. We're not spies. We're saboteurs. We'll get shot. Not tortured. Go on, lads, help yourselves.'

No one did.

'I'm taking mine,' Rose called encouragingly.

York glanced back over his shoulder.

'Now?'

A glass of water and a capsule followed the question.

9

Dugi Otok was outside the range of allied bombers, and the Dalmatian's disinterest in the war was evident from the numerous lights which clustered about the foreshore and dotted the hills. It could have been any village on the north coast of Cornwall. From the Axis point of view, the only danger was the thousand to one chance of a British submarine deciding to snoop around the islands for an easy prize. The vessels in harbour therefore remained darkened, though not strictly. Cigarettes glowed in the darkness on the E-boat decks. A torch had been seen to flash as gunners inspected their weapons or, perhaps, boastfully displayed a latest pin-up to a drooling friend.

Then there was a haunting melody, sung softly in German, which drifted across the twinkling water and down through the circular, star-studded hole in the deck of the empty oil barge. Twenty-five pairs of eyes were focused upwards on that hole through the glass goggles of gas masks worn to prevent death by fumes from the black and slimy coating of crude oil that boxed them in on six sides.

Everyone was listening to that song.

'Lend my your 'anky, Nobby,' someone mumbled from under his mask. 'That bastard's got me in tears.'

'He'll still be singing it when he cuts you up with his Spandau,' Adams growled without sentiment. 'Anyone heard it before?'

'It's called "Lilli Marlene,"' Rose said. 'That's the German version. It was sung originally by Lale Andersen, back in '39. It never caught on. It has now.'

A shaft of light slanted in through the hole and lit a gleaming circle of oil as Dunbar had the dish of bulbs on the after funnel switched on.

The Gunner's Mate, waiting at the head of the ladder, slipped the manhole cover almost into place, leaving just a thin crescent of light like a new moon.

They stood then in silence, sweat pouring from their bodies, for the barge was a stinking oven after the heat of the day. And into the stillness came the distant rumble of tumbling water as the tug approached.

York took his Colt out of the holster.

Outside they heard Guiseppe's voice shouting instructions. A moment later the tug bumped against the barge. They all staggered, clung to each other to remain upright and clear of the treacherous viscous oil. Running feet sounded above. Wires scraped. The sound of tumbling water increased to a roar as tug and barge backed away from *Scorpio.*

Two and a half minutes passed.

Rose thought about the love song and of Freer ... and of his dream; but dreams, Edward had said, were a manifestation of one's own fears ... or one's own convictions?

The tug's propellers stopped churning. Engine-room telegraphs tinkled distantly. Then again the waterfall of noise. The tug had turned, was moving inshore.

With infinite care, an inch at a time, the manhole cover scraped back, and the Gunner's Mate put his head up among the stars, turning it like a periscope, then hung it down inside the tank. 'All clear, sir. There's a light inside her bridge. Can't see anyone on deck, though.'

The First Lieutenant acknowledged, his grip tightening on Rose's arm as he warned: 'No noise. One shot will bring those E-boats.'

One by one they emerged from the hole, slithered away into the night. Prior to embarking they had studied a sketch of the tug. Everyone knew exactly what to do, where to go. All they waited for was York's signal.

Rose flinched when a spotlight pierced the darkness from the bridge, fell on the shore and water ahead.

'He's checking his bearings before anchoring,' York whispered. 'Not to worry, Professor, this is kid's stuff.' He sounded utterly bored with the whole thing.

A low whistle preceded the attack. Fourteen pairs of feet made only the smallest patter as they landed inboard. Gorman's section covered them from the barge.

A ladder led up to the door behind the bridge.

In the dimly lit interior, the Tugmaster and three men were concentrating and their awareness of an alien presence came in the form of four flitting shadows and the hard jab of a Colt in the small of the back.

The Tugmaster was thick-set, not tall. His scalp gleamed dully between strands of hair, for he'd had his head out of the front windows and lost his cap during recoil. Being the one man most likely to raise the alarm, York took him from behind, hand over mouth, lifted him bodily, carried him through the door behind the helm and dumped him on an untidy bunk in a cabin strewn with empty bottles, discarded clothes, and tattered naked ladies. The other three were shepherded in as well. Yates stood guard.

Engines were stopped and the helm put hard over to allow the vessel to lose way in a tight circle.

A Leading Seaman of Section 1 set up his suitcase-size radio and kept a listening watch on a pre-arranged frequency.

All this had hardly been done when Gorman strutted in and reported that another eight men below decks had put up no resistance and the tug was theirs. But one more oddity: 'No Gestapo, sir. Not a sign of them. We've searched.'

'That's strange.' A surprised York considered, then turned. 'Ask the Tugmaster what happened to the Gestapo, Professor!'

Yates was gloating over the ladies when Rose slipped in. Alas, they were not real.

The question was put in Italian. The swarthy face looked up from the bunk. One would have expected belligerence, anger at least, in those dark eyes; but instead there was fear.

'They went ashore at dusk,' he answered sullenly.

'Do you know where and why?'

A shrug. 'Would they tell me?' It was a fair answer.

As the Navigator dived back on to the bridge he was conscious of the hiss and crackle of static from the radio, of the Leading Seaman mouthing words at the First Lieutenant, and then York, who'd been squatting by the set, climbed to his feet, hand to his forehead. 'Dunbar. He's just been on. Durand's escaped.'

'Escaped!' echoed Rose.

'Escaped! Escaped! Escaped!' York thundered. 'Are you bloody well deaf! He's gone. He jumped over the side.' He stood breathing heavily, undecided.

The Gunner's Mate knew his master's moods, he approached cautiously. 'E.R.A.'s on the blower, sir. He and the two Stokers are in the engine-room now. They're ready when you are.'

York nodded, raised his eyes from the deck, stared at the Navigator or a full five seconds. He didn't have to say anything. Once off the ship, Guiseppe could vindicate himself with the Gestapo. But there was no turning back.

'Let's go!' York barked.

After three minutes of hurried preparation he took command, and had just asked the engine-room for enough speed for steerage way only when a commotion sounded on the decks below, feet sounded on the ladder, and the bridge door crashed open.

Guiseppe lumbered in, clothes clinging wetly to his fleshy torso. He stopped in front of the First Lieutenant.

'The Germans,' he gasped breathlessly, 'they notta see me. I swim under water. My brothers. I help them escape. You take me please.'

York was relieved. But he was sceptical. 'You mean you're joining us? Changing sides? You! I don't believe it.'

'My father fought with the British in the

last big war,' Guiseppe said grandly. 'It is not my fault that Mussolini takes the Third Reich as his ally.'

That was true. Nevertheless...

'Don't believe him,' Rose said urgently, coming over. 'He's up to something. Men like him don't change sides.'

'I'll decide that!' snapped York. He then eyed the Italian for a long moment. 'All right. Come if you want. Who cares.' He turned away.

The engine-room telegraph jangled.

Keep close to the rock face, to be invisible against the blackness of towering hills, they crept from harbour.

Scorpio still had her funnel light on, floodlighting her starboard side. Hammering and the metallic crashing of sheet metal drifted across the night. Edward was creating the promised diversion by getting busy on an imaginary repair.

It was curious, Rose reflected, that Dunbar's clue to the airstrip had been provided by the Gestapo themselves. Odd that they should have silenced the Tugmaster so openly...

Bridge fittings included two broad shelves at the rear, one supporting the tug's old-fashioned radio, the other acting as a table for charts, all of which were filthy and dog-eared except one; and that one, oddly, lay at the bottom of the pile and was identical to the one supplied by Lenz, back at Catania, though someone had filled in a great deal of vital information with a mapping pen: important details like minefields, depths, smaller islands and rocks – and a pencilled course drawn from harbour E24 to another island which was labelled: 'EXPERI-MENTAL AIRFIELD', in English.

Incredulous, he called the First Lieutenant over. 'Look at this. Tell me what you see?'

'I'm looking,' York grunted. 'All I see is clear proof that the Gestapo is dumber than I thought.'

'Don't you see anything odd, for God's sake?'

The grey, hazel-flecked eyes flashed with momentary anger at the disparaging tone. 'Should I?'

'It's a highly confidential chart,' Rose said heavily. 'It revels top secret information on the defences of a top secret weapon. It *must* be absurdly stupid to give it to a Tugmaster. And the Gestapo are not stupid.'

'Nonsense! They make mistakes like us. Let's go.'

And so they went, leaving *Scorpio* but a fuzzy glow far behind in the night. But Rose was not fit. His arm throbbed. His head still hurt. He went in search of a drink.

The tug moved towards the beach and the barge was freed, allowed to drift in towards the rocks.

The manoeuvre had just been completed when the Navigator, refreshed by a cup of tugman's coffee, returned to the bridge. If there was anything in life designed to put a man on guard, it was, he reflected, the simple fact that things go absolutely according to plan, when, by all the laws of human frailty, they should go wrong. Not drastically wrong, perhaps, but at least there ought to be one mistake. But no mistakes had been made. Not one. Edward's hunch has been uncannily correct. It was just too good to be true.

Was he thinking of himself? It was the first time he had posed that question since leaving Alexandria. Perhaps it was important now that he should. Help others while helping himself. A good philosophy. All men were selfish.

He decided to alter the course of events.

But York was one of Nature's bulls. Born to breed. A good bull to have around, but also a stubborn one. And he could be violent.

The bull was leaning out of the bridge window.

'Excuse me, sir...' Rose said.

He received an eye-over-the-shoulder glance. 'Hullo, Professor, feeling better? Fifty minutes grace and you can start to sweat again.'

'I'm sweating now,' Rose answered pointedly. 'I want to talk to you urgently. Right now!' He deliberately moved away to the far corner of the bridge.

York followed. 'Come on, then. Let's have it.'

'That course on the chart,' Rose said, turning. 'Let's just follow it so far, then find our own way.'

'One good reason?' York was snappy.

'I have a hunch–'

'You mean you had a dream,' York sneered. 'Dunbar told me. One question. If they knew who we were, why did they let us get this far?'

'I don't bloody well know.' Rose tried to keep his temper. 'Look, why is our radio being jammed? Why were the Gestapo hiding on the tug this morning? Why was the Tugmaster jovial this morning – when now he's frightened out of his guts?' He caught York's arm, pointed with his other hand at the cabin door. 'Go and look at him! See for yourself! His fear shows.'

'So does yours,' York retorted contemptuously, and pulled his arm away. 'And don't tell me to go and see anyone in future. I give the orders. And while we're at it, I'd appreciate a little more "sir".'

Rose made one last desperate bid.

'Look – sir – there is one good reason. The enemy need a fast ship to test the glider bomb. Does it matter what nationality the men on that ship are?' It was a lousy reason, but there was just a chance that dumb York wouldn't know that. Wrong again. York did.

He stopped in the act of turning away. 'I discussed that with Dunbar. Very soon we'll be at the airstrip. By the time we leave there won't be any plane and no glider bombs.'

'There *must* be a reason,' Rose pleaded at the receding back. 'There's something – something they know and we don't. Or something we've forgotten–'

'There's something I haven't forgotten,' York said in a loud voice for all to hear.

'What's that – sir?'

'You fell on your head!'

Not funny. But some day, Rose vowed, he was going to strangle Leading Seaman Yates with his own bare hands.

He went and had another chat with the Tugmaster and got nowhere. The fear was still there. Strong.

Because the bridge was in semi-darkness to avoid York's night sight being impaired, the gloom added to his frustration by leaving that Gestapo-marked chart in a tiny island of vibrating light. It was a trap. He sensed it. He sensed it as a man senses the approaching edge of a cliff by the almost imperceptible up-draught from the sea ... a blind man.

Then came the hiss and crackle of static from the radio.

'Bluebell calling Primrose. Are you receiving me? Come in, Primrose. Over.' It was Edward Dunbar.

York strode over, knelt down.

'Primrose answering. Primrose answering. We are receiving you. Static bad. Have important message. What you lost, we found. G is with us. I repeat. G is with us. Your hunch was right. All is well. No casualties, proceeding phase two. Over.'

'Your message gratefully understood. Will maintain listening watch. Good luck. Over and out.'

Phase one had ended.

The twenty-knot wind of the tug's rampaging passage steamed through the open stormproof windows out of which the First Lieutenant leaned, watching along with Durand the channels of darkness that ran between the dark masses of overlapping islands.

Discovered to have been christened *Juliana,* the sturdy vessel was now an hour and ten minutes steaming from *Scorpio's* berth, fifteen minutes from the southern tip of *the* island, and one hour ahead of the moon. She was wearing her red, green and white navigational lights to avoid ramming the many fishing boats whose one candlepower lanterns rocked violently in her deeply corrugated wash.

Most of the time had been spent reproducing pocket copies of the chart, removing crude oil from hands and clothes with petrol, getting weapons ready, dishing out hand grenades, Troy's explosives, and drinking ERSATZ coffee that made the oil smell like violets in comparison.

The island charted was only four hundred yards from the towering alpine coast of Yugoslavia. Like all the islands, it was elongated, had a spine of hills, and lay parallel to the coast. Mines had been laid from the southern tip to the mainland, and likewise from the northern tip, thus creating an oblong 'box' of water from what had been a through channel. The pencilled course zigzagged, for the mines had been laid in such a way as to make direct entry impossible, and with the same simplicity that the enemy had engineered the security of the airstrip – it lay on the west side of the 'box' – Simon York had planned its destruction. They would, he had said earlier, pass through the minefield and then alter course and seek a cove or inlet within one mile of the target. The platoon would go the rest of the way on foot, in moonlight, and time would be well on their side; but not so Lieutenant Rose's unspoken comments! Simplicity was a fine thing, the right thing –

if the element of surprise was assured. But York had not spoken to the Navigator for one hour and ten minutes: being a fearless, practical man he was sulking at having been confronted by doubts on his own ability to master what seemed a straightforward if dangerous task, and the Navigator's theories amounted to little less. Because everything had been as meticulously timed as the constant plotting of stars and cross bearings on mountain peaks had to be accurate, it was all the more surprising when, ten minutes early, the First Lieutenant suddenly retracted his head and shoulders, turned, glared angrily at Rose, crashed his fist on the nearest telegraph mounting, and bellowed: 'Stop engines!' The order marked the end of eighty minutes of unaccustomed introspection.

The racket of telegraphs and vibration died away.

York's eyes were on the Gunner's Mate behind the wheel. 'I'm modifying the plan, Adams. Your section and Gorman's go ashore here. It will mean rowing for two miles to the south tip of the island and hoofing it for another three over hellish country. You'll be lucky if you make it. That's why I'm going on as planned. We'll probably have done the job before you get there – but at least we'll give you a lift back. Right?'

'All right, sir.' A puzzled Adams nodded

slowly. 'But why – why the change?'

Every face on the bridge followed the First Lieutenant's glance at the chart shelf. 'Let's just say that one of us missed being a man by a few hormones!' He strode across to the door, slammed it behind him.

Under his soot, Rose was scarlet, and Yates' snigger made it worse. The quiet voice at his side was Adams. 'He didn't mean that, sir. He's said worse things to me. He's a good man to have with you in a tight corner.'

'Yes. He is. And he's walking straight into one. The trouble is, he's too bloody proud to listen to anyone else.'

'He's too worried about all the men who'll die if he doesn't make it to consider himself,' Adams retorted stiffly.

There were many angry things the Navigator would like to have said. He said none of them. He took the Gunner's Mate's arm, drew him close under the light and pointed at the chart. 'You don't have to do what I suggest,' he began. 'But at least you can listen and decide for yourself...'

Juliana had two boats turned in on davits, one on each side of her squat funnel. It took ten minutes to turn them out, load them, muffle the oars and rowlocks, lower them to the water. Adams took one, Gorman the other. They had copy charts, compasses, experience and guts. The splash of their oars was audible long after they were lost in the night. But their exit left only eleven men on board.

All lights were extinguished and York rang for slow speed. In the KANALI navigators had to become pilots and, with the proximity of the southern minefield, every terrestrial cross bearing had to be double checked against the stars, and checked again, time after time, and rancour had no place.

However, one other man might have caused discord, and that was Yates; he sat on a chair in the cabin, heels on the table, studying the exciting poses of the naked ladies and taking little interest in the three tugmen who played cards on the same bunk as their Captain sat with his head in his hands. Apart from being a glib, cynical tough, the Leading Seaman was bone lazy. The Navigator went in once, because firstly he was trying to put himself in the Gestapo's place and secondly the tugmen's indifferent behaviour puzzled him. It had been expected that the men would be armed, but no arms had been found, not even a knife, and there was no concealment under the multi-coloured shirts and slacks. During that one trip he took another look round, but Yates affirmed sneeringly that there was 'nowt'. The only other hiding place was the untidy bunk on which the men were sitting, and he made to order them to rise when Guiseppe called him from the door to say that the minefield was four hundred yards ahead. As it happened, the minefield was nearly a thousand yards ahead when Rose checked the chart; and six hundred yards was a big error in time at slow speed. But then Guiseppe wasn't piloting and there was no good reason to suspect contrivance, so suspicion was put down to nervous tension – even when, while crossing the bridge from port to starboard to check bearings on the other side, he noticed Yates going off with an empty mug for coffee; and on the Navigator's way back to report to York he saw Durand hand the Colt back to the returning Yates, and emerge.

'*You* were keeping guard?' Rose challenged.

'They do notta seem to need much guarding,' Guiseppe shrugged. 'They are merchantmen. The war means little to them.'

'It means something to the Tugmaster.'

'Like all captains, he worries about his ship.'

'I wonder.'

Besides the three officers, there were on the bridge three ratings, and one was the Leading Seaman by the radio. He was doing nothing. So why hadn't Yates asked him to guard the tugmen? – instead of a senior officer who was virtually a prisoner-of-war on parole! There could only be one answer to that: not even Yates would have asked Durand, and therefore the Italian *must* have volunteered. But why?

As he gave the careful alterations of course that conned the tug into position to enter the minefield, Rose considered this. 'A daring and resourceful officer and a patriot,' Edward had described the Italian. But an hour ago Guiseppe had made a decision which automatically turned him into a traitor...? Or was he being resourceful? He had heard Rose's theories, seen the oddities like everyone else, and he certainly looked less desolate than he had during the morning. At that moment Rose stopped thinking, for he suddenly knew beyond any shadow of a doubt that before jumping from *Scorpio's* decks Guiseppe had guessed the real reason for all the oddities for which he himself was desperately searching.

'You know!' Rose blurted it out.

Durand said nothing, gave no sign that he'd even heard. He had settled by the front windows out of which York leaned, concentrating hard.

'You know! What it's all about! You've guessed!' Rose exploded again.

This time Guiseppe turned a heavy face, and in the eyes was that old hate. 'I do notta know what you talk about.'

York withdrew his head, glanced first at the Italian, then past him at Rose. 'What the bloody hell's the matter with you now!'

The Navigator willed himself to calm. 'He

knows the answer. He's guessed. Ask him. He didn't come here to help us rescue his brothers. He knew it was a trap, and why, and he's playing along with the Gestapo–'

The Italian staggered in the semi-darkness as York lunged past him, caught the Navigator's overall lapels and half his flesh as well, impaled him against the bridge front. 'Thirty seconds!' he snarled. 'Thirty seconds and we'll be slap in the centre of a minefield. Do you know what a mine will do to this tug?'

'Listen – for God's sake listen,' Rose pleaded through his agony. 'We've got to get the answer from him.'

'Yes. I'll listen. To you doing your job!'

'You stupid fool–!' The sentence was cut short by a vicious scything stroke of York's hand.

Rose was plucked from the bulkhead, spun round to face the back of the bridge, sent staggering against the chart shelf, over which he hung winded, breathless, watching the blood from his mouth drip on the parchment. Then, desperate, he half turned, made to speak again, saw Guiseppe's triumph, heard Yates' soft snigger; and he knew it was hopeless.

He turned his head back to the chart, smeared away the blood from his calculations. 'We will enter the field in ten seconds,' he said, cursed the tremor in his voice. 'Steer three-two-oh degrees!'

'Course three-two-oh degrees, sir!' The helmsman's face was flushed by the glow of the compass card.

The mines were anchored to the sea bed by weights, and being buoyant they stood erect, straining on the long wires which kept them a few feet below the surface, where they waved gently in the warm, dark, silent waters, as do anemones; but they were black, and one touch on their evil horns would bring disaster, so *Juliana* had steerage way only, and not a sound of a ripple could be heard, nor a flutter from the wind, and all was quiet but for the muted rumble of her engines. The smell of petrol and oil hung on the clothes and turned the stomach. No one spoke. Rose had his eyes on the second hand of the watch that would tell him precisely when to give the next order to the helm. According to the chart the field was a mile and a half in depth and sown in separate concentrated strips, each approximately a quarter of a mile apart. In each strip was a gap, called a gate, and they were staggered, not in line.

11.17 p.m. 'We're passing through the first gate. Now,' Rose said sullenly. In one minute and thirty seconds they were clear. 'We should be through,' he said. 'All clear for three-fifty yards. Steer three-three-five degrees!' The tug turned the few points necessary to bring her bow in line with the next gate.

'Course three-three-five degrees, sir.'

'Very good.'

11.21 p.m. 'Next gate coming up – now.' Sixty seconds this time. 'All clear for four hundred yards.' Rose also gave the next alteration of course, then, because his body was painfully taut, tried to relax by looking up and around. Yates, he noticed, had got off his fat bottom and now leaned out of the cabin door, back to his apparently indifferent captives. He had the furtive look of a nervous man; but who hadn't? Guiseppe hadn't: he had moved back from the front windows and into the shadows on the other side of the helm, leaving York half out of the bridge front, eyes straining into the night. But the Italian seemed relaxed – waiting? For what – and what defence had they? Apart from the three men down in the engine-room, non-combatants, only three of York's section were missing from the bridge; they were manning a Lewis gun on the decks below.

11.27 p.m. 'Next gate coming up!' Rose called. 'Your head, helmsman!'

'Three-four-two degrees, sir!'

As the second hand ticked round the face of the watch, Rose was conscious of his swelling lip, of the controlled anger that still burned from the First Lieutenant's childish behaviour, and then – ? – then he was conscious of a noise: a very, very slight sound that seemed like a scrap on the tug's metal hull and lasted no more time than it took to glance round and see that everyone else had heard it too: and then it stopped – suddenly – as if the wire it had sounded like had parted. And Guiseppe was faintly smiling... It couldn't have been the wire of a mine or he wouldn't have been... The only other kind of wire it could be was the kind that stretched under water and trips an alarm.

But they were dead in the centre of the third gate. Unable to turn. Unable to retreat. And it could be imagination.

There were forty seconds to go. No time to speculate. No margin for error. 'Sixty-six, sixty-seven.' He looked up again. 'All clear for four-fifty–' He broke off.

A searchlight lit every corner of the bridge.

'*Danger!* Heave to! You are in a minefield and off course!' The order had come in German, booming on a loud hailer.

The trap had been sprung.

He dived for the engine-room telegraphs, stopping the tug before York could respond to the translation.

Their dash to the side window was automatic.

The searchlight was being directed from shore, without doubt backed by guns and itchy fingers.

'I can hear a boat somewhere,' York whispered.

'Aw, shut up!'

The Tugmaster's cap skimmed across the bridge, was caught, clammed down on Rose's aching head.

'Bluff 'em!' York hissed.

'How, for Pete's sake!'

'Tell them we're on our way through to Zadar to pick up a barge of aviation fuel on Gestapo instructions!'

'They can check that in minutes.'

'Do it!'

Rose used the tug's megaphone. There was no reply. He tried again with the same result and then gave up. 'It's no use. They're stalling. They're waiting for something–'

'They are waiting for my signal,' announced a voice from behind.

They wheeled round, found themselves staring into the muzzle of an Italian Breda machine-gun. Behind it stood the stocky Tugmaster, flanked by two of his men, armed likewise, the third tugman having just throttled Yates, who slumped to the deck as the helmsman raised his hands in surrender. But it was the mocking grin on Guiseppe's face which got York panting with fury. 'You stinking traitor!'

'On the contrary, he's just being a resourceful patriot,' Rose objected dryly, and looked the Tugmaster straight in the eye. 'So you had your weapons under the pillow. I nearly found them, you know. I suppose the Gestapo have your wife and kids...?'

The Tugmaster didn't say; he didn't have to. The Breda poked Rose to silence. The bridge lights flashed on. In less than ten seconds a boat bumped the tug's side, was followed by pounding feet on the decks below, barking voices, feet on the ladder. The door crashed open. York's three Lewis gunners stumbled in, hands clasped above their heads. In their wake came men dressed in greenish-grey lightweight battledress and forage caps. Their trousers were tucked into their boots, their tunics heavily pocketed, held tight to their bodies with belted ammunition pouches.

The uniform badges caught York's eye.

'Paratroops,' he whispered.

'Nothing but the very best,' replied Rose glumly.

A tough, tanned, lace-booted officer, pistol in hand, barked orders. Being the biggest menace – in every sense – his men pounced on the First Lieutenant, trapped his arms, stripped off what little he had on.

York protested violently, glared at Rose. 'Tell them to lay off, will you. What the hell are they looking for?'

'Your cyanide capsule.'

They didn't find it, of course, but they

searched high and low, and York finished up purple.

Two men with brown shirts, black breeches, and arched caps with white piping strode through the door. They were Gestapo. To the Italians they showed the same contempt that the Ju88 bombers had shown to *Scorpio*. But they ignored the prisoners and spoke in Italian to Guiseppe and one of the tugmen. That conversation explained the jamming of the radio and all the strange events of the day. It also brought a soft, bitter laugh to Rose's lips.

'Where's the comedy?' York demanded acidly.

Rose cleared his throat. 'The S.S. *Earith*. It must have been the ship carrying *Scorpio's* Italian crew. It went aground in the storm we had. One prisoner escaped. That's him. The smallest of the tugmen. Guiseppe must have guessed something was up and started figuring. He got the answer I failed to get... It wasn't that the enemy knew something we didn't. It's the other way round. We know something they don't... We steamed into a trap. It was set to catch – alive! – the man who was organising the resistance fighters in Yugoslavia and Greece. The man who knows the names of partisan leaders.'

'Major Troy!' The whispered name exploded on York's astonished lips. 'But – but he's dead.'

'Silence!' barked the paratroop leader.

'Oh, shut up!' York snarled back at him, and turned desperate eyes on Rose. 'Tell them to ask Guiseppe. He knows. He saw Troy die. Tell them!'

'That's the comedy,' admitted Rose quietly. 'They have asked him. Guiseppe has just denied it... About those cyanide capsules you refused to take... Have you ever been tortured to reveal a truth that you know won't be believed – not even when you scream it at them in agony?'

10

The enemy's searchlight moved over the water with purpose, scanning an arc of two hundred degrees. It was obviously mounted on some half-track vehicle, for it had moved to the very south tip of the island after Guiseppe had revealed that fourteen men had disembarked. If Adams and Gorman were where they should have been, then it was quite impossible for them to remain un-discovered, and occasional torchlight on the hillside made it certain that more troopers were astride the goat, sheep and dirt tracks among the vineyards and the trees.

'They haven't found them.' York's voice

was low, filled with worry and disbelief. He, like Rose, stood on the tug's port side with the nine other men, hands tied behind their backs, 'chained' together with ropes which were also reeved through handrails on the bulkhead. 'They couldn't have landed,' he went on. 'They couldn't have landed already, could they?' He paused for a comforting reply, got none, then said: 'All right, Professor, so I was wrong. You don't have to go in the huff about it.'

'I'm not huffing. I'm just praying your ramrod stiff Gunner's Mate had some common sense.'

'In what respect?'

'He could have crossed the channel and slipped along under the cliffs on the Yugoslavian side, then crossed at the other end of the island and come in from the north. It's the last thing they would expect. The Gestapo, I mean.'

'Talk sense. It would take them nearly three hours. Anyway, Adams had no reason to change my plan.'

'He had.'

'What d'you mean?'

'I told him to.'

'You told him...' York echoed incredulously.

'I also told him his boss was a great, hairy, bone-headed ass,' Rose said mildly. This, of course, was a lie; what the Navigator had actually said was obscene, unrepeatable and, in practice, physically impossible.

A gun butt put an end to the discussion for some minutes. It wasn't the first indication that they were not to be treated as prisoners-of-war. The paratroops were surly, offensive, and Rose had already seen the contempt in their eyes; and not only for the British, but for Guiseppe, too. If there was any irony in the situation it was that, irrespective of Durand's cruel denial, as far as the Gestapo was concerned, Troy, like Edward, was immortal and couldn't be dead anyway: and Yates was immortal as well – he alas had recovered from well-deserved strangulation and stood coughing and wheezing near by.

A nudge from York. 'Professor, you've got to get out of here. And you've got to make it before they lock us up and put the screws on.' A pause for reaction. There wasn't any. 'Adams and Gorman can't fight blind. They've got to know the lie of the land. They won't have time for reconnaissance. You'll have to do it and then contact them... Ever played rugger?'

'Not since I broke a finger at conkers,' Rose scowled. 'Don't tell me. You have another plan...'

Neither friend nor foe was infallible, and the *time* changed sides from hour to hour, being sometimes with you, sometimes against you; so also the elements, the prevailing circumstances, and only the rotation of Earth, that brought sunshine, moonshine or darkness, was constant – like the fast rhythm of fear.

Since balls and chains were in short supply, the Wehrmacht paratroops had used ropes. Had the bonds on two or more wrists been tampered with, the enemy's frequent torch inspection would in all certainty have foiled the plan. As it was, only one pair of hands had been loosened and rebound with a nautical slip knot by the time *Juliana* rounded a hook and turned into a harbour under a half moon. This time they passed through an anti-submarine net before tying up alongside a jetty where they were led over a gangway in single file and marched, still united by the guide rope, up between trees and sleeping houses and along a dusty, winding track that kept ascending, now parallel to the sea and high above it, until they had almost reached the brow of a hill.

Everyone knew what to do, and all they were waiting for was the right time, the right place, and luck.

York was leading the way, with Rose just behind him, and the column was guarded by the Wehrmacht Captain and one trooper ahead of them, two troopers on each flank, and two behind. It was difficult going. The tree-lined, one-car road had been deeply rutted with caterpillar treads and wheels. It was dark and shadowy because foliage met overhead and obscured the moon. But opportunity came in the form of an approaching military vehicle with slotted headlights which, on the shouted commands and gesticulations of the Wehrmacht officer, drew half off the track to allow passage.

'This is it!' York hissed the words over his shoulder and altered course a couple of points to make sure the column brushed past the vehicle.

Being mortal, the two guards on the right flank had to mark time, for their way was suddenly barred by the truck. For a few seconds the right flank was therefore unguarded.

York fell over his feet. One after the other, against all the laws of velocity, the column piled on top of him; and on top of Rose who, under the scrum, cast off his bonds, selected a pair of legs, and dived through them and under the truck. Five seconds was all that was needed, and at the end of that time the First Lieutenant was upright, cursing, dragging in the surplus rope where Rose had been.

Would they count the bodies?

The Navigator held his breath. Above him the Germans in the truck were laughing. Incensed by their mirth, the guards laid into

180

the column with their gun butts, lashed them with words that were oaths in any language.

He lay on his face between the wheels and watched the feet line up, watched them move off but could hear nothing now with the rumble of the vehicle's heavy diesel as it revved up. Would it move and expose him before the column's rear guards passed? A glance revealed a pair of legs wandering on the other side of the truck; but they disappeared upwards as the owner reboarded. The last legs in the column were abreast when the vehicle lurched forward, stopped, lurched again, and stopped dead. Its nearside rear wheel had bogged down in soft earth.

Above the big, idling pulse of the motor could be heard the restless thuds of Wehrmacht feet on the planking above. At any moment those feet were going to jump down and their owners would start pushing, arms outstretched, toes dug in, eyes on the ground where one prostrate British body would appear when the truck moved forward.

Rose slithered out from under on the woodland side, but had covered only ten feet when, in response to staccato commands, the truck's tailboard crashed down and men leapt out.

He lay still, face down and to one side, that he could see. Against the background of dead leaves and starved grass he was not invisible, but a fallen log near to him lessened the chances of discovery – until one man climbed down from the driver's seat, swaggered towards the back of the truck, but stopped six feet from where Rose lay, put his hands on his hips and barked: 'Come on, then! Don't look at it – push it! One, two, three – push!' and the men at the rear bent their backs while the truck driver revved his engine, making dirt spray from the spinning, smoking wheels. The vehicle bucked and swayed and jolted but refused to budge. Finally the Sergeant called a halt and the men rested, panting with exertion in the warm, shadowy darkness.

It was the moment Rose feared.

The N.C.O. was only as far away as he was tall and he suddenly turned half right and faced the fugitive and would have seen him had not someone yelled, 'There's a bunch of twigs back a bit, Serg. That would shift it.'

The tucked in trousers stopped two feet from the Navigator's nose. The toes were facing him but an upward glance revealed that the Teutonic face was diverted. 'All right. Kurt, Hans, and you, Walter – fetch them!' One more pace. Rose could hear his heart pounding the leaves. 'I'll tell you. Webber, you nip back to the camp and fetch the KUBELWAGEN!' A pause. The feet turned slowly until the heels were foremost.

'Where *is* Webber?' Silence from the men. There was soft menace in the Sergeant's next words. 'He's in the village with that woman again. Isn't he!' No one spoke. The N.C.O. took an angry breath. 'All right, you go. Yes, you, Kurt. And make it fast. And you can tell Webber he's on a charge when you see him. If he's poxed up I'll have him shot.' As the threat was delivered the feet turned fast and strode past with a snapping of twigs and the crunch of leaves.

They stopped about, well, five or six yards behind Rose, and he was afraid to turn, to move, for the driver had stopped his engine and the forest was quiet and every breath brought a rustle, every drop of sweat plopped on the withered leaves like a stone into a pond. The footsteps of Kurt, Hans and Walter receded. He heard the Sergeant sigh somewhere behind, the quiet guttural tones of the men in front, and then – then as the smell of urine tainted the air, he heard the rustle of clothing and the feet turned and started back towards him from the rear, and he held his breath because discovery was inevitable. And it was incredible that he wouldn't be seen and so he turned his head and tensed his body as the Sergeant approached. Seven feet away the man stopped in his tracks, seemed to stare straight at Rose as if disbelieving what he saw. Then a rustle. A click. A scrape and a flash and the German face was lit by the fire of a match which blossomed and went out as the feet strode forward again and tripped over Rose's outstretched arm. 'Donnerwetter!' – the expletive burst from his lips as he staggered, recovered, dropped his cigarette, picked it up twelve inches from the Navigator's face, straightened and soldiered on. It wasn't a miracle for the Sergeant had been blind, his night sight destroyed by the flash of the match.

Nearly four minutes had passed by the time the men returned with the twigs and pressed them under the rear wheel. On the first try the truck jolted out of the rut and on to the track. Then the forest grew silent as its high-ratio engine faded in the night.

Lieutenant Rose, who had been built more for comfort than speed, was not the kind of man to go romping about in the night like the hero of a silent film, and his next move was dictated both by circumstances and the memory of a certain civilian in a certain naval port who had, by purchasing a naval uniform, walked in and out of a certain R.N. barracks and treated himself to free meals for nearly eighteen months, being only discovered when some fool had tried to draft him on to a cruiser.

He selected a stout fallen branch, broke it into a two-foot length, and waited for Kurt.

The KUBELWAGEN came over the brow

of the hill and bumped down the track. It stopped in front of the Navigator who had the stick at his back and his hand in the air.

'Who are you?' Those were Kurt's last conscious words.

Typical of the excellent German equipment, the Volkswagen, as Rose preferred to call it, was a patrol vehicle or Commander's car in the desert. It was armoured, had light machine-guns, and a spare tyre on its sloping front bonnet. He had seen them in Egypt, where they abounded because the 8th Army went out of its way to capture them.

Clothes truly make the man. It was quite astonishing how different Rose felt in the paratrooper's uniform. Though the trouser legs were a little long, it otherwise fitted. Because what little he had possessed, including the carefully concealed cyanide capsule, had been taken from him on the tug, he put on Kurt's wristlet-watch, climbed into the open 'wagen and drove out of the woods, leaving his unconscious prisoner, gagged, bound hand and foot to a tree.

How far was the airstrip? How far ahead was the column? Had the enemy yet counted the bodies?

Moving as fast as the rutted road would allow, he passed over the brow of the hill, down out of the trees and across the floor of a shallow valley, called a POLJE, where maize, barley and hay were generally grown. A silent village, a second wooded hill, and the airstrip lay in the next POLJE. He saw the column ahead, descending towards the roofs of huts, and tents on which the moonlight glinted. It was extraordinarily bright, like a day seen through heavily darkened sunglasses. He could see the runway angled across the floor of the basin to where mechanical diggers had breached its far end to allow planes on take-off to soar out over the KANALI. Whitish patches on the hills told of the presence of limestone and erosion by overgrazing. It was a place, typically Dalmatian, where rain didn't lie around long, being drained away through the soft rock in a network of subterranean channels and caves formed by the solution of calcium carbonate. It was a place that would have excited even a half-baked saboteur and had worried the Germans into withdrawing a crack paratroop regiment from Crete to defend it. The strip had originally been built to support the Wehrmacht's invasion of Yugoslavia and Greece, and would now be used to hunt down partisans led by Communist leaders like Josip Broz Tito. Parked on the aprons, in front of the huts, were Ju88 bombers, Me109 fighters: and one other aircraft, standing apart, with what looked like a petrol tanker at its side. That plane was different. It was larger. It was fatter. It had a greater wing span. That plane was *it!*

The air was warm, contaminated by aviation fuel, scented by foliage and flowers and filled with white dust from the 'wagen's racing tyres.

As he approached the rear of the column he saw on the right, on high ground, what looked like a gasometer. It was actually a camouflaged tank of fuel holding millions of gallons. But round the petrol tank, sentries lurked, alert, watchful, some walking about openly, others invisible and their presence detected by a shadow that seemed at first inanimate until it moved. It was indeed a formidable place, and the 'wagen might well have stopped to allow its driver to reconsider – but the man at the wheel was no longer the inept wartime sailor who had joined *Wildcat* at Alexandria a few days before; but a man who not only spoke the language of the enemy but understood his ways; who not only was a bachelor and a scholar with an ear for music and a photographic memory, but possessed a brilliant strategical mind to go with it. In short, on land, he was – well – not so dumb. And he could sing, too!

Rose cleared his throat and tuned up his larynx. What he was about to do was to provide hope where hope was needed, nothing more.

The rear guards glanced over their shoulders when the vehicle slowed down behind them, showed no surprise at all that the lone occupant was singing lustily, then called ahead to the paratroop Captain, who turned and started to walk backwards, waving the column over to one side, at the same time beckoning the patrol car to pass, which it started to do, slowly, its inquisitive driver peering insolently at the prisoners and still singing. As it drew abreast, the trudging York glanced sideways at it sourly: a glance that froze into comical permanency as he recognised the song.

A smart salute to the Captain and the Volkswagen picked up speed. 'Only a Rose, I bring you... Only a Rose – da, da, dum, dee... Only a Rose...'

It wasn't a bad song, even if the paratroopers hadn't swooned. At least it had been in tune.

But his escape, Rose knew, was a bare fifteen minutes from discovery, the point where the tides of time and circumstance would perhaps be turning.

Ahead lay the camp. It had been built on uneven ground on the edge of the POLJE. The dominant feature was a house, gleaming pale in the moonlight, on slightly raised ground and amid half a dozen trees: the only trees, for the hillock was semi-encircled at a lower level by the small town of huts.

As he drew closer, the ten-foot-high chain

fence became visible, the bark of guard dogs audible, and the gates were open, a sentry on each side, and on one side, inside, stood the guardroom.

He slowed down.

The sentries ported arms and started forward, intending to converge on either side of the 'wagen. They would know Kurt had gone out, where he'd been going and why; they would also be expecting him back.

Forage cap well over his eyes, the memory of Kurt's Westfalen accent in his mind, Rose threw up a friendly hand. 'They got the thing out of the ditch before I got there – but watch out. Warn Webber. He's with that whore in the village an' the Captain's right behind with the English swine.'

He kept the car moving at walking pace as he called. Both sentries were level with the bonnet. One had his hand up. Then, as one, they both laughed and turned away, waving him through at the same time.

The huts were in rows with avenues between, and in the manner of all such camps, each revealed its purpose by a printed notice or by character. Those for living in had windows with anti-blast wire netting in the glass and blackout curtains. So had the offices, but they were marked. The radio hut had its mast. The telephone exchange glinted with insulators and wires.

There were no hangers, only parking aprons, but the windowless building beside the workshops was new, with double steel doors and two sentries – the only sentries off the perimeter other than those guarding that very interesting house on the hillock.

The tour of the silent avenues took four minutes, and with a mental picture of the layout well established he turned across the aprons and drove straight down the runway towards the far end. There had been a light in the traffic control tower and he knew that someone would be watching the patrol car's progress, possibly even picking up a telephone to warn the north gate – *if* there was a north gate.

Far ahead he saw the wedge which had been cut out of the side of the basin by the mechanical diggers. Through it lay a patch of sea. The runway would end in a sheer drop like the edge of a table; a fair assumption because there was no fence.

He turned off through the extinguished runway lights, crossed grass, came to a side road which led him to the north gate. One sentry. He stopped the car and leaned out. 'This is a hell of a dump to be stationed in. You haven't got a cigarette, by any chance?'

The man removed a carbine from his shoulder and came round the bonnet, out of the headlights. He flashed a torch, killed it. 'Sorry,' he said. 'Thought it was the Captain trying me out... You're new?'

'Came in this afternoon,' Rose sighed. 'Our outfit's chasing this Communist bloke. Tito. Over there on the mainland.'

'I've heard.' The sentry shouldered his carbine, took a packet of cigarettes from his breast pocket, held it out. 'You're welcome. The name's Barte.'

'Mine's Lemke. Peter.' Rose accepted the cigarette, lit it from the flame in the guard's cupped hands. 'Thanks. Didn't have a chance to get any.'

A few yards away stood a silent sentry box, the white insulators of its telephone wires plainly seen. York and his column would be approaching the guardroom.

'On your own?' Rose asked.

'No. Goppel – that's my mate – he went down to the gun emplacement at the end of the strip for a can of coffee. He'll be back soon... What did you come here *for?*'

'I was told to go and find a Sergeant some-thing-or-other. Forgotten his name, now. At the north end of the island, the Captain said. Go through the north gate and along the track and I would find him, he said... What *was* his name, now ... I've got a heck of a memory...'

'It'll be Sergeant Helmut–'

'That's it!' Rose exclaimed, snapping his fingers. 'Knew it was something like that. It's just that I feel lost when I'm anywhere new. They used to tell me I was dumb back home. The Captain explained the whole layout of the northern defences – but he speaks so flipping fast... Oh, well...'

Trooper Barte was young, little older than Freer, and, not unlike Freer, his whole manner betrayed an uneasy shyness. He glanced at Rose almost eagerly, as if pleased to be able to help a man twenty years his senior. 'It's really quite a simple layout,' he began with the quiet solemnity of a London policeman, and pointed. 'There's three 88mm guns at one mile intervals. Above each, up the hill a bit, there's three observation posts. And that's it – except for the patrols. Two of them. A Corporal and six bods in each. They picket in opposite directions, arriving here every two hours, on the hour, an' have a rest.' He seemed to smile then, and said, 'If you want the Serg, he'll be playing poker with the gun's crew in No. 2 bunker, but don't mention it around: he's decent to the lads.'

'Maybe it won't be so bad here after all,' Rose chuckled. He took a long drag at his cigarette, yawned, then said: 'One of the lads told me about those new bombs in that security building back there. Have you seen them yet?'

Barte shook his head. 'They don't let anyone in.' At least his answer confirmed the purpose of the new building.

After several negative probes, Rose said, 'Reckon they'll put an end to the war inside a month, though.'

This time the guard laughed softly.

'One of the scientists – they live in the house – he says they have other things up their sleeves as well. One of our lot says he was talking about rockets. Big ones.' A pause. 'Jet – jet propulsion?'

'Yes,' Rose answered absently. 'A little more deadly than the bomb with wings.' It was a piece of information he had not bargained for. Something for the future. It would certainly interest Intelligence.

He glanced at Kurt's watch. It was vital not to raise any sort of alarm at the north end of the island before Adams and his men landed. What the hell was the matter with the Gestapo – couldn't they count! Rose wanted to be exactly where he was when that telephone rang.

Then, thank God, the telephone did ring.

Barte turned away, entering the sentry box, stood with his back showing as the Navigator removed Kurt's Luger from the holster, slipped off the safety catch.

He watched the guard who, significantly, stopped talking, turned his face out of the box into the moonlight, glanced at the Volkswagen then away again, went on talking, now inaudibly.

Rose's finger curled round the trigger.

The telephone bell pinged once.

Barte emerged unhurriedly. Casually he removed the carbine from his shoulder, came over, stopped five feet away, the muzzle pointing at Rose. The upper half of his face was shadowed by the forage cap, but the puzzlement was in his voice. 'One of the English prisoners has escaped.' A pause. 'The Sergeant of the Guard says Kurt Brandt had this KUBELWAGEN…?'

A long drag at his cigarette and Rose flicked it away in a shower of sparks. Because the 'wagen was open and had a left-hand drive, he was sitting at the same side as the guard stood, his left arm over the door, below the level of which was the concealed Luger he prayed he would not have to use. Everything depended on the free-meals theory of that certain R.N. barracks being non-fiction.

He looked first at the carbine then up at the guard's face. 'What's up with you? Do I look like an Englander?' He sighed and looked away. 'So I lied to you. So I'm sorry.' He twisted and flung an imploring hand at Barte. 'Look, I don't even know half the blokes in my own outfit. I was coming through the camp minding my own business when the KUBELWAGEN drew up beside me. It must have been this Kurt. "Will you do me a favour," he said. "There's a bloke called Webber. He's out of bounds with a

194

whore in the village. I got to warn him."
Then he said he was on his way to meet
Sergeant Helmut because he'd run out of
cash playing poker. "For goodness' sake
don't tell anyone or you'll get me an' Helmut an' Webber all in the cart" His very
words … I told you I was dumb. I know I
shouldn't have done it. But – well – someone did as good for me once.' He hung his
head miserably.

The next twenty seconds were the longest
on record.

He heard the guard's feet move away, and
when he looked up, one of the double gates
was swinging back, then the other one.
Barte came over. 'I'll cover up for you,' he
said, and raised a hand as he turned again
towards the box.

'Auf Wiedersehen!' Rose called, and let in
the clutch.

The cliffs on the north-east side were whitish
in colour, brittle in texture, treacherous to
the unwary. In places they were sheer, though
not high, and deeply indented by coves and
bays, channelled with caves, topped by trees
and scrub which climbed steeply with the
land to a thousand feet, broken only by the
pale horizontal scar of the single winding
track: it, like every other blemish, showed up
in the moonlight because of the lime content
of the soil. From the rock outcrop where

Rose lay, he had an uninterrupted view for nearly a mile, and felt relieved that nothing visible was out of the ordinary.

He turned over on his stomach and watched the sea. Had he not known otherwise, it would have seemed impossible that any boat could have crossed that narrow channel without being seen; but the pale-grey, misty, eerie quality of the surface, accentuated as it was by the complete blackness of the near mountains on the other side, was very deceptive, and his first sight of York's depleted platoon was the small, careless glint of the moon on a dipping oar.

Y-O-R-K ... Y-O-R-K... The German signal torch was well hooded, but Rose kept it down in a cleft a foot above the water. The message was sent five times in slow Morse. All he could see himself was the small flush of blue it cast on the surface; but Adams would see it and read it and follow it in; and Adams did.

They came straight for the rock formation the Navigator had specially chosen, their boats materialising out of nothing, ghosts but for the small glint and splash of invisible oars. He caught the bow of the first one, guided it in among the rocks. The second followed.

'Oh, it's you,' Adams whispered, and added 'sir.' The disappointment was strong. 'Your hunch was right. We saw the searchlight. What happened?'

But he didn't tell them what had happened; not until they reached the cave. It was situated half-way up the cliff face, accessible only by the rope which had been tied to a tree high above. It was a place to talk. When all fourteen of them were inside, plus their radios, the bottom half of the rope was hauled up.

'Fine.' Rose dusted his hands. 'We're only twenty feet from the top.' He turned to the semi-circle of worried faces; York was their idol. Navigating officers were two a penny and classified with ministers of the church.

'I don't want to be rude, sir,' Adams said with difficulty, 'but this isn't the job for you, sir. Honestly. Supposing I send out a patrol to reconnoitre...?'

'I already have a complete picture of their defences and the layout of the airstrip.'

Adams and Gorman exchanged glances.

Gorman said: 'An *exact* picture?'

'A *precise* picture – including the movement of patrols, their strength, and the times they move.'

Again the glances.

To avoid being knifed, no questions asked, Rose had left his Wehrmacht jacket and forage cap at the rear of the cave, and Adams now leaned forward and peered closely at the singlet and baggy trousers.

He was smiling when he straightened. 'I

see,' he said. 'You knocked off a sentry. Well, sir, you can take it from me he told you a pack of lies. They always do.'

'Not quite accurate, Adams. In fact, I knocked off a patrol car, drove round the camp taking notes, spoke to a sentry, borrowed a cigarette from him, got him to cover for me, had a look at their 88mm gun emplacements, spoke to a Sergeant Helmut – he was playing poker by the way – and then I knocked off some sandwiches for you chaps.'

Silence.

'Poker? Sandwiches?' The Gunner's Mate swallowed. In his grey eyes there was something akin to terror. 'You – your head – it's still, uh, bothering you, sir?' He was trying desperately not to be rude. Unsuccessfully.'

Rose turned, switched on the torch, pushed his way through the bodies. The cave was twenty feet deep, with white pitted walls. He led the way to the rear where he'd passed some of the time.

He showed the Petty Officers the map he had drawn. 'That look all right to you?' It should have done. It was drawn to scale and contained some degree of artistic talent. They didn't seem to notice the sarcasm.

Their reaction was anticipated.

A low whistle from Gorman. 'We'd have less chance in there than a virgin in Morgan's mess.'

'Or Rose's cabin,' Rose reminded. 'However, as it has been planned, we're not going in. Not, that is, until they are in no position to stop us. Then we get York and the rest – if they're still alive.'

'Your kidding us now.' But Adams was grave. 'How?'

'You chaps have a hobby,' Rose sighed, folding up the map. 'You're always boasting you can sling field guns around cliffs and mountains, I believe. Well, I can't supply field guns – but I can supply what has proved one of the most devastating weapons of the war, so far... One guess?'

'The 88mms!' Adams and Gorman said it together.

'Right first time,' Rose smiled. 'Now I'll show you how Major Troy would have planned it. Sit down. It's all right, the floor's dry.'

Rose picked up a parcel from under his jacket, squatted down cross-legged in front of them. While Gorman held the torch, he opened it and spread it out. 'According to the historians, this is the most vital part of any plan,' he said, and pointed to the contents. 'The ones on the right are egg. Those are cheese. That, I think is tomato.'

11

Clouds had begun to blot out the stars and lightning flashes deep in the mountains exposed the Yugoslavian peaks in jagged silhouette.

As should any sensible mortal, the Professor had made himself as comfortable as possible, but not Adams: Adams lay at attention even when prostrate like an undertaker's dream.

It was now 2.51 a.m.

Rose took a dose of fresh air to steady the nerves and again raised the binoculars. They focused first on the superb Flak 36 88mm general purpose gun which sat on a moonlit shelf on the hillside below, its slim barrel pointing seaward. Unlike the old-fashioned field guns the Chatham Rats played with, it had tyred wheels – unfortunately they were off at that moment in time – stood twice the height of a man, or so it seemed in comparison to the three paratroopers grouped around it, one of whom was scanning the channel with night glasses. Like the Ju88 bomber, that gun was one of the best reasons for Hitler's success; it was simple, accurate, mobile and versatile. At the rear of the shelf two 'tin' huts had been built into the hillside; one for ammunition, the other for men. The vehicle for towing the gun was parked beside them. It had wheels in front and caterpillar treads behind and was called a half-track. All round, a wide area of trees had been cut down, except three immediately behind the huts, and those were of special interest: on the limb of one lay Less Harrington, an A.B. with red hair and freckles, and a self-confessed hypochondriac who did violent exercises every morning on deck and upset everyone. As God willed it, the branch stretched out over the back of the hut and almost above the stove-pipe chimney into which would go two hand grenades.

This was No. 3 bunker, two miles from the airstrip and sited near the northern tip of the island.

On the other side of the huts, behind a ridge and screened by scrub, lay Gorman and L/Sea Frank Smith. Both were crack pistol shots. Twenty feet uphill from where the G.M. and the Navigator lay was John Golly, A.B., with hair to match and known as 'Wog'. Telephone cable in hand, a pair of cutters in readiness, he was waiting for the signal. Above him, at three points on the two-mile skyline, the observation posts were covered by the remaining men.

No prisoners would or could be taken.

Four minutes. Where the devil was the patrol?

'They're coming now, sir.' Adams had just seen them. As Trooper Barte had said, there were six bodies and a Corporal. They were marching briskly in single file, heading for a cup of coffee, a rest, a smoke – and death. 'Three minutes and they'll be at the hut,' the G.M. estimated.

'They're sticklers for punctuality.'

'I know.' Adams took out his Service revolver and toyed with it moodily. 'It's going to shake Old Nick when they clock in a few years ahead of time,' he sighed.

Two minutes.

Just one hundred and twenty seconds – and in the next fifty-five minutes the Chatham Rats had to move as they had never moved before, or die; they had to capture No. 3 bunker with the minimum of men, jack up the heavy gun, put the wheels on, tow it at breakneck speed along a rutted switchback of a road only six feet wide where one mistake could mean plunging a hundred feet or more to the rocks below; while the men on the skyline had to knock out the observation posts, converge and rendezvous at No. 2 bunker, go through the same routine again, cover the last mile with both guns, kill Troopers Barte and Goppel, capture the north gate and bunker No. 1 … because, at precisely 4 a.m. the guard was

202

due to change: but the guard would not change because the guardroom would then know the telephone cable had been cut and the troops searching the south end of the island would be switched north; and then would come the running fight, and failure. Could they do it? Rose thought they could. But the real questions were: would the thunderstorm that would turn the track into a bog hold off? Would the Wehrmacht find Kurt's trussed-up body and switch the search north long before 4 a.m.?

At least Edward and *Scorpio* were all right. Rose had told him only that all was proceeding according to plan.

One minute.

The heavy tread of marching feet was three yards below and five yards away.

Thirty seconds – and the Corporal had forked away from his men to approach a box on a stick that held the telephone, which he lifted and spoke into for ten seconds as his men filed past and grouped in the shaft of light from the opening hut door.

The phone pinged once.

As the receiver clicked into place Adams twisted and flashed his light up at Wog. Another ping as the wires were cut and the retreating Corporal stopped, looked back, shrugged and went on. Adams was flashing his light up at the skyline. One flash answered him. He then swopped the torch for a hand grenade, removed the pin with his teeth, waited till the last man had finished a bit of backchat with the three at the gun and passed out of sight, then took a huge breath and held it.

The hut door banged shut.

There was a small, tinny rattle, silence for five long seconds, then – CRUU-MMP! – as both Harrington's grenades exploded inside the stove.

Two pistol shots, then as two of the three men at the gun fell to the ground the third started to run, staggered to a halt on the third shot; he dropped his carbine as his hands went to his stomach. It seemed he would never fall. Then a fourth shot as Adams and Rose reached the hut door, kicked it open, flung in two more grenades, slammed it closed, counted four – and dived flat as the grenades exploded and the dying man took three more steps and fell on his face.

Harrington abandoned his branch, leapt down from the roof, ran past. On his heels was Wog, having slithered downhill in an avalanche of loose scree. They converged on Gorman and Smith who were already jacking up the gun.

The hut door creaked open under Adam's hand. He signalled Rose. Together they went in, sprang to one side, flashed their torches.

It was a stinking, smouldering, blackened

slaughterhouse, choked with acrid visible fumes from burning coke and cordite, filled with the stench of human excretion from ruptured bowels. Grenades one and two had exploded the cast-iron stove into a thousand lethal pieces, pitting the bloodstained walls and roof, shattering the lights. There were bunks at one end, but the men had been standing round a deal table with long scrubbed stools only feet from the explosion, and some lay in grotesque attitudes on the floor, though not all were dead. Some moaned. One still sat at the charred and splintered table, head turned towards the torchlight, his bloodied fingers clawing for the Luger at his belt when Adams shot him, and he fell sideways, thudded to the floor and lay still; and his very stillness and the silence it brought made their torches swing on a scraping sound: a second man was feeling his way towards them along the hut walls, but he was blind, had only half a face, and he decided to die before the G.M. could pull the trigger.

Sickened, Rose made to turn away, saw a movement. He stopped, flashed his torch in a far corner where a third lacerated creature had risen on one elbow, his free hand drawn back behind his head. It was the sight of that drawn-back hand which chilled his blood and he fired three shots in quick succession.

The man grunted, fell forward on his face.

Then came the metallic sound as of a spring clip being suddenly released and hitting the roof.

Something rolled noisily across the floor and stopped in the pool of light at the Navigator's feet. He knew what it was, had known before he fired: it was a live five-second hand grenade. He just stared down at it, immobilised.

It had taken three seconds to roll over, one second to stare at it – and in the fifth explosive second Adams scooped it up, flung it to the rear of the hut and sent Rose crashing to the floor by kicking away his legs.

Shattering in the confined space, the blast emptied their lungs.

Adams climbed back to his feet.

'You – you – we should have died,' Rose gasped.

'It was a seven-second fuse,' Adams said breathlessly, helping him upright.

'How the hell did you know?'

'I didn't.'

It had taken only two and a half minutes to kill eleven men. Own casualties: nil. There was no time to think which of the enemy had been fanatics, or which had been innocents like Barte, caught up in the relentless tide of war; no time to think of the widows, the fatherless children only time to move, and move fast, to slam on the lock the wheels of the gun, to back the rumbling half-track and hitch it on, to curse, to sweat, to select Wehrmacht jackets and forage caps, not too bloody or torn with shrapnel, for the five men without ... and yet Wog found time to stand and stare.

'What the blazes are you supposed to be, you perishing golliwog! Come on, man. All on board!' This from an enraged Adams, because Golly was standing between the purring truck and the hut, binoculars to his eyes and scanning the hills. He bellowed again and the rating turned, ran towards them.

'A mother's gift to a nation,' Gorman sighed. He was at the wheel, raring to go, Adams standing up beside him hanging on to the windscreen.

'He reckons the Jerries are on to us,' Harrington called from behind. 'Says he saw movement when he was cutting the phone wires.'

'Bloody rubbish!' Adams bent down, caught Wog's hand, hoisted him inboard where he climbed in beside the Navigator at the back.

3.7 a.m. on Kurt's watch. Gorman let out the clutch. They swerved on to the track and south in a cloud of dust. The approaching clouds were low, densely black, lit with flashes, silver where their misty edges approached the moon. A peal of thunder rolled and tumbled through the mountains.

Only a corporation dust-cart being driven across a marshalling yard at right angles to the railway lines at fifty miles per hour could have been more unstable than the pitching, swaying half-track and its bouncing gun behind. Had the vehicle had four wheels, instead of two at the front and caterpillar treads in the rear, it would have leapt from the road, plunged down the one-in-one gradient, ricocheting from tree to tree like a pin-table ball before emerging in free fall. But when they skirted the bays and inlets there were no trees, no gradients and just a tiny margin of grass and scrub lay between them and the rocks and a sea a hundred feet below.

Golly watched the hills with puzzled certainty, but Rose was in no mood to comfort him; anyway, he was waiting for the sudden silence as his ear-drums burst.

Adams, bouncing: 'Gaaw, my bum ain't aff numb!'

Gorman, smugly: 'I gotta air cushion, Fred.'

The gun weighed tons, and – once – on a corner it swerved right over the edge, pulling the back end of the half-track with it. All that saved them was the road – it decided to turn on the opposite tack and they couldn't miss it.

Adams, crouching, hand on cap: 'Oooaah! Where ya learnt t'-drive, fer cri-sake!'

Gorman, circus-born, pleased with road. 'Dodge-ems, Fred.'

The slotted blackout masks on the headlights produced a feeble glow. Rose watched out for a special stunted tree. It appeared black and petrified against the sky.

The whole contraption shuddered to a halt in suffocating dust, to be met by four panting Rats called Fergie, Mac, Tiny and Happy – Tiny being tall and Happy sad – who had cut the telephone wires to No. 2 bunker seventy yards ahead and disposed of two of the three skyline observation posts with the silent use of short bayonets. Or so it had been planned, and so it seemed until Happy climbed up beside Rose.

Happy wasn't only sad, he was breathless, excited, puzzled. 'The observation posts. The Jerry lookouts. Both dead, sir. Mac and Tiny, they found the same. Both killed. Knifed. Bodies still warm, sir.'

'Suicide?' ventured Fergie.

Adams faced Gorman. 'You know what?'

'Muscles,' Gorman said dismally, and looked over the back of the seat. 'It's Muscles an' his lot, sir. Dead dumb an' stooped, that's him. He's knocked off all three posts on his way to the north gate.'

'Surely not. His orders–'

'He misunderstood his orders,' Adams raved. 'All brawn an' no brain. A'll kick 'im inside out. A'll – A'll…'

But it didn't make any different, and time did.

'Let's go!' Gorman broke every tooth in the gear box and heaped his passengers.

The attack on No. 2 bunker was to be made on the free-meals theory, there being no convenient tree for the stove-pipe act, and this time there would be no patrol, just six men and Sergeant Helmut.

The clearing was just ahead, the gun on the left, the huts on the right as before. What the enemy would see was one of their own half-tracks stop in a cloud of dust between themselves and the huts. It was here that Rose had helped himself to the tin of sandwiches.

Because Fergie and company had still to acquire uniforms, they lay out of sight on the floor.

Pistols were drawn.

The thunder was closer, the lightning now over the channel on which Rose had heard the loud sizzle of torrential rain. One raindrop trickled warmly down his face.

They burst into the clearing at twenty knots, and Gorman slammed on his anchors as the moon vanished into the silver lining and caused a shadow to pass over the land at the moment they stopped, peered, waited, breath bated.

Not a movement. Gorman, Adams and Smith watched the gun while Rose and Harrington watched the other side, waited for the hut door to open. Wog had two hand grenades ready, pins out. 'There *was* someone watching me back at No. 3,' he said stubbornly. 'I could *feel* his eyes on me.'

'You'll feel my toe up your backside,' Gorman forecast.

It grew darker. The gun, unmanned, ten yards away, was barely visible. A square of light, thread-thick, lined the door.

Wog's remark had made everyone shrink.

A precious minute passed.

Lightning hissed and lit the scene like day, and they saw no one: no one by the gun: no one anywhere on the ledge.

Wind rustled in the trees.

Rose winced as a hand touched him. It was Adams. 'I'm going in, sir.'

'We're going in,' Rose corrected.

They climbed down, circuited the vehicle on tiptoe, met in front of the hut door. Men in the half-track covered them. Flattening themselves one on each side Adams put his hand on the knob, turned it slowly, stopped, held his breath, pushed the door inward, and drew back.

The hinges creaked as the wedge of light grew into a square shaft which reached to the truck's caterpillar tracks; then the door banged against the wall, shuddered.

No sound from within.

Adams glanced across at Rose and

nodded. Like Rose he had a revolver in one hand, a grenade in the other. To leap in could have meant death from a burst of machine-gun fire, and the G.M. knew it, so, with speed, he peeped in, drew back, stared at Rose in astonishment, peeped again, and then stood forward in the shaft of light.

'God's truth,' he gasped softly; and he had every right, for at the hut table sat seven men. In front of them were playing cards and coffee mugs. All were sitting back on the same long stool and propped against the wall. All were dead, and in the centre of the table lay an ace of spades, a dagger through its black heart.

Without moving his torso, the G.M. turned his head very slowly, very cautiously, until his narrowed eyes had searched the bunks and shadows behind the stove, then brought it back and peered over his other shoulder, then at Rose.

'Fairies?'

'Yugoslavian fairies.'

'In which case...?'

'They're on our side.'

They glanced at their watches, glanced at each other, then dived out the door. God saw them coming and pulled the trigger. The blinding, sizzling flash and crash of His 16-inch water cannon fired in their faces. It left on the retina a red fading image of a fork of lightning and nought else. With it, like all the best firing squads, same kettle-drums of rain. It filled every hole and rut with chalky slime, turned the ledge to an ice rink which turned out to be a warm mud bath; but the Chatham Rats were amphibious.

3.34 a.m. on Kurt's watch – and both vehicles, each with their guns in tow, stood ready, the pulse of their engines barely audible above the storm.

Adams counted the bodies, gave the order to board. He climbed up and took the wheel of the second half-track, beside Rose. Gorman led the way with the first vehicle. With him went Fergie, Harrington and Tiny.

No. 1 bunker lay one mile ahead.

Without the caterpillar treads they'd not have moved twelve inches; without them the gradients would have been unclimbable; and even then they slithered down hills, crabbed wildly on hairpin bends.

What was happening under his bottom, Rose could feel, but what was happening to the vehicle in front, he could *see*, and that was enough. Gorman, like Adams, had his whole body weight down on top of the steering wheel to reinforce his hands and arms in keeping the waltzing front tyres on the river of mud. The thunder was endless, the gods now taking twelve flashlight photographs a minute, and the island was lit from north to south in stark relief. High above them much of the rain soaked through the perforated rock, but that which didn't careered seaward down every dried-up stream and crevice; raging water, that sluiced across the track and bounded whitely down among the trees, leaving behind a treacherous surface strewn with sticks and stones and full-grown branches; gears screaming, the half-tracks crushed them like pistol shots.

But then the trees thinned on one side and left a void of utter blackness, in which the only thing visible was driving rain glinting in the meagre headlights' side-glow – until the lightning flashed and revealed the creaming sea a hundred feet below, revealed a torrent gushing across the road ahead of Gorman and spurting out in a steaming jet from the cliff edge, where it curved and fell thinly away like white sugar. It wouldn't be deep, perhaps a foot or less, but it would have speed and strength and the road surface had little grip. On the other side of it, lit in the next flash, was a steep bank of rock and scrub round which the road, on the very edge of cliff, turned invisibly to the right; that fact being certain by the empty darkness beyond.

Adams slowed, only to curse and accelerate again because the vehicle ahead did not slow; the intrepid Gorman had in fact increased speed and the torrent reared up and over him as he crossed it, the current slewing the half-track obliquely to the road, slewing the lighter gun that its wheels ploughed sideways on the narrow margin between life and death: but Gorman made it crabwise, and Adams followed likewise.

All were half-drowned, blinded, clinging for dear life when the torrent subsided.

Ahead was the sheer drop, and there wasn't a sign of Gorman because he had, presumably, turned the corner as Adams was starting to do right then, his vision impaired, his headlights showing nothing for they were sweeping round through empty darkness...

Rose saw it first.

'Look out! Look out! Look out!'

The meagre headlights arrived as Adams stood on the brakes and the tracks locked: locked in a foot of mud and didn't stop them, and all they saw was the slim barrel of Gorman's gun, the black hole of its muzzle coming straight at them: it crashed through the windscreen, through the back of the seat between them as the vehicle stopped.

Shock was the worst thing, and it shook Rose bloodless, shook him to anger, that he might have stood up and shaken his fist at Gorman and cursed him for a fool; and he would have, had he not seen that Gorman was about to die.

A landslide had fallen on the road. The leading vehicle had rammed it, its speed and caterpillar tracks forcing it right up on to a mound of loose rubble where it was balanced at an angle of fifty degrees, on the point of toppling; and worse – a quarter of the road and all the seaward margin had vanished for ten yards, leaving nothing, nothing but a short fifty-degree slide, and the half-track was sliding, slowly but inevitably, foot by foot, as the torrential rain undermined its tracks: and what was Gorman doing? Gorman was not one bit worried that he had all but stove a hole in Rose's eye – Gorman was sitting at the wheel bawling orders at three muddy beavers who had between them one of the towing wires all military vehicles carry and, having hooked it to the side of the sliding half-track, were dragging it up the incline knee-deep in mud; but not to the nearest tree that *might* have prevented imminent disaster, but to a tree on the other side, whose position would allow a pendulum motion – *if* the wire held across the slope to safety.

The wire was thrown round the trunk and hooked to itself. It went slowly taut, started to sing under the strain, but the death slide was checked. Gorman, alone and struggling with the wheel revved up his motor and jerked forward. The gun barrel at Rose's side unexpectedly went with it, and the rest of the windscreen as well; so did years of his life as he watched the half-track slewing and sliding on the cliff edge, watched the avalanche of loose grit gradually break up and shower away into empty space, listened to the rising pitch of that stretched, singing wire, waited for it to snap in any second as the vehicle described a shallow arc, drew closer to the broken road at the other side. So tense, so utterly nervebound was he that only Gorman, his half-track and gun, held as they were in the meagre light of Adams' carefully positioned headlamps, were visible to his captive eyes; and he saw nothing of what was happening at the perimeter of the lights, nothing of the danger that muddy Fergie, Les and Tiny were sharing with their boss – for standing on the crumbling slope above Gorman was hazardous enough, but if the wire parted it would cut all three of them in half.

Nor did he see what was happening behind; and Adams' cry, 'Out wire! Same tree! *Move!*' did not register; not until, in the same moment that Gorman reached safety, the G.M. let in the clutch...

What followed was exactly like being on the underside of a steeply banking aircraft with serious engine-trouble and taking flashlight photographs of the beach below.

Rose closed his ears to the inane cries of insensitive fools. Like: 'Think these hooks will hold?' or 'This wire is a lot thinner than his, P.O.' Then, only half-way across the slope, Adams was saying, 'Gorman an' his lot are getting soft. Took 'im four minutes. I timed him. Too much horizontal time, that's what. Bet we do it in three, sir.'

It took three – hundred years.

On reaching the other side, the G.M. stopped to pick up muddy Wog, Happy and Smith. He actually looked at his watch. 'Two minutes, fifty-one,' he chortled in triumph.

'Congratulations,' Rose said, unlocking his teeth.

Goosy Gorman hadn't waited to concede victory. The small glow of his headlights bounced along through the darkness and between the rocks. They had lost five and a half minutes and now started to regain two by attempted suicide.

Once round the bay they branched from the cliff and drove fast over flat land and between trees. Somewhere ahead was a fork in the track, leading left to No. 1 bunker and right to the north gate.

They reached it at 3.48 a.m.

Gorman changed down indelicately. Adams slowed behind him. The plan was to go left, straight for the bunker.

But two Able Seamen, Arthur Lawson and Victor Shaw, were supposed to rendezvous at the fork. They were not to be seen.

'Maybe they've fallen asleep, waiting,' suggested Happy.

Gorman stopped. 'Go past him!' Rose ordered. As Adams bumped and jolted off the track, the Navigator cupped his hands, waited till both vehicles were abreast, then shouted: 'Follow us, Gorman! Whatever happens, don't use your weapons!'

'Another hunch, sir?' There was a trace of sarcasm in Adams' voice. He conned the half-track back on to the road, took the left fork. From behind came the crash of gears.

If there was anything worse than heavy rain, it was dripping trees. Rose turned up his Wehrmacht collar. 'I think we are just about to drive into a friendly ambush,' he answered.

'Friendly, sir?'

'The partisans are Communists. We're still on the same side, but we're Capitalists.'

'Speak for yourself, sir. After deductions I get about two quid from the Navy, and my total piggy-bank balance is eighteen and sixpence. On *Wildcat!*'

No. 1 bunker was twice as big as the other two and was sited at the end of the runway at the edge of the cliff. Only the chain fence separated it from the grass verge and tarmac. The gun, facing the sea, had only to be turned round, lined up with the other two, and aimed at the targets Rose had selected. He saw all this at a glance as they burst through the thinning trees and ground to a stop outside the huts.

Again, the place was deserted, and because the hut door didn't open, Rose and

Adams jumped down and opened it, this time without caution.

It was no surprise.

Blood on the floor, a heap of dead Germans, and five sorry-looking Chatham Rats sitting at the table under the guns of six darkly dressed and rugged partisans with belts of ammunition – ex-Wehrmacht issue – diagonally across their chests and what looked like rolled-up Balaclava helmets – ex-British Expeditionary Force – on their scruffy heads: that was the first thing they *saw*. The first thing they *heard* was Able Seaman Victor Shaw, nearest to Rose, head on one utterly dejected arm. He sniffed and said, 'You can get busy with the sign language, sir. He' – he jerked a dirty thumb over his shoulder at an advancing partisan – 'can't speak one word of English. But his fingers told us he'd got fifty-three men. They're outside. Covering your trucks. And the best of Chatham luck to you, sir. And you, Chief.'

Adams sighed, followed Rose's example and put his Service revolver on the table. He then held up his hand grenade to the light, screwed up his eyes, and threaded the pin back into the hole like he was about to start a sewing class.

The man who stopped in front of Rose had a black beard which would have brought an instant sneer from York. It was wild. Untamed. And the face was nut-brown and parched.

He took the Navigator in his arms, kissed him on both cheeks. Rose kissed him back. The action brought the Gunner's Mate's eyes from their almond norm to full circles.

'Stone the crows!' he said.

'It's the custom,' Rose explained sourly.

The partisan's name was Kosovac. He spoke passable Italian. Because time was flashing past, the discussion was brief. But Adams was curious.

'What's he talking about, sir?'

'He's going to co-operate with us,' Rose answered. 'I've got a plan, and I'm trying to explain it to him.' Rose went on talking in Italian, then said: 'I'm going into the camp, Adams. They're going to cover me along the hills above the north fence.'

'What's he smiling for?' Adams was highly suspicious of men who went around kissing each other. There was a name for that kind of thing!

'I just told him you were hopping mad at his men for leaving no Germans for you to kill.'

'Are we?' Shaw had no such thoughts.

The verbal exchange lasted one minute, thirty seconds.

'Okay,' Rose said when he finished. 'He's sending some of his men south in the boats to capture the tug, Adams.'

'You must be very persuasive, sir.'

'I'm oozing charm,' Rose smiled.

Adams just glanced at the ceiling and sighed.

Petty Officer Gorman was not the kind of fellow to waste time looking for a key. He opened the front of the ammunition hut with his radiator, then tore around flattening thirty yards of chain fence that the enemy had thoughtlessly erected in the line of fire. 'The Germans are all the same. No vision,' he said after roaring back to safety behind the already sighted guns.

They were to use star shell. But flash after flash of lightning revealed the camp at the south end of the runway. It was pointblank range for the 88s. The house on the hillock and the shed where the bombs were stored were both visible. So was the huge tank of high octane aviation fuel on the hillside behind. Only the plane itself could not be seen; it was screened by the Ju88s and Me109s.

Three vehicles laden with paratroopers raced down the runway towards the north gate. Someone had used the phone and failed. A siren wailed in the camp.

'All right, lads, take one truck each,' Adams called. 'This is for practice. Take your time. Get your cross-wires between their headlights...'

Rose took his place behind the wheel of the half-track, revved the engine. What he was about to do was a job for one man.

The time on Kurt's watch was 3.57 a.m.

Then there was a peculiar silence; a numb, thunderless silence in which a fork of lightning touched the ground, its stark light gleaming on the shells in the arms of a chain of men, on the motionless guns and their crews – on Adams, who stood behind them, ramrod stiff, not jubilant, yet knowing he had won his race against time and circumstances: a proud man, who had risen to the top of his profession by his own personal effort alone: a family man, who knew that to fail his family and friends was to fail in all things.

He was not alone; nor where they without fear.

The headlights were two hundred yards away.

The Gunner's Mate raised his hand – dropped it.

'OPEN FIRE!'

12

A triple flash lit the clearing, lit the guns whose slim barrels recoiled instantly, retracted slowly. The three explosive shock-waves came as one, at the same time; at almost the same time as the enemy trucks exploded in flame and debris.

'No. 1 gun switch to star shell! Lay 'em right over the house, Tiny! Range one-five-double-oh...' But the strident voice was drowned out by the clanking of metal treads and high-ratio gears; for Rose had let in the clutch and started forward along the muddy track. Driving a normal vehicle with a wounded arm would have been painful enough, driving the jolting half-track was agony. He lay half-over the wheel, steering with his chest and one arm, appearing – by sheer coincidence – exactly what he intended to appear: as one wounded, escaping German.

He negotiated the hairpin bend at the fork in the road, pressed the accelerator into the floorboards, roared through the north gate, swung right, zigzagged down the grass strip between runway and fence in the manner that any escapee would. Adams' well-aimed shells whistled overhead. Tracer bullets from stolen Schmeisser machine-pistols tore up the grass yards from the caterpillar tracks, on purpose; but was there such a thing as a friendly bullet? And had he ever done anything mean to Happy and Wog? They were firing them!

A pool of flaming fuel covered the runway, the heat wafting in his face. In its centre lay the shattered remains of the trucks. Men, a dozen or more, fanned out from the fire, running or crawling away in the night, like flaming torches on two legs, screaming as they went.

But Rose's eyes were on the house where, behind darkened windows, the men who designed the bomb would now be awake, panicky, bawling at one another and grabbing their dressing-gowns; for above the stone-built house two star shells hung swaying on their tiny parachutes, tinting the black and scurrying clouds, and in the pale and shadowy light shell after shell pounded the soft rock foundations: and then it happened as he knew it would, sooner than expected: it was as if a fire without flame had been lit in its cellars, for what looked like dense smoke – it was actually dust – rolled out from its base, spread across the hillock on all sides; and the house was shrinking, tilting a little to one side as it did so: collapsing: and then it vanished in a mushroom of dust that climbed into the sky and enveloped the star shell, defied the rain: the noise of its lost cohesion came only then, matching the thunder.

Adams switched targets immediately, his shells passing dangerously close and exploding among the parked planes. One exploded, set two others on fire. Black smoke started to obscure the rest.

One hundred yards to go.

The fifteen-hundred-yard dash had taken two precious minutes. Only now did the enemy start to return fire; so far, with light machine-guns from the fence patrols.

He drove diagonally across the runway, turned half-right and made for half a dozen parked Me109 fighters, zigzagged through them, reached the open space between aprons and huts.

Organised chaos.

Men, mostly Luftwaffe personnel, were manhandling fire extinguishers towards the blazing planes. Other men ran about with no obvious purpose, getting in the way of those who were heaping sandbags for spread eagle sharp-shooters.

One stood up and waved angrily.

'Get to hell out of the way!' he yelled. 'Sheer off! Get that vehicle out of here – you're right in the line of fire!'

Rose swerved, went round the back of them. For a terrible moment it looked as if no one was going to stop him. There was nothing in the world Rose wanted more than to be stopped.

Then someone did. A sergeant. He stepped out in the centre of the approach road to the huts.

Up went the hand. 'Stop!'

The Professor applied the brakes. He didn't have to look exhausted, he was. Nor did he have to look nervous. A moment before the vehicle rolled to a halt he stood up behind the wheel, pointed frantically back down the runway. 'All hell back there, Serg. Two thousand partisans. Fully equipped. Looks like a full scale landing.'

The N.C.O. danced round the bonnet, jumped on the running board. It was difficult to see his face, the upper half being in shadow below the forage cap, the lower half being heavily tinted by flame from increasing fires. 'Two thousand,' he barked. 'How d'you know?'

Rose subsided into the seat, shrugged hopelessly. 'I – I just got through. My arm.' He held it up. 'A bullet. Sergeant Helmut sent me. He said I had to go straight to the Gestapo. I had to tell them...' He let his words tail off, groaned, nursing his arm.

'Tell them what – you pig-witted fool!'

'Sergeant Helmut said I'd to tell them the Yugoslavs are massing for an attack on the north-west fence,' Rose said, cowering. 'He said the Major would be in the hut with the British prisoners – but I don't know what hut that is. Do you know, Serg? Or better still, would you tell the Major, Serg?' No more gentle or timorous request had ever been made in the German language.

There was no instant reaction. The Sergeant still had his face all puckered up at one side; the way a man listens through the din of men yelling, the near chatter of small arms, the piercing whistles and explosive crashing of shells. Only one thing was certain: he was thinking.

Stimulate the process. Rose engaged top gear, revved his engine. 'I've got to go, Serg. I'll ask the guardroom.'

'Wait! – Why the Gestapo?'

'The partisans. Their leader is Major Troy.'

'Gott in Himmel!' The Sergeant slapped the door twice. 'Right!' He'd made a decision. 'I'll tell them.' He jumped down, ran off.

He didn't go far. Five yards and he stopped, hovered on tiptoe, turned, raced back, again jumping on to the running board. 'Hut 52. *Move!'* He had merely discovered that caterpillar treads were faster than legs.

Hut 52 lay on the other side of the camp, last on the right in an avenue and next to the south fence. Two guards in dripping camouflaged capes stood at the door.

The Sergeant ran up the three steps and

vanished inside. When he came out, the half-track wasn't there. *'Mein Gott!* Where did the pig-witted fool go?' Rose heard the question from the small passage between the huts, heard the guards proclaim that the vehicle had gone 'off back', which it had; but it had also come back, this time on the parallel road behind the hut where it was now stopped and silent.

Time was running out at about the same speed as the cursing Sergeant ran off down the avenue.

Schmeisser tucked under an arm, Rose removed the pin of the hand grenade, allowed the spring clip to recoil against his hand, drop silently into the grass.

One second – two – three – and he tossed it over the hut like a cricket ball, diagonally.

It exploded in the air above the road.

A glance. Both sentries had fallen, one writhing in agony, the other motionless, face down, his spread cape like a dead bat in the shaft of light from the opening door.

Two men came out. Then a third. A torch flashed up and down the roadway as Rose drew back, transferred the Schmeisser to a horizontal position at his waist, slipped off the safety catch. Were the other huts empty? How many more were inside *this* hut? Too many questions. No answers.

More feet. 'A shell?' It was the puzzled voice of the Gestapo Major. 'Where on earth did it land, Ludwig?'

'It burst in the sky, Ernst. See the pock marks on the hut walls?'

'So the miserable pigs are firing anti-personnel shells,' said Ernst wrathfully. 'But wait. Just wait. Troy will not escape us this time.'

'I'm much afraid he already has,' Rose interrupted, and stepped out into the road-way.

All four turned together; died together, their faces expressionless, lit by flickering gunfire from the wicked little muzzle as it swept through a quarter circle in one deafening burst. They fell in a heap in the light from the door. Rose leapt over them, leapt deliberately through the light. But nothing happened.

He approached the door now from the other side of the shaft of light, knelt in the darkness at the side of the steps, face level with the top step.

He glanced in at floor level, drew back. Instinctive caution. For one tenth of a second his retina held the image of wooden walls and rafters, the vacant desk at the far end, the special chair between desk and door that was set under a powerful inter-rogation lamp and supported the man whose ugly hairy face was twisted back over the broad shoulders and filled with hope; God knows why! On the desk a telephone started ringing shrilly as Rose put his foot on the step – and no further: no further, because Simon York had suddenly flicked his head away.

Why? Why should a man, eager to be rescued, suddenly turn his head away? There was no one else in the room…?

The door! It hinged on Rose's right, stood open, inwards, though not right back against the wall.

Damn the telephone!

Two steps and Rose was silently on the top step, gun reversed, safety catch on, right foot inside the hut and taking his weight, left foot free and describing a slow anti-clockwise circle to the rear of the right one, where it paused briefly, then returned clockwise with all his weight behind it.

The door juddered back against the wall. A Mauser pistol skidded across the floor. A grunt of pain came from behind the panels, then another one as Rose wrenched the knob, exposed one cowardly interrogator.

'Kick his face in! For me!' York barked.

'With pleasure.' The Schmeisser butt came down – *Whack!*

From tossing the grenade, all this had taken barely one minute and York had now to wait to be cut free because the telephone had been ringing for fifteen seconds by the time Rose had checked a second door behind the desk, found it locked, and pounced on the receiver. 'Hut 52. Interrogation.' He was conscious of York's curious gaze, aware too that the First Lieutenant had not been beaten up but tortured with the electrodes whose cups and wires lay in a tangle on the floor.

'Put Major Schwarzhaupt on the line!' a voice demanded.

'The Major stepped out, sir. This is the sentry here. Can I give him a message?'

'Where is he?' A tempting question.

'Down the road, sir.'

'We are evacuating the camp. Immediately. Colonel von Ungern wants the British officer taken to the guardroom. Now. I'm sending a car. Tell him that!'

'Yes, sir. Right away.' Rose hung up. He didn't have to puzzle about the imminent evacuation. Adams' third target was the ammunition hut with the bombs; his fourth, the petrol tank. He explained this to York in one breath as the ropes were slashed, received in return the sickening news that the location of the other nine men was not known.

But Rose was now listening for the car, worrying about the bodies in the roadway.

He gave the Schmeisser to York, who, though unmarked, was hardly able to walk at first. 'You take this.' He helped the First Lieutenant down the steps. 'Easy does it. This way.' The huts were built a foot off the ground, sitting on squat brick columns, and they were half-way or more along the narrow passage when they heard, above the din of battle, a splintering noise, close at hand.

They both stopped.

'Sounds like splintering wood,' Rose frowned. And it was coming from under the hut they'd just left. 'That door – the one at the side of the desk – what was behind it?'

'I haven't a notion,' York breathed. 'The Major went in once–'

'It couldn't be Yates and company?'

'No, he'd have crowned the Major. Anyway, they were at the guardroom when I was taken here.'

'I'm going back.' Rose pointed ahead. 'There's a half-track parked at the back. Get in it. Stay in it. And lie down, because any minute there's going to be one hell of an explosion. Off you go!'

'But the car–'

'To blazes with the car. If you hear shooting, it'll be me. Don't worry.'

A glance up and down the roadway revealed, as yet, no approaching car. Three bounds across the hut and a bullet removed the lock of the door beside the desk.

It creaked open under its own steam.

A prison – dimly lit, with bare walls, rafters, barred and shuttered windows, a rough-hewn table and two chairs and an iron bed: that was all – except for two dead bodies, side by side on the floor; both dressed in the desert uniform of the famous Italian Ariete Division: that was all – except, of course, for Guiseppe, who got up slowly from his knees, gave up the task of prising loose one floor board in an attempt to escape.

'Great God!' Rose whispered. 'Why – in God's name – why?' As he spoke, he slipped off the forage cap, saw the recognition in the no-longer-cold, but hurt, Italian eyes. 'Why?'

Guiseppe said nothing. He just stood, still in his white shirt and uniform trousers, beaten, hands hanging limply at his sides, one holding the piece of rusty iron which now clattered to the floor. But he didn't really have to answer, for the tragic answer was there on the floor. Captain Durand and his country had come into the war on the wrong side.

The hands elevated slightly, palms up. 'They did notta believe me. They say I help the British, then change sides when it suited me. But you know that is not true.'

'Yes, I know. But that was a dirty, lousy trick you played on us – on York. You bloody well *saw* Troy die.'

Kill him? Run off and just leave the door open? But squealing brakes at the hut's outer door made Rose's decision for him.

'Remain still!' he hissed at Guiseppe.

Yells sounded outside as the bodies were found. Heavy feet thudded on the floor as two or three men entered the hut. But before Rose could turn, someone behind jabbed their fingers into his ears with numbing force, hit him full in the back with a sledge hammer, then brutally kicked in the whole north wall of the hut, causing the roof to fall on top of him. The man responsible for this remarkable feat was Petty Officer Adams, who had just demolished his third target highly explosively.

He found the Italian among the rafters, dazed and shaken. He helped him up. Doors were obsolete. The newly arrived car was upside-down, wheels spinning.

'W-what-a happened?' stammered Guiseppe.

'Rats,' Rose replied truthfully – but dryly, too, for there was no elation. Nine men were still in captivity. Star shell over the camp had fizzled out on the wet earth. Three more now burst above the petrol tank, beyond the fence. Tracer criss-crossed the sky, fuzzily luminous in the dispersing smoke; but in minutes now the partisans would retreat, live to fight another day from their mountain caves. Within the same time, Adams would retreat, too, but not unscathed; only two of his three guns were firing. The flash and crack of enemy-manned 88mm guns, on the south slops of the POLJE, was the obvious reason. Had it not been for the smoke between the enemy and No. 1 bunker, it would have all been over long since – like the thunderstorm, itself retreating westwards, taking the rain and lightning with it.

The heavy half-track was still the right way up. Not so the First Lieutenant. He was sucking air like his windpipe was a straw; a phenomenon associated with crouching in semi-confined spaces during vacuum-producing explosions. Sad. Sad, too because Guiseppe's arrival beside him justifiably caused another, smaller explosion. '*You!* Where the hell! *You!* Durand. You – you...' The rest was obscene.

The driving seat was still warm, though wet. 'He's coming with us. So shut up, York!' To hell with the 'sir!' Rose started the motor, engaged the clutch. York and Guiseppe were behind him. 'Would you pick up one of the Schmeissers, Captain Durand! There are three in the back somewhere... Found one?'

'I have found one, Lieutenant.'

'You're letting *him* have a gun?' York was incredulous. 'You must be nuts. What the devil are you playing at?'

'You've just been a prisoner of the Gestapo, haven't you?' Rose asked mildly, turning left on the perimeter road.

'Yes' – thoughtfully.

'You've just escaped, haven't you?'

'Yes' – worriedly.

'Fair enough, then. Captain Durand has just recaptured you. Any objections?'

York had, all the way to the guardroom.

It wasn't far. The perimeter road led along the fence. The journey took less than one minute. Most of the time, Rose's eyes were on the three star shells that drifted slowly to earth above that great camouflaged petrol tank like street lamps in the mists of evaporating rain. The tank was just above the guardroom. If it burst, it would burst like a dam. Like a dam, its contents would leap and bound down the hill and engulf the camp. It was no longer a race against time. It was a race against being roasted alive. But even as he explained his plan to the two men behind, he was conscious that only one of Adams' guns now fired, that its shells were bursting in all the wrong places on the hillside, the gunner's visibility being badly restricted. Because the southern perimeter was uphill, and many of the huts had been flattened by blast, he saw to, on the airstrip below, that the runway lights were on, the glide path stretching away into the smoke. He heard the aircraft engines, knew then that some of the planes had been salvaged, their pilots scrambled. The aero engines faded, came again, only to fade again as each plane raced down the runway on take-off.

Ahead lay the guardroom, its front facing the half-track as it approached on the boundary road. The main gate was on the right. One of the vehicles evacuating non-combatants had just passed through, its headlights bouncing uphill. Had the part-isans recaptured the tug? That was the key question.

One truck stood in front of the guardroom. From the telephone conversation, Rose had known it would be there. It was waiting for Simon York. A big, six-wheel vehicle, it was fully enclosed with green and brown camouflaged canvas. Exhaust fumes eddying in the red glow of its tail light said the engine was running. One man sat in the driver's seat, watching the half-track approach. The two gate sentries were nowhere to be seen; no one was likely to enter.

He turned left a few yards short of the truck, down the left side of the broad entrance road, made a U-turn to the right, started to come up slowly behind it. The manoeuvre revealed – with relief – that the truck's rear flaps were drawn back like curtains; and inside were the missing Rats, the nearest face, lit in the half-track's head-lights, that of 'Taxi' Yates.

'They're inside. All nine of 'em,' York hissed, quite unnecessarily. 'But watch out. That's von Ungern. One lamp.'

The 'one lamp' was a monocle, reflecting star shell as the Gestapo Colonel, darkly conspicuous, detached himself from the group of lighter uniforms on the guard-room's covered veranda, tripped stiffly down the three steps, and strode over as Rose stopped. To give the Colonel his due, he had taken no guards with him, nor did he appear one bit worried that Adams' shells were whistling overhead.

He looked up at York, sitting bolt upright in the back, then at Guiseppe, who was standing up and covering the prisoner with a Schmeisser, then at Rose, after which he then removed his monocle and arched his eyebrows in mild surprise. 'Where is Major Schwarzhaupt?'

'Dead, sir,' Rose bleated. 'All dead. All of them. The whole lot.' He had his left elbow over the door, almost in the Colonel's face, hand idly on the steering wheel; but in the other hand, now rising slowly from the empty passenger seat, was the Luger auto-matic, its black barrel heading across his chest, unseen, for the underside of his elbow. When it arrived, it would be dead in line with the Gestapo chest. 'They were killed by the explosion, sir. The Italian officer saw the Englander trying to escape. He recaptured him. Bravely, sir.'

L/Sea Yates couldn't understand German, so he believed his eyes. 'Ya rotten lousy swine!' he bawled at Guiseppe. 'Ya bloody rotten Eye-tie–!'

'Silence, dog!' A voice from the veranda.

Von Ungern replaced his monocle and frowned.

'Hmmmm,' he said – sceptically! Rose couldn't be sure.

The Luger barked.

As the Colonel fell, two Schmeissers opened up a foot from the Professor's right ear-drum. The veranda cleared like a skittle alley. One, two, three hand grenades went in through the guardroom. Nothing came out but dust.

The driver of the truck jumped down to see what was going on. He did. Rose jumped over the body and arrived in the driving seat as York came in the opposite door.

'Guiseppe?'

'Hanging on to the tail-board.'

The truck roared through the south gate. Three miles ahead lay the harbour and the tug, their only possible chance of reaching *Scorpio* before the dawn – their only chance of escape from the natural trap of the Adriatic Sea, and a small one indeed … and they might have made it but for Able Seaman Golly, a long way behind at No. 1 bunker, who pressed the trigger of the remaining 88mm gun for the last time; perhaps in memory of his boisterous friends, most of whom lay dead around his feet...

The shell followed a slightly parabolic flight, spinning on its axis, whistling down the runway and over smoking planes, over the deep-red fires of burning oil: it passed to the left of the hillock of rubble where the house had been, over the huge scar in the earth where the bombs had been, then screeched over the guardroom, the south gate, the bouncing truck that was as yet but thirty yards beyond: and dead in line with that spinning, conical nose, high on the breast of the hill, sat the huge cylindrical petrol tank, blacker against the lighter blackness of the sky ... and York heard it coming, glanced at Rose as the whistle faded...

It had no beginning. It was there. Suddenly. A gigantic splash of brilliant crimson and gold with jagged edges of flame that pierced the clouds and curved out over the land like solar flares. It seemed momentarily suspended, illuminating with a soft and yellow light the scattered trees and scrub and their fear-filled faces. Then it fell, dropped, showered down from clouds of red and gold to form a thousand yards of fire across the curvature of the hill like the sun's edge at total eclipse. The shock-wave came then; small like the gust of wind from the opening door of a white-hot furnace and it singed the canvas and shrivelled the laminate between the twin layers of glass in front of their eyes and distorted Rose's vision that panic made him crash his fist through the screen as he swerved from the track with but one frenzied thought in his mind – could he outflank the leaping, bounding tidal wave of flame that approached at forty feet per second?

The answer was *No!* – he knew it even as he turned the wheel, even as York – the bloody idiot! – trying to turn it with him, bawled, 'Turn round! Turn round! Turn round!' at which Rose screamed back, 'What the hell do you think I'm doing! Get out of the flaming way!'

Then they were at right angles to the road, tossing and swaying, the primitive suspension crashing against the under side of the chassis as the heavy-treaded tyres crushed the bushes and climbed the boulders, but still turning: turning until they were parallel with the road, but still ten yards from it, on soft mud into which the tyres sank, lost grip, whined and smoked because Rose pumped the accelerator frantically time and again in a futile effort to supplement the revving vibrating engine with his own physical strength and power of will – until they stopped, jolted forward, stopped again and saw while stopped that the twenty-foot wall of flaming fuel was but fifty yards away.

Someone jumped out of the back and started to run. York cried at him to come back but he paid no heed, kept running towards the camp. Two others jumped down, jumped in again as York leapt out, left the door swinging on its hinges; and all this little while Rose pumped the accelerator, juggled the wheel, jumped up and down on the seat in the hope – the utterly absurd hope – that his momentum would add weight to the rear wheels which were spinning stationary, gouging sideways in the slime, first one way, then the other, causing the truck to slew: but each turn of the rear wheels caused the tyres to sink ever deeper until without warning they found a lost branch on which the tyres caught: the truck catapulted forward, careered towards the road, reached it, swung left down it as York, who had crossed the base of a triangle like a greyhound, came in through the door at the end of a world record leap. 'Gaaawwwooo,' he said. But Rose was concentrating, conscious of the picture of fire in his wing mirror, conscious of the heady motion as the wheels raced in the ruts like a train on tracks.

The man who had jumped off was one of the Stokers and they caught up with him at the main gate, slowed sufficiently for the lad to jump on the running board beside York, where he hung on.

The gates flashed past, then the guard-room.

Their speed increased on the smooth

avenue and down the incline. The road narrowed between the huts. Yards behind, the leading edge of the tidal wave of flame shot into the air on hitting the buildings like waves on the beach reach for the sky on hitting the rocks.

So intense was the heat that sweat poured from Rose's body, blinded his eyes like a swimmer risen from the sea; it ran into his partially open mouth from which each breath was the brief gasp of barely-controlled panic – for steam drifted up from the wet road, mingled with the undulating layers of smoke that thickened in the misty beams of the slotted headlights with each yard covered, reducing visibility to twenty feet – fifteen – ten – and then the wall of a hut came rushing at him at an oblique angle; and he swerved, skidded, hit the wall on his own side with an appalling crash that was followed immediately by the crash and crunch of bodies in the back as he bounced clear. 'All right, son, don't worry. Hang on to me. Nothing to be afraid of. Our Navigator's the world's lousiest driver but he'll make it.' This from funny York, crooning comforting fibs to the terror-stricken lad who crouched on the running board, head and shoulders in through the cab window; but brave York, who spoke softly like a mother to her child, while the tremor in his deep voice belied the bravado.

A little weaving to pick up sight of the hut walls on either side and Rose again had his bearings.

The intersections were at right angles to his line of flight. All the time there was the dread that some frantic lunatic might cross his path in a heavier vehicle; but the crossroads flashed past on either side, so far empty; so far, or as far as he could see.

Aviation fuel engulfed the camp like red-hot volcanic lava but moving many times faster: so fast that it ran like a river of molten steel between the huts and leaving them skeletons in instant combustion for the briefest moment before the force of the tide sent them askew and tumbling like flotsam on the oceans of hell: so fast that it was about five seconds behind the racing truck and turning the mist and smoke ahead into a red and terrifying glare shot with leaping shadows ... and they were not the only ones to race for safety ... but most did it on foot, impossibly, and Rose saw the back of a running paratrooper loom suddenly in front, saw in the next quick intake of breath the heads and fiery backs of twenty others, all tight-packed in the avenue, all in his path, some already glancing back over their shoulders in abject terror. To stop was to die, and yet he put all his weight instinctively on the brake pedal and the wheels locked: locked and skidded and screeched and failed to stop on the cushion of recent rain. Brutally and thankfully York kicked that instinctive foot from the brake. He held on to the lad at his side and put a protective arm over his own face in the same way that Rose himself did, and ducked: ducked and closed their ears and minds to the ghastly *Thud! Thud! Thud!* of human bone and flesh being struck at fifty miles per hour by the angular bonnet of the ten-ton truck; but they could not close their eyes. Like the cowardly hit-and-run driver, Rose looked not back, looked only ahead at the trickling blood on the screen, at the youth impaled on the radiator, whose body had been torn open to release the blood that flowed on top of the bonnet and rippled in the fierce wind of their forward motion which brought some of it through the fist-hole in the screen, where it spotted his face, filled his mouth with the warm taste of salt and iron, brought with it revulsion, then nausea; and he vomited over the wheel, all but lost control as the truck bounced over the dead and dying, bounced so much that the carcass, glistening bright red and pinky raw in the light from the fires, fell away, left behind a huge segment of rag and flesh.

Unseen, two avenues away on the right, but two intersections ahead, paratroopers – far too many of them – were clambering into another truck from the guns they'd been manning. Their escape route lay north as well, but their way was obstructed by fallen huts and they headed west at speed for the main avenue down which the Chatham Rats were driving.

With blood on the windscreen and smoke streaming into his face from the hole, Rose could see next to nothing, and what little he could see was on his own side. The left side. And York was on the right, still clutching the lad on the right-hand running board. Rose subconsciously knew that the young Stoker's name was Hunt, for the lad had told York who was still molly-coddling. But Rose was also searching his memory of the camp layout. Somewhere, not far now, the main avenue was obstructed by huts and the road swept left to the aprons. That bend in the road he must not miss.

One intersection came and went. The next was the length of two huts away. Ahead of that, deep in the smog, he saw a fire. It appeared to be right in the centre of the road.

The next and last intersection was upon them.

With the corner of his eye he saw headlights on the right. Then their beams were in his path, at right angles to his line of flight.

York cried – 'Look out! On your right!'

It was too late.

What happened, happened so fast that

each event, though separate, happened within the span of a human scream.

Again instinctively Rose swerved left, only to swerve back again to avoid going straight through the hut on the far corner. At the same time the Wehrmacht driver, already commencing his right-hand turn to go down the same avenue, slammed on his brakes. His wheels locked. Rose kept going. Both vehicles were turning into the neck of the same 'bottle', the enemy from the right, Rose from the left merely because he'd swerved and re-swerved. But the enemy, now virtually out of control was, turning in a skid, juddering sideways. They would crash side on, nose to nose, tail to tail. Both vehicles weighed ten tons and were full of men. Stoker Hunt was between them. His was the scream.

Only God could have lifted that boy off that running board in time; only God and Simon York.

The cab was fully enclosed, the windows eighteen inches square, and Hunt came through it. His head and shoulders landed at Rose's back, like a wedge. The two vehicles married in the same instant. Adams must have heard the din a mile away. Together they careered down the road.

The tidal wave of flame was three seconds behind. One hundred and twenty feet. The cab was an oven.

It was now seen that the fire in the roadway was a blazing hut that marked the end
of the road. Invisible in the mist would be
the bend to the left Rose sought. While both
vehicles were locked he could never turn
that bend, for he was already trying.

In York's hand was the Mauser he'd picked
from the hut floor. Across his chest, through
the open window that Hunt had come in,
sat the Wehrmacht driver, hanging on to his
wheel, casting panicky glances across at
Rose. There was no enmity on either side.
They were soldiers not Gestapo. Fire was
the common enemy.

'Shoot him!' Rose barked. 'Quick! Quick!'

But York didn't – couldn't or hesitated –
and Rose's right hand shot out and grabbed
the Mauser by the barrel, wrenched it from
his hand, tossed it, caught it by the butt and
fired it three inches from York's face. The
bullet hit the Wehrmacht driver between the
eyes.

A hard kick of the wheel to the right, a
swerve to the left, and the enemy truck
veered away, ploughed into the hut on the
right, tore down the wall, burst into flames.
But Rose hit the hut on the left a glancing
blow and he found the steering impossible
because the truck tyres were racing flush to
the wall – and the wall vanished – ended –
and it was too late to turn, impossible to
turn, and right in his path sat the blazing hut

– empty? – full of machinery? – but there was no way of telling and he hugged the wheel with hands and arms, and crouched: crouched in the same split second that York crouched too and they went through the wall like a motor cyclist going through a flaming hoop – *Crash!* – and it was no hoop; all the domestic accoutrement for the entire German Army had been packed into that hut, Rose was certain, and not least was the red-hot iron bedstead that ripped the roof from the cab, let in the blazing rafter, and remained on the bonnet like a glowing cage when they burst from the other side in fire and sparks and zigzagged crazily on to the aprons, canvas and tyres aflame, their clothes aflame.

They had lost two seconds. The heat was almost unbearable. A tyre burst like a shotgun and Rose fought for control, unable to see, aware of flames licking his face from part of the blazing rafter in his arms which York, now on his feet, lifted with bare hands as the truck lurched and crunched over the wing of an Me109.

Then – the runway lights! – stretching into the smoke, and they were now gaining on the fire, or the fire was slowing, spreading out over the flat floor of the POLJE.

Someone squirted a soda siphon on Rose's clothes, on his face as he opened his mouth. 'What the–!' It tasted like fire extinguisher.

Then the strength of panic ebbed, left him limp, exhausted and in agony ... and the truck rolled on, its burst tyre flop-flop-flopping along the tarmac, York now in the back and heaving his men out like sacks, for the vehicle was hopelessly on fire ... and Rose went limp over the wheel...

Adams, one arm useless, got to his feet slowly. Gorman lay dead. Golly, Harrington and Smith staggered about trying to comfort the wounded. Happy was all in, staring down at the body of his best friend, Tiny, when eleven charred and blackened creatures stumbled unseeingly upon them.

'Who's that?' Adams' voice was soft with weariness.

'It's us,' York said. 'Where's everyone?'

'There's only seven of us, sir. Alive.'

No. 1 bunker lay in darkness, the darkness tinted pink, the air hot, and light from a sea of flames glinted on the shattered guns, on the empty shell cases that littered the whole clearing, revealed the shell holes as black patches on the ground.

They stopped, staggered, leaned breathlessly on the guns, heads hung in sheer exhaustion. York and Adams knelt by the wounded, talking softly.

'Better make – for – boats,' Rose said stiltedly. 'The tug. Must get – to – the harbour.'

Adams got up. 'No use, sir. The partisans shoved off. They sent a runner. He's over

there. Dead. He said the rest got shot up.
Never got near the tug. They *did* try.'

High in the sky the moon entered the
silver lining of the receding storm, then
burst into full brilliance and lit the clearing.

A small chorus of sharp, metallic clicks
made them turn slowly, carefully.

Round them, two deep in a wide semi-
circle, were fifty men at least, all dressed in
the light desert uniforms of paratroopers.

The moon glinted on the rising barrels of
the Schmeisser machine-pistols, as all took
aim.

Happy, himself badly wounded, had given
all he had, and lost his friend. He started to
shake uncontrollably. He was crying.
Strangely, brave men sometimes do.

That was the moment when time ran out.

13

Dawn came. Mist swirled round the islands,
drifted from the water's surface. Of this,
Rose had caught only a glimpse as they were
shepherded on board the tug.

Now *Juliana* was under way, romping
along.

Where were they being taken? 'Either to
Zadar, on the Yugoslavian coast, or across

the Adriatic to Ancona, on the east coast of Italy.' That was York's suggestion. Rose thought Zadar the most likely.

They were tucked in the Tugmaster's cabin behind the bridge, could see nothing, and speculation was damped by the guns of two guards. Those present were the First Lieutenant, Adams, arm bandaged, Guiseppe, who had said nothing at all, Yates, greedy eyes back on the naked ladies and Rose himself. They were drawn, haggard, blackened, charred and blistered; and what were they doing?

'Kings over tens,' York cried triumphantly, and placed a neat semi-circle of playing cards on the bunk.

Adams had his cards in one hand and was sorting them out with his teeth. Having completed the operation, he laid them down on top of York's. 'Sorry, sir. A straight.' His face was deadpan, his voice tight with pain, but his eyes were twinkling with delight. The trouble was, none of them understood why they hadn't been shot on sight. In fact, the enemy had been coldly polite, uncommunicative, and not unkind to the wounded.

They laid down their cards and looked apprehensively at each other when the engine-room telegraphs tinkled and speed was reduced. Two minutes passed. Again the tinkle of the telegraphs. This time the engines stopped. Silence for one minute.

Then came the bump as the vessel came alongside a jetty. 'It *must* be Zadar,' York said. He had to be right, for they'd only been on passage fifty minutes.

Distant voices shouted in Italian. Rose couldn't make out what was said. Then comparative silence reigned for nearly five minutes, broken at last by jack-booted feet.

The door opened.

In came a paratroop Major, his laced knee-boots and uniform caked with dry mud. He stopped, motioned them upright with his hands. 'Get up!' He spoke in English.

'We're going somewhere?' York inquired, glancing at Rose, then at Adams.

'Don't try anything,' Rose whispered. 'Not now.'

'Wise advice,' the Major interjected silkily. 'You will note that your hands were not tied. And it would be a shame to die when you are about to be set free.'

'Free?' York echoed. There was a moment of stunned silence. Then he flung his head back and laughed. He stopped laughing with the suddenness of a man who is really bitterly angry. 'Who the hell do you think you're kidding, Herr Major von whatever your name is?'

'You will follow me!' The Major turned on his heels.

Schmeissers made good sheep dogs redundant.

Escape had been planned during the game of cards. They were alert for opportunity as they filed through the cabin door, turned left, started to cross the gloomy interior of the small enclosed bridge. This first glimpse out of the grubby stormproof windows brought disappointment; their guess had been wrong. It was instantly apparent that they were about to be transferred to the shores of Italy or even Germany, via the grey warship that lay alongside.

York leading, they stepped out into a cool grey morning light, stood very still on the small platform, prior to descending the iron ladder to the deck below.

Very still.

This, Rose knew, was another moment like that one three hours previous when time had run out – for the warship lying alongside, was *Scorpio*, and staring up at them from the starboard waist, was Edward Dunbar.

It was harbour E24.

No mental confusion, in any other circumstances, could have equalled that which he felt. He didn't speak, because speech was not possible, and no one else did.

As he descended the ladder, his feet were quite literally leaden with unreality; dragging – like living in one of his own dreams. So stunning were the implications of what was happening, that his mind refused to entertain the truth: and rejected it utterly in fact because the truth *could not* be true. That, for the moment, was the end of reasoned thought. Then there existed a stupefied atmosphere, in which voices were distant, remote, strangely clear, but without real meaning – like the gentlemanly Major's guttural English after he'd strode on board *Scorpio*, clicked his heels and saluted Edward. 'Good morning, Kapitan. You have my respect. After my radio message I thought you might have sailed.' Unlike the Gestapo, there was no sneer in his words.

Edward, looking his own handsome self, though pale and drawn, returned the salute. He was immaculate in a white Italian uniform but there was no attempt whatever to disguise his very British drawl. 'In the same position, Major, I feel sure you would have waited for your men. Thank you for taking them back. However, since I presume it wasn't entirely your own idea, may I ask whose it was – and why?'

'I regret, Kapitan, I can tell you very little because I know nothing. We had just come across from the Yugoslavian mainland when we captured your men. My orders came from the Gestapo.'

'To set us free…?' It was barely a question.

'To set you free, Kapitan.'

'I see…' But Edward didn't. Nor anyone.

While this absurd conversation was taking place, the guards on the tug had casually shouldered arms, and Cruikshank's medical men were scuttling back and fore between the vessels with stretchers, transferring the wounded who had been below decks with the remaining men. Happy and Wog were, however, gazing open-mouthed at their hairy boss who approached them in front of Rose and motioned them irritably to cross the gangway, nearly going headlong over the coil of rope as he did so, because he too was watching and listening to the Major: '...and you will kindly get under way as soon as you are ready, Kapitan,' he finished.

Edward wasn't finished. He took a red bundle from under his arm and held it out. 'You will have *my* respect if you would see that those of my men who have not returned, are buried with the usual honours...?' It was a Union Jack.

Even Cruikshank stopped.

There was dead silence.

Suddenly the Major took the flag, took one pace to the rear, clicked his heels and saluted. 'It will be done, Kapitan. You have my word.' He turned on the exact spot and crossed the gangway. Had the Major not been a man of honour, or if he had been a member of the Nazi Party, the scene might have been quite, quite different.

They stood bewildered, watched the tug draw away into the morning haze, saw then that the E-boats had gone, that the two U-boats were no longer there.

Kind, considerable Reece-Davis took Rose's arm. 'Nice to see you back, sir. You look as if you've just been through Hell itself.' That was the understatement of the war ... though no one knew it ... except York ... perhaps.

It was also premature.

Edward didn't care about anchors. The cable was broken. *Scorpio* slipped out of harbour. And it was a beautiful morning for those who cared, with green and white islands lying on a milk-chocolate sea, in which their rising bow-wave foamed not white but shot with amber light.

An anti-submarine zigzag was worked out, the times and legs handed to Edward. All the guns were manned.

'What the devil's going on!' York demanded. 'I'm not dreaming. This isn't war. This is plain fantastic.'

He was right.

No one answered him. No one knew the answer. Edward knew only what the Major had told him. They were being set free. Why? Why? Why? There was one answer, and it brought Edward to the chart-table for the umpteenth time, brought the same question again and again. 'The glider bomb. Are you dead certain that all the airfield installations were destroyed? For God's sake think, Pilot!'

'Utterly.' There was no other adverb in the book that could so adequately suit what had happened.

'If you are wrong, we're dead,' Edward said quietly.

He was right, too.

But there was, of course, one other answer. The obvious answer. Reece-Davis put it in words. 'They're going to make us run the gauntlet from here to Crete,' he forecast. 'They'll throw in every plane they've got, from both sides of the Adriatic, to avenge what we've done. Even if we are lucky enough to reach the Strait of Otranto, we'll find the Italian Fleet waiting – in force.'

He was right as well. But it was the young man's theory, made without the knowledge that aerial attacks require a great deal of organising; and time was passing. Time was passing and Otranto and darkness were only four hundred miles ahead; ten hours at forty knots.

So the speculation went on.

An hour passed. It was more than ever sinister because nothing happened. Tension mounted. Rose washed himself from a basin of hot water on the chart-table. Cruikshank came and dressed his burns, and York's, while all the time the funnels droned, smoked a little, and the Asdic pinged; but no black periscopes appeared, nor aircraft, nor E-boats.

Ninety minutes.

Edward's second cup of coffee arrived.

The Doctor left.

'His speciality is circumcision, you know,' muttered Reece-Davis, staring after him. This was true.

Then – suddenly – 'Aircraft! Aircraft! Bearing Green two-four! Angle of Sight – seven-five!'

'Seven-five!' York echoed. Back went his head. Every head on the bridge went with it.

One aircraft flew in the pale blue heavens, almost invisible at four miles above the sea. It crossed the ship, started to recede, leaving behind bits of a vapour trail. But then it started to alter course, to begin a semi-circular sweep that would bring it over *Scorpio's* long foaming wake.

York bounded across the bridge, clambered up the ladder to his 'mushroom' tower.

The telephone was in Edward's hand.

Where was Adams? The fear which stimulated that question in Rose's mind, also brought the conviction that the truth *was* true, and he went down the bridge ladder, two at a time.

The Sick Bay was warm, stinking. The Gunner's Mate sat in a chair having his wound dressed.

'Adams. That plane. Did it get away?' It was the most futile of questions. Adams had been in the boat, not with York and the column when they entered the camp. He hadn't seen the plane. Nor could he have seen it from No. 1 bunker, for it had been obscured, first by the other planes and then by that damned smoke; and all this Rose realised in that terrible moment when Adams shook his head and said: 'Some of them took off, sir. We saw their landing lights, like car headlights, coming down the runway in the smoke, straight at us...'

The 4.7 guns opened up as Rose reached the bridge.

'I'm afraid I was wrong, sir. The plane—'

'That's all right, Pilot. You did your best. I think I've known all the time,' Edward smiled. 'Just let's pray.'

Although the plane appeared to be almost overhead, it was actually a mile astern, overhauling *Scorpio* at two hundred and seventy knots. Round it, but hopelessly scattered, were the very tiny, dark and fluffy shell bursts of the 4.7s, the only guns on the ship whose shells could reach to that height and angle of sight. The chances of a direct hit were next to nothing. All depended on shrapnel from a near miss. Down below decks lay a compartment called a Transmitting Station, which accommodated a mechanical computer, called a Fire Control Clock, into which a vast amount of complicated data was fed continuously, and out of which came the estimated point in the sky at which the gunners aimed. To complicate matters further, the shells had to be fused by hand to burst at the estimated height. And after all that, it was still like hitting a high-flying, fast-moving swallow with a .22 rifle. That, therefore, was the sum total of their hopes of survival.

After one minute, that last hope was snatched from them when all three turrets ceased to fire. Like the smaller weapons, they were not designed to fire vertical, and their slim twin barrels stood hard against the turret roofs, silent, smoking, useless.

Sitting in the aircraft, the bombardier would have a telescopic view, not only of *Scorpio* herself, but the vast arrowhead of white foam which stretched to port and starboard on a blue sea, for the islands had gone, and with them the silt. He would also see the white thread of foam that was the destroyer's two-mile-long wake. These factors would help him to define his target, and the aiming point would be the bridge. In one hand would be the control lever, linked manually to his radio transmitter, in turn linked by radio pulses to the receiver in the bomb which would operate the tiny wings; and thus he would guide it down, alter its course if *Scorpio* altered course; and he had plenty of time, because four miles was a long way for a bomb to drop, and drop it would: fast: like a parachutist who can pin-point the spot on which he wants to land by waving his arms and legs while in free fall. The plane's height and the time it would take the bomb to drop would, Rose knew, have been carefully worked out to preclude any possibility of *Scorpio's* escape.

All this, Edward also knew. He knew, too, that the bomb would penetrate the magazines, that his ship would inevitably blow up, disintegrate together with men and machines. But although his knowledge was shared, the unenviable responsibility for taking evasive action was his alone.

When the 4.7s stopped firing, a curious mortal hush fell on the ship. The purring of the funnel exhausts, the hollow ping … ping … ping of the Asdic, and the soft and endless crashing of the bow-wave all receded from conscious hearing; and when Guiseppe reached Dunbar's side, and stopped, there seemed to be no other sound in the world but Edward's voice: 'Hold her on one-eight-four, Coxswain! No matter what happens, hold her dead on course.'

'Course steady on one-eight-four,' confirmed the voicepipe gruffly, and – for once – said no more.

Edward straightened, glanced round, raised his voice: 'There'll be two U-boats and three E-boats somewhere ahead,' he warned the lookouts. 'After we dodge the bomb, they'll be waiting. Keep your eyes peeled!' Having fooled no one, he reached with unseeing accuracy for his cup, a drug addict to the last sip.

The ack-ack guns' crews were motionless along *Scorpio's* length, all wearing their grubby anti-flash hoods and gloves and deep Italian helmets. Freer was there, too, by the forward funnel and partly obscured by the searchlight. Rose shook off the inescapable conviction that Mrs Ann Freer was about to become a widow, and moved closer to Reece-Davis, who stood so still by the chart-table he could have been dead, except for the sweat which trickled down his face.

Guiseppe said nothing, did nothing.

Grey against the blue-grey haziness of the heavens, the plane looked almost transparent.

'The bomb's bin released!' York yelled.

'I can't see it,' Dunbar argued.

'You will.'

Rose did. It was just a black spot, seeming stationary in the sky, and the plane was moving ahead of it; an illusion caused by its height. It was actually curving down, gathering speed, and – yes – wobbling, wavering distinctly from side to side as its controller conned it down towards *Scorpio's* bridge.

But even in the face of death, man deceived himself.

'Make smoke!' York bellowed.

'Smoke wouldn't do any good,' Edward called back. 'He'd still see the front of the ship.'

'The bomb is notta foolproof,' Guiseppe advanced.

'Get out of the way!' Edward pushed him aside, put his head in the voicepipe. 'Hard-a-starboard!'

'Starboard wheel on, sir.'

Scorpio keeled over to port. They all staggered. Fear turning into anger as their attention was distracted from the bomb. Then their eyes were back on it, fascinated; but not before Rose had accidentally seen what no one else had seen.

'Aircraft! To port!' There was no time for bearings. He just pointed. 'There! Look!'

A squadron of Ju88s. Three miles. Two thousand feet up. Waiting. 'They're going to be disappointed,' Reece-Davis said. The hope drained visibly from his eyes as he looked away.

'Port thirty!'

'Thirty of port wheel on, sir.'

There was no better Coxswain than Morgan. He spun his wheel instantly on the command. The ship answered her helm with alacrity every time. The sea was a heaving, foaming mess. They went round in a tight circle. They turned sharply left, sharply right. It was near impossible to stand up.

All this happened in enough time to turn

a man's hair from black to white – already a proven fact in the war – and if the bomb had had eyes it would have seen one grey warship, a quarter of an inch long, going stark raving mad inside a circle no greater than a tin lid; and so the bombardier would aim for the centre of the circle, knowing he could afford to ignore *Scorpio's* reactions until that last three thousand feet, when then he would glide the missile on to its final goal.

No one bothered about the waiting Ju88 bombers.

Yet there was more tension than fear; more a disbelief that any bomb could hit a ship from such a height.

They were terribly wrong.

At least one Chatham Rat was determined to die fighting and he'd removed his 20mm cannon from its pedestal. With the barrel held between two other men he opened fire vertically and orange tracer climbed into the sky. York did nothing to stop this brave but futile reaction; instead he abandoned his perch and leapt down on to the bridge, making for Edward's side on the theory that two useless heads are better than one.

Then came the short period when disbelief was swept aside, when all could see the black and hideous missile – saw its wings cant first one way and then the other as the bombardier adjusted its final course.

Captain Guiseppe Durand still stood at

one side of the bridge where he'd been unceremoniously pushed. He was very pale, fists clenched, eyes alternating between the bomb and the backs of Edward and York, who were trying to be very cool and very British and failing miserably. Then – so quickly it barely registered – he pounced forward, brought his huge hands down – *Slap!* – on York's shoulders, jerked him back, chopped him in the stomach and then on the back of the neck as the First Lieutenant folded; a preliminary to going flat on his face. Edward straightened, astonished, received a straight right on the chin.

Lieutenant Rose went instinctively for his gun. It wasn't there. He tensed and sprang at Guiseppe, only to catch Edward as Guiseppe threw him.

Both crashed to the deck.

'Hold your course! Stop both engines! Both engines, full astern!' Those commands – Guiseppe's commands – reached Rose's ears as he tried to struggle out from under Dunbar.

The engine-room telegraphs jangled down in the wheelhouse. Vibration stopped as the engines were stopped. Then they restarted and *Scorpio* shuddered, juddered, vibrated until teeth chattered and her speed dropped … forty … thirty-five … thirty knots as the powerful propellers clutched at the sea.

The Italian had lost all. He was taking the

honourable way out. Suicide. Rose knew that as he heaved Edward aside, struggled to his feet. And York knew it, too – he was scrambling to his feet 'You – you – you – you...' He couldn't get the word out so angry was he as he lunged forward, dragged Guiseppe back from the voicepipe, fist already raised to deliver the retaliatory blow ... but it never landed, remained suspended – frozen – and all noise was drowned out by the approach of death.

There was nothing more fearful than the hissing friction of that bomb as it parted the air with its conical nose and vampire-like wings. It was a black bat. They heard it, saw it, knew it was going to hit the bridge. Then they knew they were wrong and it was going to be a direct hit on A turret. Then it swished past their faces and their eyes closed.

A column of water shot fifty feet into the air and ten yards ahead of *Scorpio's* slowing bows.

'Stop both engines! Both engines, full ahead!' It was Guiseppe who gave the order immediately to increase speed. In the same breath he picked up the phone. 'Aircraft attacking from port! Open fire! Open fire!'

The twelve Ju88s were finished waiting; they had seen the bomb miss. Hardly had the column of water dropped back into the sea when they banked, turned to attack.

Guiseppe laid down the phone. Every gun on the ship opened fire. Dunbar, who had climbed to his feet, walked unsteadily to the bridge front, a trickle of fresh blood winding down his chin from tight lips. He joined York, Rose and Reece-Davis. But Guiseppe turned, pushed his way through them without a word, grew small as his huge figure descended the steps, and vanished. In his face there had been pride, triumph, contempt – but he had saved their lives, for he'd seen the one flaw of all machines: the human error. Up in the plane the bombardier had observed every move *Scorpio* made, and promptly countered it. But there was one move he could not see – a sudden and drastic reduction of speed, which because he was aiming-off ahead of the fast-moving destroyer in order to hit it, had caused him to miss ahead. The only mystery was why Captain Guiseppe Durand had done it – for minutes later he was found dead in his cabin, shot by his own hand. A man of honour? 'He did it because he wanted us to live through this day, and suffer,' York said bitterly of this: but it was the kind of cynical remark men did make under stress, and didn't mean ... though he might well have been right, for there is no sentiment in war...

If there was anything worse than being on a

ship under aerial bombardment, it was being the pilot of a plane attacking a heavily armed ship.

Being unable to attack from opposite directions for fear of collision, the Ju88s came in from port. Because Simon York had chopped down the mainmast, sheered the stops on the gun mountings, they were met by a barrage of two-thousand-plus shells per minute, of all sizes, but all lethal, and one fifth of them visible because of the tracer. The men behind the guns were York's men; superbly trained; and they had one aim which the Luftwaffe had overlooked: *To live!*

Clearly acting under orders to destroy *Scorpio* at all costs, the pilots came in low, bravely and eagerly, their sleek twin-engined machines setting up a whining and snarling that made the nerves cringe. As controlling officer, York switched every gun, including the 4.7s, on the two leading planes and ignored the others. The bright morning sky became dark with shell bursts, streaked with white and orange tracer. Both aircraft were coned in concentrated fire for four seconds. Some gunners, like Happy, were out for vengeance.

The first Ju88 exploded, bombs and petrol blowing it to smithereens in a huge ball of black expanding smoke and flame. Blast removed the wing of the second plane, which fell in a spiral and splashed whitely into the sea to the accompaniment of a Chatham cheer. 'Two down and ten to go!' yelled trigger-happy York.

'Starboard ten!' Edward ordered smugly.

'Ten of starboard wheel on, sir,' confirmed the voicepipe, and then added, puzzled: 'Whatever happened to the glider bomb, sir?' Poor devil, no one had told Morgan!

After that the attack was cautious. An estimated fifty bombs were aimed at the ship. None hit. Many dropped so far off target, they were probably jettisoned, perhaps because the bombardiers had been wounded or just because pilots were human and the barrage was frightening to any man.

All through the attack, Rose could see the high-flying plane which had dropped the glider bomb dwindling in the northern sky. It left behind one question: had the events of the night failed to hinder development of that deadly bomb? But that was a question that only the future could answer.

The Ju88s flew off westward, one trailing smoke.

Edward altered course due east, and due south again when the mountains of Yugoslavia appeared on the horizon: this he did to dodge the U-boats and E-boats. The enemy strategy, he said, would be to cripple *Scorpio*, then sink her.

Immediately after that, one submarine contact was made by Asdic, then quickly lost astern.

At noon, nothing more had happened.

In anticipation of the massed attacks expected, Reece-Davis suggested a radio message to Dorman or the C-in-C, for the radio frequencies were no longer being jammed. But Dunbar wisely refused, knowing that the enemy could – and very readily would – use *Scorpio* as cheese to trap any Fleet units which ventured to their aid.

It was 12.34 p.m. when a panting Telegraphist arrived on the bridge, stuffed a signal into Rose's hand.

That signal was addressed to Edward Dunbar, and came from the desk of ex-chicken farmer, Heinrich Himmler. 'My orders are that all units of the Italian Fleet shall put to sea, that all available aircraft shall take the air, that the vessel *Scorpio* shall be sunk with all hands.'

It was the sentence of death.

'He's angry about last night,' York growled, and cast a reproving eye on Rose. 'This is all your fault, Professor; you and your damned 88mm guns.'

'He's just a big-mouth,' Reece-Davis scoffed.

'Me?' York glared.

'No, sir – Himmler.'

Both!

And yet, incredibly, time passed and still nothing happened. Men washed and ate at

the guns. Nelson, strangely worn-out looking, staggered aft to his scupper, staggered
back again and vanished.

3.50 p.m. on the chart-table clock. Position: 110 miles north of the Strait of Otranto.
Rose scribbled it down in the log. He heard
the lookouts cry in chorus: 'Aircraft! Aircraft!
Aircraft!' He noticed that no bearings were
given but didn't budge until the dreaded
cries: 'Stand to! Stand to! Stand to!' Then he
glanced over his shoulder. Edward stood at
the front of the bridge, head twisted, eyes on
York's tower; and the blood was visibly
draining from his handsome face.

Rose ran to his side.

Without a word, Dunbar pointed ahead.

The sky to the south was densely speckled
– dark – as if from some swarm of giant bees,
whose multitudinous droning reached their
ears, swamped the funnel exhausts, made
the air quiver. It wasn't necessary to count
… for eight hundred to a thousand aircraft
were approaching, flying at roughly ten
thousand feet; familiar Ju88s, the deadly
Ju87 Stuka divebombers, Dorniers 17s and
215s, HeIIIs – they were all there, cruising in
scores of near perfect V formations. Above
them, only discernible by the criss-crossed
and curving vapour trails, were hundreds of
protecting fighters, Me109s and Me110s.
The whole aerial armada spread through an
arc of a circle from south-east by south to

south-west by south; and there was no escape.

The twin barrels of A, B and Y turrets took aim.

'Hold your fire!' Edward ordered.

That huge armada approached them slowly. Not once did the Captain lower his glasses. They covered the whole sky. The day seemed darker. It was fearsome, deafening.

Lieutenant-Commander York made no attempt to dispute the order not to fire, for he, like everyone else – except Edward Dunbar – was immobilised, stunned by the futility of offering any resistance whatsoever.

'Saturation bombing.' It wasn't a question, it was a fact that removed every trace of colour from Reece-Davis's face. Like so many others, he was staring at Dunbar, his hero, *their* hero; and it was the moment when Rose knew that the real secret of the Chatham Rats lay in *faith:* faith in the man who calmly lowered his binoculars and smiled encouragingly, said quietly, 'Not saturation bombing, Subby. No one – not even Himmler – could dislike us that much.'

It took a long time for the sky to brighten.

As the armada passed, Rose saw that the rear formation consisted of huge Ju52 transport planes, undoubtedly carrying thousands of troops from Greece, Crete – the island had fallen two days before – and

Sicily. It was a withdrawal from the Mediterranean theatre of war. The battle was won:
won except for a small group of men, called
the British 8th Army, who were still stubbornly holding the gateway to Egypt at El
Alamein; nothing for the mighty Wehrmacht
to worry about. But those Ju52s explained
vigilant Edward's negative orders, also the
impish smile on his face when Simon York
climbed down from his tower, stumbled
over, face ashen, gulped and said: *'Gott in
Himmel!* I nearly had puppies when I saw
that lot.'

He wasn't alone!

'Wonder where they're off to, sir?' asked
the Signalman.

Edward shook his head sadly.

'Hitler knows,' he said ... and so, twenty-
three days later, on June 22, did the people
of the Soviet Union.

Radio silence was broken, a sighting
report sent.

The anti-climax equalled a hot bath after
a hard day. But it was the fortune of war.
The odds against them had been slashed by
one insane stroke of Hitler's pen.

Hopes soared like a thermometer in an
oven.

By evening, only light attacks by Savoia
Machetti torpedo-bombers had been made
on the ship. The intent was to cripple. They
didn't succeed. One man was killed and

three wounded by cannon fire. Mrs Ann Freer still had a husband.

So *Scorpio* hissed through the water at forty-four feet per second, the tides of time and circumstances flowing with her. But Heinrich Himmler was not given to idle threats. The 44-mile invisible bottle-neck called the Strait of Otranto began to close. Brindisi, on the heel of Italy, lay on the starboard hand, well below a horizon on which the sun sat like a great flaming orange, its nuclear fire turning the mare's tails from white to pink.

Fifteen minutes later, radio silence was again broken:

From Officer Commanding H.M.S. *Scorpio*, to C-in-C Mediterranean Fleet. Repeated D.N.I., Alexandria. Repeated Admiralty. T.O.D. 18.40 hours. 9/6/41. Mission accomplished within bounds of possibility. Being heavily shelled by concentrated units of Italian Fleet. Some casualties. Still maintaining speed. Have hoisted white ensign. Proceeding to attack.

Typical of the naval war, the cheerful if slightly incredulous reply came back: 'The Italian Fleet. Impossible. I sank them all at Matapan. Well done. Good luck.'

14

The sun sank. Dusk deepened. Seconds flew. Visibility was five miles. Flashes in the gloom revealed the exact position of one Italian cruiser. An irregular wavering sound of rushing air made faces tighten as another broadside of 8-inch shells shuffled across the sky and exploded in their wake, too close.

Handy above the voicepipe Edward held the telephone with one hand, adjusted his 'tin' hat over a wry face; his coffee days were over. He was attacking like a skier zigzags on a mountain slope, and *Scorpio* keeled from one side to the other, time and again, dodging the shells that lifted the sea to port and starboard and astern. Stiff in the breeze, above and behind their heads, a huge battle ensign fluttered and cracked, starkly white and red against the dark blue of the sky. Her twin stacks belched black and oily smoke, its purpose not to hide in, but to conceal from enemy eyes the fierce flames that licked the wind from a ragged tear in her after deck. Two shells had entered the ship's side below the gunwale, exploded in the cabin flat. One other had exploded on the empty forward mess-decks. But her torpedo tubes were standing out, waiting. York was in his tower, hating. A and B turrets were trained where the enemy would appear, right ahead. Itchy fingers waited sweatily for the range to close.

Edward was grumpy. The cruiser was in his way. It had long out-ranged the 4.7s.

The Italians had stretched a screen of two cruisers and a dozen or more destroyers across the 44-mile wide northern entrance to the Strait. This cruiser was the key to the front door.

The range closed at the rate of one mile in each eighty seconds. Now Rose could see the enemy distinctly, grey and sinister, her raked outline blending with the gloaming.

'*Open fire!*' York just couldn't make a noise quietly.

With a blinding, deafening quadruple flash and bang, A and B turrets opened up, B firing over A, both firing over the bow. But the cruiser was travelling across their line of sight, her port guns blazing, and the 4.7s missed badly astern of her. 'Lost your spectacles?' This was thrown up at York over an irritable Edward's shoulder. The reply was obscene.

'Stand by for torpedo attack!'

Mr Chaplin – 'Charlie' to his back – didn't have to be told. He'd been waiting, he said, since Matapan. He wasn't going to miss. A quiet fellow, a grandfather at forty, he was saving up all these rare moments for bed-time stories.

The vibration shook the chart-table. The chart was illegible. The darkening sea creamed level with *Scorpio's* gunwales as she leaned first one way and then the other. To the enemy she appeared as a grey and narrow pyramidal shape, approaching head-on against a halo of black smoke.

Two miles. One mile to go. Eighty seconds. For Edward and Mr Chaplin, working in unison by telephone, were going to fire the torpedoes at two thousand nautical yards.

But to do this, Dunbar and Chaplin became like pilot and bombardier of an attacking aeroplane; for Edward had, very soon now, to stop dodging the shells and hold *Scorpio* straight and level to give Charlie a chance.

That enemy Captain knew it.

The cruiser's two port 4-inch batteries joined the four twin 8-inch turrets and her whole port side was lit with gun flashes. Then she opened up with her ack-ack guns. Multi-coloured tracer curved out over the sea ten seconds after Dunbar ordered: 'Steady on one-six-four, Coxswain!'

Scorpio steadied, a sitting duck until Charlie fired his tin fish, her bows aimed slightly ahead of the cruiser's bow. Both vessels were travelling at a combined speed of seventy knots, closing the distance between each other at thirty knots because of the angle of approach.

The computer in the TS supplied data to guns and torpedoes. Men followed pointers on dials. But the 20mm guns opened fire visually. So did the two 50mm guns aft.

Y turret joined A and B.

Tracer crossed the sky in each direction, whined from the superstructure as they ricocheted, pocked the sea for miles around, and the air shuddered with projectiles.

Then – and it seemed that *Scorpio* leapt out of the water under Rose's feet – once, twice, three times 8-inch shells struck them in quick succession, and he fell, was pitched from his feet by the whip of the elastic steel deck. Then he was up, helping Edward up too, blinded by smoke and lungs emptied by concussion. Face blackened by blast but apparently unhurt, the immortal Edward was back at the bridge front. 'Hold her steady, Coxswain! Hold her steady!' The Damage Control telephone was buzzing. Fires glowed on the cruiser's decks as the 4.7s scored hit after hit: but only A and Y turrets were firing, and the bridge lay dark and shadowy in what seemed an island of leaping flame, most of which came from B turret, directly hit, gaping open, roofless, like a fire-filled can. 'Sick Bay hit. Cruik-shank dead.' That was a breathless Reece-

Davis reporting to Dunbar. And the shells and tracer still came. A lookout on the port side died behind his binoculars. The Signalman tried to pull him free, turned then and stared at Rose in blank astonishment, then died himself, fell face down at the Navigator's feet.

'Hard-a-starboard!' Edward cried.

Scorpio keeled over to port in quick retreat. But Charlie had fired his whole outfit of torpedoes. Somewhere in the sea eight sleek missiles streaked under the water.

They turned now into their own smoke screen, for Edward had started to describe a figure 8 in order to give Chaplin a chance to reload.

The firing stopped. Smoke enveloped them. The bridge had become a pot sitting on a naked fire. But everyone waited, prayed, listened. They even smiled when they heard the two distant CRUMP! CRUMP! Charlie's bedtime story would be true.

In the four minutes that followed, they could see nothing but flame-tinted smoke in which silhouetted men fought the flames from B turret, the canteen flat, and aft, sorting out the dead and the dying as they worked. Hoses had been run out on deck. Spray drifted across the bridge and turned to steam in the heat. But the damage was what the Navy called 'superficial', and most important of all – the engine-room was still intact. For most men, death came with heart failure. For the Chatham Rats it would come with engine failure.

Chaplin reported his tubes ready.

'Stand to! Stand to! Stand to!' The gunners clambered back on their guns. The First Lieutenant, who had turned over his tower to the wounded Adams, went about the job of keeping the ship afloat and the wounded from dying.

Speed was reduced to twenty knots.

Edward came out of the southern loop of his figure 8 to find the cruiser stopped and listing, vomiting smoke that had in its centre the deep red glow of internal fires.

The Italian guns remained silent.

Scorpio held her fire, passed close to the cruiser's stern. Then Edward bent to the voicepipe, ordered revolutions for maximum speed.

They were inside the front door.

Smoke was shut off. Night closed in. Somewhere behind, the destroyers of the northern screen would be chasing after them, their binoculars focused on the fire and sparks which sped through the darkness at forty knots.

Under the flickering light of the hooded chart-table Rose had the local chart for the Strait; a pencil in one hand, he listened to the telephone from the W/T office. On a tiny platform at the rear of the foremast a small metal hoop like a tricycle wheel without spokes revolved slowly: it was a radio direction finding aerial, called a D/F, and was the best reason why all warships in peril kept radio silence. In the phone's ear-piece was the small voice of the radio operator: 'Enemy radio transmissions at one-six-oh degrees ... also at two-double-oh, sir...' and the Navigator plotted each tell-tale transmission on his chart, then asked: 'Any idea of distance, Anderson?' A good operator could guess. Leading Telegraphist Anderson was the best outside his native Scotland: 'Forty to fifty miles, sir,' his voice answered. 'I'm charting them down here, sir. Looks like they're going to box us in.'

The cruiser's fate had triggered a spate of frantic radio activity from which a rough picture emerged: it looked as if *Scorpio* was inside an oblong trap, forty miles wide by sixty long.

Edward agreed.

Darkness was their friend, but the worst enemies were the flames and the wind of their passage.

Morgan had been relieved from the helm. He and an E.R.A. arrived on the bridge in a flap, followed by York. They circled Dunbar. 'We've got to stop the ship,' York said tersely. 'The flames are gaining hold in this damned wind. It's like a furnace down there.'

'It's the canteen flat – but B turret mostly,'

Morgan chipped in. 'The ammunition hoist was damaged. B magazine is far too hot, sir.'

'The sprays were damaged,' explained the E.R.A. 'We can't flood it. It'll be critical inside thirty minutes, sir.'

Dunbar took a deep breath and turned his eyes on Rose, half his face lit by the flames from B turret. He was waiting for the answer to the unspoken question; and that answer was *No! No! No!* Don't stop!

But Rose shrugged, lifted his palms in a timeless gesture: what did it matter when they'd blow up anyway?

The engine-room telegraphs tinkled distantly.

Inside five minutes, *Scorpio* was stopped.

But how many of the enemy had not used their radio? How many were out there, unseen on the port or starboard beam? Were there bombers in the sky, unheard above the cursed drone of the funnel exhausts? With the fires burning, *Scorpio* could be seen; but the only thing her crew could see was flame-tinted darkness: darkness that was blacker because their night sight had been ruined by the light ... and in night actions, he who fired first, won. All this and the knowledge they'd lost their doctor, lost young Pascoe who'd been 'getting on fine', lost all of the wounded except Adams and Happy; all this brought a morbid dread into the eerie, flickering, shadowy night.

Some were lucky, they worked. But those without option, like Freer, whose glistening face showed clearly in Rose's binoculars, had to wait and watch and listen and sweat. But what of those who were down in the warm and stuffy TS, or in the blistering heat of the engine-room, or in the explosive confinement of the cell-like magazines, sitting on fifty tons of live ammunition, with half an inch of steel that reacted to the slightest sound from friend and foe without telling you which? What of them...?

The seconds fled and the minutes dragged.

A telephone buzzed.

Rose lowered his binoculars, tiptoed to the chart-table. It was Anderson. 'The ether's gone quiet, sir. All of a sudden. The last broadcast was above five or seven miles.'

Motionless above the voicepipe Edward had his eyes on the diminishing flames from B turret.

He turned. 'Yes, Pilot?'

'I think the enemy has spotted us, sir. They're keeping radio silence.'

'How long do you think we've got?'

'Five minutes. At the most. Perhaps.'

'The First Lieutenant tells me you did a good job last night, Pilot. A very professional job – *he* said. I'm putting you up for a D.S.O.'

'Posthumously?' It seemed a hell of a good

answer. 'Tell you what, sir – put young Freer up for a D.S.M. instead...?'

'Why, for goodness sake – what for?'

'Restraint!'

Water was being sucked inboard. Hoses hissed. Steam sizzled and clouded the bridge and the night. Twenty tiny rivers flowed noisily back into the sea from the bilges. Inch by inch *Scorpio* sank by the bow as the pumps failed to cope.

Voices were whispers. Feet were on tiptoe. A dark shadow climbed down from York's tower. Another shadow climbed up. The bridge grew darker as the last flame from B turret flickered and went out. Only the faintest glow from the cabin flat remained, and the smell, which would live in the memory unto eternity.

Five minutes had gone.

'Aircraft!' A big whisper from a lookout.

'Any idea where?' Dunbar challenged softly.

'Starboard beam, I think, sir.'

Rose heard it faintly. He also heard Adams instruct the guns' crews: 'Watch the sea!'

At the same time, Dunbar ordered full speed.

But as the vibration started up underfoot, the aircraft passed immediately overhead, began to recede. What happened then, happened so fast that each event was indistinguishable in time. A flare exploded and lit a square mile of sea, not however above them but over an identical grey destroyer that was steaming parallel on the same course, her guns pointing at *Scorpio*. In Y turret, the gunlayer found his wires crossed precisely on the Italian's waterline, saw too that her guns were ready to fire and pulled his own trigger before A turret was even on target. A tongue of flame leapt straight into the sky from the enemy's bridge and fo'c's'le. Y turret's two shells had scored a direct hit on a magazine. The explosion destroyed the Italian's two forward turrets but *not* her after one, and *it* fired in that same explosive instant: in almost the same instant that *Scorpio's* forward funnel, searchlight, and Freer's gun platform vanished in flame.

The Navigator grabbed Reece-Davis. 'Take over!'

Down the ladder two at a time. Unlit, gutted, blackened, the canteen flat was ankle deep in hot evil-smelling water, strewn with soft resilient things that no man would dare to touch. Yards of wiring hung in the blackness like steel cobwebs. A smouldering glow was the starboard blackout screen. Rose dived through it, tripped over a body. It was the E.R.A. in charge of Damage Control.

Scorpio was picking up speed. The enemy destroyer was a blazing hulk, receding astern, the tiny figures of men leaping from her decks in the light of the flare.

Somewhere in the sky on the port side an aircraft was diving. The guns opened up, firing blindly. Then the rush and whistle of armour-piercing bombs.

The sea erupted as if from depth charges.

All this, Rose hardly noticed. Arm shielding his face from the breath of fire he picked his way over the hoses, watched each shadow lest it be a hole. Above he could now see the forward funnel pitted by shrapnel, torn open like a Wellington boot from top to bottom. No searchlight. No gun platform. Just a hideous vista of black saw teeth which was in fact ragged, jagged metal in silhouette against leaping flame. Men, fiery demons, were up there struggling with jets of water, almost invisible in pink drifting steam.

More flares burst in the sky. Wood crackled. Men bawled. More piston engines. 'Torpedo bombers! Watch the water! Watch the water! Open fire! Open fire!'

Another body. Dead. Leave it. The starboard boat had gone, its davits twisted by blast, the twisted ropes burning like smouldering string.

Freer! Where the hell was he! Rose cursed himself for a fool. Freer was dead.

A third body. In deep shadow. He turned it over. It was Freer. 'Freer? It's me. Rose. The Navigator.' Arms under Freer's arms he dragged him two or three feet – so very gently – propped him against the boat's davit. That was better. He could make out Freer's face in the flickering firelight. No blood. The eyes were open, reflecting flames.

'Hullo, sir, what happened?' Freer's voice was husky, tired, sleepy, 'What happened?'

'Are you okay?' It was incredible. 'Any pain? Are you wounded?'

'I – I don't think so. Just – just a bit numb.'

'Where?'

Freer didn't say. He pointed instead. 'Over there, sir. Happy. Help Happy. He needs help, sir.'

'O.K., I'll help him.' But why was Freer numb? A glance around. No one in sight with a torch. Damn the guns! He put his hands on the lad's shoulders, ran them down the trunk in the way a policeman frisks a gunman. Still no blood. More bombs. Freer's eyes closed. Then they opened. Another plane was diving on the starboard quarter. The forward turret had swung round, fired aft all but over their heads. The flashes lit Freer's face, lit his body … and then Rose was on his feet, running, tearing off his shirt as he ran…

'Chaplin! Chaplin!' Charlie was there by his tubes. 'Chaplin! I need two marline-spikes. For God's sake, Chaplin, two mar-line-spikes – where?' Rose had his shirt off, tearing it into strips.

'Here.' Charlie stuffed two spikes into his hands. 'What the devil's up?'

But Rose was off. He tripped over a hose,

picked himself up, ran on. The 4.7s blinded him. He collided with the davit, cursed, knelt, felt. *No Freer!*

'Freer! Freer! Freer!' A pause. No reply. *'Freer!'* Wait. Someone was close. A flash lit Happy's face, his bandaged chest. On his feet, he was leaning gasping against the davit, dripping blood. 'Where the hell's Freer?'

'I tried to stop him, sir. He – he seemed to be dragging himself deliberately over the ship's side. I couldn't believe it. But he did. He's gone.' Happy's voice was high-pitched with sheer disbelief.

In the flash of the 4.7s, Rose saw the trail of blood and palm prints from davit to gunwale. The marline-spikes he'd brought for tourniquets clattered on the iron deck, rolled into the scuppers. He put an arm round Happy's waist. 'Hang on to me, son. Must get that wound redressed. Don't worry about Freer. He didn't know what he was doing.'

'He was looking over his shoulder at me, sir. Desperate, like. Like he was afraid I'd stop him, sir.'

'Forget it.'

'His legs – he had no legs, sir.'

'And Jesus wept, yet again,' Rose muttered softly.

Damn the guns! Damn the war! Damn bigotry!

Of course, Happy didn't understand. Nor

would anyone else. None had read Freer's letter. But no one life was any less important than any other. Happy had fought all day with a hole in his side as big as a fist, which had bled ceaselessly from firing a 20mm cannon that kicked like a pneumatic road drill. Still a little worried, he died at midnight from loss of blood. 'Know his name?' asked the S.B.A.

Rose shook his head. 'The First Lieutenant knows, I don't. They just called him Happy.'

The temporarily unknown warrior – immortal, too. Like Edward Dunbar who, white with fatigue, fought the enemy all through that terrible night. Like Simon York, who kept the guns firing and the wounded from dying. Like the Engineer Officer, who kept his engines turning until an enemy shell stopped them at first light and left *Scorpio's* decks awash. Like Andy Butterworth who, with his seven remaining 'boats', hove out of a grey and misty dawn, battle flags flying, and chased away the enemy coming in for the kill...

They were all immortal – immortalised in the bedtime stories of men like Charlie.

15

The discussion took place in the lounge of Alexandria's Hotel Cecil. *Wildcat's* officers were sitting round a low table, sunk in basket chairs, faces uptilted at a whirring fan, and being generously supplied with pink gins by Ali, a brown-faced waiter with a red fez and a white robe from which sandals peeped. Edward had just finished telling the long and exciting story of how he fought a U-boat and became immortal; it proved beyond doubt that sex was wildly exciting rather than sinful. At least, that was the view of the Sub-Lieutenant Reece-Davis, who recorded the discussion, as it unfolded from that point on.

Some months had elapsed since Lieutenant Rose had been whisked from the sinking *Scorpio* on that morning in June by one of Andy Butterworth's Fleet destroyers. Alas, Lieutenant Rose had not been seen again, for the destroyer carrying him had, to everyone's consternation, made off on its own to places unknown.

Lieutenant-Commander York lumbered across the lounge, intercepted Ali, returned the greetings from the now upstanding officers, and as one they all flopped back in their chairs.

York took a long, long drink.

'Well, what's the news?' Edward asked impatiently. 'How did you get on in England?'

'It's a new secret weapon,' York said, eyes afire with enthusiasm. 'They call it Radar—'

'About Rose. Not Radar.' Edward was peeved. His officers and ratings *always* came back. Lieutenant Rose had not come back. 'Did you call at the address I gave you?'

'It was a phoney address, sir. I knew damned well it would be.' He waved away Dunbar's objection. 'From the moment Rose rescued me in that camp I *knew* he was no more a wavy-navy Navigating Officer any more than my Aunt Sally.' Another long drink. 'Argument won't get us anywhere. Let's talk about this Radar. It's a wonderful invention—'

'About Rose,' interrupted Charlie, leaning forward. 'You said he made a mistake, or something. You didn't say what...?'

The glass clinked on the table.

'All right, Mr Chaplin. Let's get it off our chests and forget it, eh?' York was keen on Radar, irritable because he knew very well that all this would get them nowhere. He took a deep breath. 'Rose made one mistake. It was just after the petrol tank blew up. We were trying to race that damned fire. We collided with a truck. For some seconds both vehicles were locked together. For some reason – God knows why – I hesitated to shoot the driver. It was our only chance. Rose knew that, too, and he grabbed the Mauser pistol. He grabbed it from my hand, gentlemen. By the barrel. Then he tossed it, caught it by the butt, and shot the Wehrmacht driver clean through the forehead.' He paused. 'Gentlemen, only a professional saboteur could have done that.'

Silence.

'Luck?' suggested Charlie.

'Oh, come…' rebuked the Paymaster Lieutenant. 'You are not really trying to suggest that Rose was some kind of secret agent… Are you?'

'I'm trying to talk about Radar,' retorted York angrily.

Mr Chaplin was not so sceptical. He glanced at Edward. 'Mind you, sir, it was funny the way Rose was whipped away in that destroyer.'

'It wasn't a bit funny,' replied Edward mildly. 'As a matter of fact, Rose picked up some vital information on new missiles. From a German sentry, he said.'

'Yeah. *He* said,' York said.

Edward sighed. 'Rose had one secret, Number One. He was an accomplished linguist. That enabled him to deal with the enemy and the partisans. And that address you say is phoney was given to me, after considerable trouble, by Vice-Admiral Dorman. None other.'

'Rose *knew* those partisans were going to be there,' York growled. 'Adams was certain about that. He said Rose showed no surprise. He even forecast they were walking into "a friendly ambush". It's true that Adams didn't understand one word of what went on between Rose and Kosovac, but Adams said Rose didn't even pause at the door. He went straight in.'

'You mean, into the hut at No. 1 bunker?' smiled the Sub-Lieutenant patronisingly.

'*No!* – the lavatory on Waterloo Station!' York snarled.

'Let's talk about Radar,' said Edward tactfully.

'Damn Radar!' York snapped. Out went a hairy hand. 'Look sir, I can't prove it, but I *can* tell you *why* it happened.'

'Why what happened?' inquired Charlie innocently.

'You wouldn't look so funny with a torpedo in your teeth instead of that cigar,' York glared.

'Gentlemen, gentlemen, please…' Edward was M.C. 'Let the First Lieutenant speak… Now, Number One…?'

The wrathful York was suddenly very calm, with – yes – just a trace of smugness. 'Once you see the point,' he began, 'you will find that everything that happened on *Wildcat* and then on *Scorpio* and finally on the Dalmatian Islands drops into place. It will also explain why Lieutenant Rose acted like a clown for half the time and like a professional agent for the other half. Once I had seen that trick with the Mauser, I began to ask myself questions. Now, I will ask you the same questions... First, who were the three vital characters on that operation?'

'Major Troy... Lieutenant Rose...' Edward paused and frowned. 'Guiseppe...?'

York nodded. 'Now tell me the name of the man who found the gilder bomb west of Trieste?'

'Major Troy!' they chorused.

'And who was the man who knew the names of the partisan leaders?' York smiled.

'Major Troy!' Second chorus.

'And who was the man the Gestapo set the trap for?'

'Major Troy!' Third chorus.

'And who knew Major Troy's identity?'

'Why, we all did!'

York sat back confidently. 'And now the key question, gentlemen... Who was the one man, apart from us – among the enemy, mind you – who knew Troy's identity and would not have hesitated to betray him?'

'Guiseppe.' Edward said it softly.

'Precisely! And that, gentlemen, is the whole point but not the entire reason for what I think happened. For Major Troy was not only worried about Guiseppe betraying him, he was also worried about himself breaking down under torture and revealing the names of partisan leaders. He was also worried about what the Gestapo would do to the Chatham Rats *if* they knew Major Troy's identity...'

Silence.

'But we *did* know Troy's identity!' Charlie gasped.

York shook his head.

'You *thought* you knew Troy's identity.'

'Lieutenant Rose! He was Major Troy!' Reece-Davis flung back his head, laughed cruelly. 'You're joking, sir.' Another cruel laugh. 'Rose was a nice, kind, gentle man. I know. He was my boss.'

'Yes, it's absurd.' Edward waved away the whole idea. 'Apart from him falling on his head, there's one thing you don't know, Number One. After Troy was shot, Rose voted to return to Alexandria.'

'I'd have been very surprised if he hadn't.' York shrugged. 'He never missed one opportunity to throw us further and further from the real truth. The Troy we knew was what they call a front man. He was there to explain the mission. He was there as a focus for attention. It was bad luck he was shot. But it worked. The clown was unsuspected – almost.'

'Almost?' Edward asked.

'When the Gestapo put the screws on me,' York said sadly, 'they didn't know that *our* Troy was dead. Guiseppe denied it. But when they shot Guiseppe's brothers, he told them the truth. Then they started asking questions about all the officers, how long we had been on the ship, and so on. One man became the focus of their attention. The man who replaced our Navigator very suddenly and mysteriously at Alexandria some days before *Wildcat* sailed. Lieutenant Rose. So you see, he came very close to failing.'

'But Rose didn't know Dorman and Troy. I'll swear to that.' It was Edward's last protest.

'Rose *pretended* not to know Dorman and Troy. Ships have ears. Everything depended on that first meeting being beyond suspicion.'

Edward sighed, beckoned Ali, ordered drinks.

'Mind you,' he said pensively, 'all this is not beyond the bounds of possibility, I admit. And come to think of it, it was Rose's idea to keep you on board *Scorpio,* Number One. And come to think of it, the Admiral hasn't said a word about that – and that's not usual. And come to think of it, it was Rose's idea to dump Lenz in the motor boat and then blow it up: not the action of a kind and gentle man, Subby... However, as you have already said, Number One, all this is getting us nowhere, for there would be only one way to prove it, and that isn't possible... It would mean going back in time to that room in Trieste, to the moment Major Troy heard the Gestapo car. For that was the moment his hand reached out across the table for the Luger automatic...'

Edward let his words taper off, eyed York.

'You know, Number One, if only we knew the answer to one question, we would know the answer to all.'

'And the question, sir?'

'The hand which rested on that Luger. Was it the wiry, sunburnt hand of the Major Troy we knew ... or was it the chubby, dimpled hand of Lieutenant John Rose...?'

Well ... was it ...?

Well...?

Historical Note: The glider bomb was dropped on British warships during the Salerno landing in 1943. But the tides and circumstances were already flowing fast against the enemy.

The publishers hope that this book has given you enjoyable reading. Large Print Books are especially designed to be as easy to see and hold as possible. If you wish a complete list of our books please ask at your local library or write directly to:

Dales Large Print Books
Magna House, Long Preston,
Skipton, North Yorkshire.
BD23 4ND

This Large Print Book, for people
who cannot read normal print,
is published under the auspices of

THE ULVERSCROFT FOUNDATION

... we hope you have enjoyed this book.
Please think for a moment about those
who have worse eyesight than you ...
and are unable to even read or enjoy
Large Print without great difficulty.

You can help them by sending a
donation, large or small, to:

**The Ulverscroft Foundation,
1, The Green, Bradgate Road,
Anstey, Leicestershire, LE7 7FU,
England.**
or request a copy of our brochure for
more details.

The Foundation will use all donations
to assist those people who are visually
impaired and need special attention
with medical research, diagnosis
and treatment.

Thank you very much for your help.

Irish Writers' Guide

1996-1997

WATERFORD CITY AND COUNTY

WITHDRAWN

LIBRARIES